"You haven'<s>___</s>
outdated birth-control pills.
Are you satisfied now?"

"Such a leading question, Ms. Harris. I find it very difficult to resist the reply."

He straightened and stepped toward her, but he didn't touch her.

"In fact, I can't resist. No, Ms. Harris, I'm not satisfied." His voice was rough and grainy as he tugged the end of the robe's tie and looped it around his hand. Letting the slippery fabric slide through his fingers onto her shoulder, he trailed the tie lingeringly across her neck, an unbearably prolonged caress of satin on her skin.

"Here, Ms. Harris," he said as he unhooked the robe and handed it to her, "perhaps you should get dressed." And let me remain unsatisfied, he added silently.

Lindsay Longford, like most writers, is a reader. She even reads toothpaste labels in desperation! A former high school English teacher with an M.A. in literature, she began writing romances because she wanted to create stories that touched readers' emotions by transporting them to a world where good things happened to good people and happily ever after is possible with a little work.

Her first book, *Jake's Child,* was nominated for Best New Series Author and Best Silhouette Romance, and received a Special Achievement Award for Best First Series Book, from *Romantic Times.* It was also a finalist in the Romance Writers of America RITA® Award contest for Best First Book.

LINDSAY LONGFORD

LOVER IN THE SHADOWS

Silhouette Books

Published by Silhouette Books

America's Publisher of Contemporary Romance

To Wes, whose courage and kindness during difficult
days have taught our son what a real hero is—
and, more important, what it takes to be a man.
Thank you.

 SILHOUETTE BOOKS

ISBN 0-373-51221-X

LOVER IN THE SHADOWS

Copyright © 1994 by Jimmie L. Morel

This edition published by arrangement with Harlequin Books S.A.

Visit Silhouette at www.eHarlequin.com

Printed in U.S.A.

CHAPTER ONE

The third time Molly woke up on her kitchen floor with the knife in her hand, she was too frightened to utter a sound.

This time the knife was spotted with blood. Dried, matte dark, it flecked the handle and clotted in the space where shining metal, wiped clean, met a wooden handle.

For a long time she lay with her cheek on the cold tiles and stared at the *thing* clutched in her white-knuckled fingers. Shadowy in the predawn, the slick black-and-white tile floor had become the color of smoke. Peaceful, this gray, in the silence. The tile felt cool against her cheek. Without turning her head, she let her gaze drift.

It would be so easy to lie here, curled up and lost in that gray blur.

So easy if she didn't have to look at the knife wavering in her clenched fist.

Silver from the handle to the sharp point that fixed her eyes. Sharp, that point, razor sharp. The sweep of metal would slice cleanly, easily, through anything, with only the slightest pressure of wrist and fingers. She knew its power.

The silver point trembled with her effort to think. Her knuckle slipped against the edge and a pinhead of bright red dotted the blade.

She couldn't move. It was only a small cut, scarcely noticeable, but the sight of her blood on that spotless metal sent her into gibbering mindlessness. Primitive instincts held her paralyzed on the cold floor, stiff against the terror washing through her in unending waves.

If she moved, her kitchen would dissolve into mist, everything familiar vanishing in a swirling vortex of motion, everything known becoming alien with each beat of her heart. Staring at the knife, she understood nothing and retreated deeper into the cave of herself, away from the howl of tigers prowling ever closer.

Something bumped against the outside door.

Metal gleamed as the knife jerked in her fist.

Molly shivered, a constant trembling running through her. Even the roots of her hair tightened with the effort of listening. Straining to hear in the thick silence, she shut her eyes, registering with every nerve in her body the sounds outside her kitchen.

But inside the kitchen, the click of the clock on the microwave oven marked the minutes, punctuation in the sentence of silence. Her heart beat loudly in her ears, louder than that inexorable click. She waited.

One minute. Two.

She waited.

For deliverance.

For horror to explode into her house once more.

She waited.

Suddenly, a thump on the open gallery that ran around the house. A rasp against the screen door, a sound light as breath against the window.

Then, once more, silence. Blood thick, heavy against her chilled skin. Heavy and insistent against her tightly closed eyelids, silence pressed down, suffocating her.

A scrape against the sill of the kitchen window.

The sound of something large moving outside on her open gallery.

Her heart banged against her ribs.

Her eyes snapped open. Heat flooded her, and her breath hazed the shiny metal in front of her.

Clutched in her hand, the knife had not changed.

She remembered going to bed earlier, with lights blazing

around her. That much was clear. She recalled the quiet of the locked house around her, the dimly lit stairwell opposite her bedroom plunging straight into the belly of the house. She had lain facing that pitchy well, watching its shadows shift into shapes that hovered near her door as her eyes burned and twitched, and night deepened outside her window.

Oh, yes, she remembered staring into the darkness.

Sleep was a demon lover, furling his cape around her, tormenting and taunting, following close on her heels while, terrified, she ran for her life from his dark seduction.

Closing her eyes again, Molly rubbed her cheek against the floor. The tile against her face. Real. The knife in her hand.

That, too, real.

Like images curved and twisted in a fun-house mirror, everything familiar and ordinary was distorted now by the knife in her hand. From a far-off place, she felt the thing vibrating between her fingers like some terrifying dowsing rod that dragged her down to sunless caverns from which she'd never escape.

Wanting to disappear, to wake up in her bedroom with this moment only a disturbing nightmare half remembered in sunlight, Molly drew her knees to her chest, curling tighter into herself. As if they'd acquired a will of their own, though, her fingers gripped the knife even tighter.

Lying there, she grew gradually aware of other sounds— her raspy breathing, the drip of water from the sink faucet, the rain chattering against her shuttered windows.

And, close to her face, the knife rattling against the floor tiles.

That frenzied clatter finally broke her, sent her whimpering and scrabbling across the floor.

Eyes still shut against the monstrous vision in front of

her, she edged back to the wall, the knife scraping the ceramic tiles with her movements.

When her hip bumped the corner of the room, she forced herself to open her eyes. With a courage she hadn't known she had, she made herself observe the instrument of her terror.

Small flecks of drying blood spotted her thumb, but there in the burnished gleam of the knife blade, the reflection of an eye, large and wild, stared back at her. Shining in the dark, that eye watched her in silvery blankness.

An eye from a dark, mad place.

Hers, she realized with a gasp. Her face. *Her* eye.

Screams pushed at her clamped teeth and made her throat raw, but she held them inside. She clenched her jaw so tightly it hurt, knowing with a primal understanding that it was important not to scream.

Too close to a border she didn't want to cross, she didn't dare look back into that metallic eye. She sat up, her teeth clicking in a frantic, uncontrollable rhythm. She was shaking all over, the butcher knife still clutched in her fingers.

She couldn't stop staring at the shining steel, the grain of the expensive wood in the handle, the splotches of blood on her hand and on the wood. As if staring at the minute details of the object would translate into understanding, she focused on the fine-grained wood.

There was no doubt about it. The knife was hers.

Just like the other times.

She'd used this knife more times than she wanted to recall. But no matter how hard she struggled, she couldn't remember coming down to the kitchen and picking it up tonight. Like those other mornings, she had no memory of opening the drawer with its carefully arranged knives and sharpening blade, no memories now to explain this spider web of blood on her palms, the clots of blood between knife handle and metal.

Shuddering, Molly fought to take a deep breath, but the thunder of her heartbeat, roaring and all-consuming, was sucking the air from the room. Dizzy in that pounding vacuum, she couldn't find air.

Tugging desperately, her fingers scrabbling at the neck of her pajamas, she dropped the knife. The clatter as it fell onto the tiles released her. Huddled in the corner of the kitchen, she inhaled, loud, ugly gulps harsh in the solitude. Tears ran down her cheeks and she scrubbed them, her fists abrasive against her cold, wet lips and eyelids.

She had to think.

She had to make sense of this latest incident.

Was she crazy, after all?

Bracing her palms against the wall, she lifted herself into a standing position. Her knees buckled, but she gritted her teeth and clung in desperation to the solid surface. Against all reason, she was relieved, *relieved* that her hands left no smear of blood on her pale gray walls.

There had already been enough blood.

Molly groped along the wall, flicking on the light switch when she came to it. Lightheaded and drunk with fear, she placed her palms on the wall, carefully, one after the other. She ended her journey at the stainless-steel double sink, where she gripped the lifeline of its curved, satiny edge.

The edge of the knife's blade was curved, too.

Sweat popped out at her hairline, ran down her spine, and she found herself dry-heaving into the spotless basin. When the wracking convulsions ended, she yanked the faucet handle up as far as it would go.

Cold water gushed out and she cupped it again and again, faster and faster against her face, her hands, her throat. Water sprayed, dripped everywhere, yet she couldn't stop rubbing her hands under the spray, rubbing and rubbing but still seeing blood on her fingers. Great rasping sobs tore through her.

But she hadn't given in to screaming. Comfort of a sort in that knowledge. She hadn't surrendered to the madness dimly seen in her reflected eye.

Her pajama top was plastered against her breasts when she finally gained control. Bent over the sink, she gripped its edge while water slithered down her neck. Damp and cold, the wet, silky fabric of her top brushed her nipples, chilling them into hard bumps.

After the first incident, she no longer slept naked, no longer left her windows open to the night lurking at their edge, to the darkness threatening now at the edge of her mind. The idea of being vulnerable was unbearable.

Whatever it was, that thump she'd heard on the gallery had been real.

Pulling the black, silky cotton away from her breasts with fingers that still trembled, Molly looked around her once-loved kitchen. Cool and serene, it bore no trace now of the violence that had splashed its walls with blood.

The tongues of both bolts on the door to the outside gallery were snug in their grooves. She'd always been careful about locking up before she went to bed. In the last year she'd become obsessed with the need to check and recheck locks and bolts, even braving the dark stairwell to come downstairs in the middle of the night and check again.

She remembered roaming the house last night, examining the locks in her gritty-eyed exhaustion, but she'd gone back to bed afterward.

She hadn't slept. Not during the night. Never then.

During those lost, lonely months after the murder of her parents, sleep had eluded her.

Wrapping her arms around herself, Molly glanced slowly around the room. She wouldn't think now about the other rooms off the shadowy hall.

Like the door, the kitchen shutters seemed undisturbed,

but she couldn't tell if the windows behind the shutters were still locked until she made herself move away from the sink.

Everything was where it should be—the red enameled teapot on the black mirrored stove, the black-and-white place mats on the table.

One thing only stood out of place...the long-handled knife on the floor.

She couldn't pick it up.

Apparently she'd gone out, roaming in the night with that blood-speckled knife in her hand, returning to lock herself in behind her bolted doors and windows.

Or someone had come in.

And vanished, leaving her locked in?

Not possible.

Molly looked away from the knife. She understood she was going to have to do something. She wished she knew what.

Deep inside her, the fine edge of control was popping, shredding in audible snaps. She wouldn't survive finding herself another time curled up on the floor. She knew that as well as she knew anything.

Turning back to the sink, she turned the water on more slowly this time and splashed her face and scrubbed her hands yet again while she sorted through her terror-blasted thoughts. Numb, scarcely aware of what she was doing, she lathered her hands over and over, soaping and scrubbing her nails, her palms, between her fingers, as she tried to reason through what had happened. Step by step, using logic to distance herself from the edge of the chasm, she considered the possibilities.

Thought was a barricade against the fears nibbling at the edge of her consciousness.

She could call the police. As much as she loathed the idea of seeing them in her house again, she probably should call them. But if she did, they'd think she was crazy.

Maybe she was. But she'd always heard if you thought you were crazy, you probably weren't. Right now she wasn't sure where that theory left her, aside from giving some perverse comfort. The police would do one of two things—either ignore her or laugh at her.

She couldn't blame them. What, after all, was there for them to check out? Her knife? Her blood in its handle?

Her outstretched fingers shivered as she looked at them.

Of course it was her blood.

Unthinkable if it were not.

Frantically she searched her hands, looking for scratches on one hand, pressing the water-pruned skin, stretching it, looking between her fingers.

She sagged against the sink when she found the deep cut at the base of her right thumb. A gouge into the flesh. She touched it, felt the flap of skin. Obscene.

In her shock at finding herself once more on the kitchen floor, she hadn't felt the dull throb of the gash in her hand. Hadn't felt anything. Until now. As if she'd turned on a switch, her whole body ached.

Maybe she had been sleepwalking.

Drying her hands against her pajama bottoms and rubbing so hard against her leg she had to bite her lips against the pain, Molly tested that idea. The pain, real in its viciousness at the bottom of her thumb, was so alarming that she panicked to think she'd been sleepwalking, wandering upstairs, downstairs, all around the town...

"Stop it." Her voice was startling in the quiet of the orderly kitchen, the single sound in all that humming silence.

She wouldn't let herself lose control.

Molly took ten deep breaths. "Okay," she said when she'd finished. Needing the reality of a human voice, even her own, she continued, "Okay. No one came in. Fact. Nobody could have.'' Thinking, she shook her head slowly, and wet strands of hair slid across her chin. "Not past all those locks. And out? Leaving everything locked behind? Only a ghost, maybe. And there's no such thing as ghosts. No such thing as the Bermuda Triangle."

In spite of her weak attempt at humor, she shuddered again in the dim morning. She would have found greater comfort if she could forget all the people who did believe in the Triangle and ghosts. In the uncertain light of these moments between night and dawn, the idea of ghosts fluttering through her home wasn't something she could cope with. Not after everything else. Ghosts who slipped through locked doors and windows. No, much better a real, tangible explanation for what was happening to her, no matter how terrifying.

That left sleepwalking.

But she didn't have a history of sleepwalking.

She no longer dreamed.

Her breath came in wheezes. On TV she'd seen a report about the behavior people were capable of while in the grip of unconscious sleep.

The reporter had interviewed a woman who "woke up" over and over in her kitchen, eating, making sandwiches. Other people discovered themselves eating cigarette butts as if they were food. Nocturnal bingeing. People did strange things in the nighttime hours.

Murder, even.

A man had, supposedly, walked out of his house, driven to a relative's home, strolled in and murdered the family.

While he was asleep.

Sleepwalking.

Madness.

Molly touched the wound on her hand.

Her blood.

She rubbed the spot over and over, trying not to think about alternatives,

Her blood.

He'd been watching her for a long time. Prowling around her house, moving silently along the gallery, watching her during the long nights. Now, he moved closer. It was time.

The small smack against the kitchen door shot Molly upright, her hands over her mouth.

A second smack. Purposeful.

She edged to the door. Worse to stay listening to that muffled sound and not know what it was.

If she wanted to keep her sanity, she had no choice.

Holding the shutter carefully so that she could look out onto the gallery, Molly saw only darkness.

Again the sound came, lower, from the floor.

Staring through the window, Molly saw a shimmer of motion, a flick of dark against dark. Something was out there.

Eyes were gleaming up at her.

Real eyes, not metallic reflections of her own fear-glazed self. A stray cat. Real. Nothing to make her hide behind locked doors jiggling with imagined fears.

Drawn to the reality of the cat, she carefully released the bolts. Damp air rushed in as she held on to the screen door and looked down at the cat staring back at her with unblinking gold eyes.

Large, with powerful muscles along his flanks and shoulders and a broad head with a bumpy, hooked nose, he was the most beautiful animal she'd ever seen. Rain-wet, his black coat was shiny and sleek.

"Hey, puss," she whispered, looking down the length of the gallery. Off to her left she thought she saw movement, but it was only a mourning dove winging off into the rain, disturbed by the rattle of the opening door.

Imperiously unmoving, the cat sat with his long tail

curled around his front paws and watched her with unwinking golden eyes.

"Looking for any port in a storm, fella?" Molly stooped and touched her nose to the screen door close to the cat, comforted by the presence of another creature. This big cat with his unwavering gaze was solid and tangible in the quicksand of her thoughts. "You're a beauty, you are." Molly looked at his neck. "No collar? That's a shame. I'll bet there's someone out there looking for you, cat."

The cat tilted his head and lifted his paw to the door. He tapped it, an arrogant demand for service. Molly pressed her finger to the door and the pad of the cat's big paw flexed. His claws pierced the screen around her finger, encircling the tip. Trapping it in the cage of his claws.

"Careful, buster. What do you want, anyway?"

The cat's eyes never blinked.

"Oh? As if I should read your mind, huh? Food and a cozy spot next to the fire?"

Unmoving, utterly still, he watched her.

"Listen, buster, this is Florida. You're not going to freeze." Molly surveyed his body. Long, muscle-padded haunches. "You're obviously not hungry. Couldn't be. Vamoose, fella." She tried to pull her finger away, but the cat tightened his grip, his eyes never leaving hers.

"Hey, this isn't funny. Shoo, go away. I can't help you. Sorry, but the last thing I need is a cat around here right now." She wiggled her finger, but the cat held it firm. "If you were a dog, maybe I'd let you stay. I could use a real big, real *mean* dog. A brute. With a nasty disposition. A dog I'd keep for sure." She pulled harder, futilely.

Uneasy, Molly raised her voice and looked around, sensing *something* ruffling her nerve endings. "Hey, listen, puss, let go. I want to shut the door, okay?" Molly thunked the screen with the fingers of her free hand.

So fast she never saw his movement, like dark lightning

streaking, the cat fastened a paw around her hand, capturing a second finger and holding it with his claws through the screen.

"Well, buster, now we're in a fine mess. Let go," she ordered, glaring at the animal.

His gold gaze held hers. There was something in his somber stare that kept her looking, looking past the darker gold flecks, as if she were moving down a golden corridor faster and faster and faster, wind and air rushing past her, golden eyes locked on hers, drawing her deeper into that spinning gold....

Molly shook her head. Light lifted the edges of gray from the gallery and she could see out into her yard, down to the bayou veiled in rain. She sighed, exhausted and wrung out.

Looking back at the sleek animal in front of her, she frowned. "So, I'm a sucker for helpless critters, cat, but you're the most *un*helpless beast I've *ever* seen. And, like I said, you're not a dog. Besides, cats are always looking down hallways as if they see something, and, puss, I don't need you seeing things that go bump in the night, you know? I'm having enough problems figuring out which bumps are real and which ones aren't. I don't need you spooking the heck out of me." Her voice dropped to a shaky whisper.

Not breaking her skin, the cat curled his claws tighter. That arrogance she'd noted earlier gleamed back at her from his gold eyes.

"You have some nerve, cat. Anybody ever tell you that? Yes, I know I like cats. Ordinarily."

The cat arched his back, his claws still hooked in the screen around her fingers. Damp heat from his large body came to her in the chilly, rain-dark dawn.

Molly hesitated. "Listen, if I let you in, you can't stay, hear? I mean, this isn't your home away from home. You can come in for a while. Just until..." She stopped. She knew what she was doing. She knew she didn't want to deal with the knife still in her kitchen. Twisting her fingers caught in his grasp, Molly continued, "Just *until*, okay?"

The cat blinked and sat back on his haunches, releasing her.

"Stinker. Bully." She unlocked the screen door. "I guess you wouldn't turn down a meal, huh?"

Padding in, his tail lifted, the cat moved across her gray floor like a dark cloud over shadowy water. Passing her refrigerator, he circled the kitchen until he came to the spot on the floor where she'd woken up.

For a long moment he stayed there.

He stopped next to the knife and looked back at her. His ears angled to the hall off the kitchen, listening. *Listening* to something beyond her hearing.

Molly watched the ripples move across his skin and felt an answering shiver move across her own. "Hey, c'mon, cat. Don't do this to me. Really." She rubbed her arms.

Smelling the handle of the knife, the beast parted his mouth in a feral baring of teeth. A low growl curled around the kitchen. His canines were long, white and very sharp.

"Stop it. This isn't funny. I mean it," Molly added, nerves twanging as he looked back at her with those wild gold eyes. He blinked again and moved closer to her, loose-jointed and muscular, stopping at her feet.

"All right. That's fair," she said, bending to pick him up. His fur was warm against her cold skin. "Unlike some guys, at least you listen. But you'd better mind your *p*'s and *q*'s, okay?" she babbled into the silky fur at his ear. "Or you're out of here. And don't count on gourmet food, either. Got it?"

Silently, he rested his front paws on her forearm, claiming her.

Molly held the heavy cat tightly to her as she walked through the rooms of her house, checking every window from top to bottom, every latch. All closed. Bolted. As they always were. She'd changed the locks, too, after the second incident. Even her brother Reid didn't have a key to the new locks.

Molly didn't realize how tightly her fingers were wound into the cat's fur until he reached up and batted her face with the pad of his wide paw, drawing her attention. "Sorry about that," she said, stroking the fur down his back and over his tail. He stretched up onto her shoulder. "Listen, cat," she said, looking at him eye-to-eye and still feeling tremors way down in the cold spot inside her, "I'm at my wit's end, and I can't figure out what to do next. I'm too scared to fall asleep, and I'm so tired I don't know what's real anymore. I'm talking to a *cat*, and you don't even *purr*."

She sank into a chair in the living room and propped her feet on the matching footstool. Clutching the cat's warm, sinewy body to her, she remembered the feel of the cold floor, the gleam of the knife. The look in her own reflected eye. Molly shuddered. "Hey, fella, I'm in over my head in really bad stuff," she whispered, "and I'm sinking fast." She buried her cold face in his fur.

Arranging himself in her lap to his satisfaction, the cat fixed her with that unwavering gaze as she muttered to him. He was so still and calm that some of her own tension seeped from her as she stroked him endlessly from ear to tail tip, the smooth, sleek fur and firm muscles solid and real against her fingers.

And all the while she stroked him, the cat was silent.

Moving closer, he watched her lean back in the chair, pale brown hair clinging to the chair fabric, her hands tangled in the black silk of the cat's fur. Saw, too, the lines around her drawn, silvery gray eyes, the smudges of exhaustion underneath. He sensed the immense effort she was

*making as her small hands moved in an endless, hypnotic
rhythm.*

She might drowse now. Possibly. Or not.

He could wait.

But he knew she wouldn't sleep.

Not tonight.

The piercing shrill of the doorbell jerked Molly to her
feet. While she'd drifted off somewhere in her mind, the cat
had disappeared, leaving long strands of black fur clinging
to her fingers. Anxiously she brushed her hands down her
pajamas, wincing at the ache in her hand.

She had no idea what time it was.

Peering through the privacy hole on the door, she saw
that rain still dripped down the eaves and spattered the gallery. Her stomach curled in nauseating twists as she looked
at the detective's shield held eye level by the man standing
in an easy, legs-apart stance at her front door.

Unlocking the door but keeping the chain on, Molly
leaned her head against the doorjamb.

Choice had been taken from her.

"Yes?" Her voice was thready. To herself as she heard
the edgy notes, she sounded guilty of unnamed horrors.

"Police." Anonymous behind the silver-rimmed, round
dark lenses of his sunglasses, he could have been anyone.

"Yes. I see." Dread was moving through her in long
rollers, gaining force, growing large and overpowering like
enormous waves far out at sea.

She saw, too, the second man sitting in the passenger side
of the black car parked in her driveway. She'd never heard
it drive up. She must have dozed off.

Trying to sort out this new set of events, Molly rubbed
her forehead fretfully against the edge of the door.

"We need to talk with you, ma'am." Florida sand in his

voice, a native, like her. She didn't recognize his tough, sharp-planed face, though.

Molly cleared her throat. "What about?"

"I'll explain. May I come in?" Against the stark black of his shirt and jacket and the sleek black of his hair, the man's face was pale.

Yielding to the authority in his voice, in the bracing of his hand against one lean hip, Molly almost removed the chain. But caution and the ever-present fear stopped her. Sunglasses on a rain-dark morning? "Look, can you give me a name? A badge number?" She was having trouble swallowing.

There was a long silence. She saw him look toward the man in the low-slung car, shrug and turn back to her.

"Sure. John Harlan." He held the shield closer to the door, his gesture somehow mocking. "Badge number 8973. You can call—"

"I'll look it up," she said through the crack, and she shut the door very carefully with shaking hands.

Racing upstairs, knees turning to syrup with fear, Molly looked up the phone number for the local police, rolling the edge of her pajama top between her fingers as she waited for an answer, trembling at each suddenly loud sound of her house, each creak and sigh of a branch against a window.

According to the desk sergeant, Harlan, badge number 8973, was supposed to be at her house.

The wave that had been building crashed around her and pulled her out to sea. There in the dark depths where monsters dwelt, it built again in slow, sickening swoops of power.

Smoothing the rolled edge of her pajama top flat, Molly unbuttoned the garment slowly, making herself go through the simple, grounding motions. She couldn't afford to think.

Skimming off her bottoms, she slid into jeans and a sweat shirt and ripped a brush through her hair. Red scrawled across her cheek as she tried to put on lipstick, and she flung the lipstick case back onto her dresser with a violence that surprised her.

Wiping the slash of crimson off her cheek, she shuddered. She didn't need any more red today.

She hurried down the stairs. "I called the police station," she muttered as she opened the door.

"Good." His voice was like hot chocolate on cold ice cream, just that edge of hardness under the smooth.

Bigger and more powerful than she'd realized, he filled the doorway and stepped into her house, wiping his feet carefully.

The bottoms of his expensive black slacks were mud spattered. Bayou mud and dried sand.

Backing up, Molly wanted to slam the door and run.

He must have seen something in her face, because he stopped. "Do we have a problem here?" He was all waiting stillness, power held in abeyance.

"No. No problem," she said, hearing the lie, knowing he did, too, as he inclined his head toward her, listening carefully. She cleared her throat. "How can I help you? What's happened?" She twisted her fingers together and sensed, rather than saw, his gaze behind the mask of dark glasses follow their movements. She stopped, let her hands lie easily along the side seams of her jeans.

And tried to breathe past the constriction in her chest. "What do you want?"

He slid a notebook from his shirt pocket. Underneath his jacket, she glimpsed his thin, black leather belt, the shine of its narrow buckle. Glimpsed, too, the edge of a shoulder holster.

As he flipped open the notebook with his long, thin fingers, Molly braced herself.

"You're off the beaten path here, Ms.—" He checked his notebook, but she didn't believe for a minute that he didn't remember her name. Something about his careful stance, his slow turning of pages told her he knew.

She let him play out his game.

"Ms. Harris." He nodded, but Molly didn't answer. The sigh of an early morning wind filled the silence between them.

She couldn't have spoken. Didn't know what to say. She only knew she had to hold on to the center of her being with every ounce of energy she had or she'd go spinning apart.

He nodded again. His pen slid along the edge of his notebook. "Ms. Harris, do you remember seeing or hearing anything unusual last night?"

She wished she could. "Nothing," she said, worrying the cuticle of her thumb with her finger. "I was asleep." The lie trembled off her lips.

His pen moved steadily across the page. "Were you." It wasn't a question.

Reflexively glancing at the slash in her palm, she stopped abruptly. "Why? What's happened?"

He reached out for her hand, turning it in his. His hand was strong, his fingertips rough. "Painful cut."

"I was peeling vegetables, carrots. For soup." Her throat gone dry, she swallowed and coughed.

"Sore throat?" he asked, still holding her hand palm up.

His fingers closed around her hand, capturing it.

"No." She was afraid to tug her hand free.

He tilted her hand toward the light and studied it. "There's a nasty virus going around." He looked at her. The glasses concealed his expression as he said, "You want to be careful, Ms. Harris. You could be coming down with something."

"No. I'm not catching a cold." Molly knew he wasn't asking out of concern for her health. "Why are you here?"

She withdrew her hand, managing not to jerk it out of his light, careful grasp.

"There's been a problem. Down at your part of the bayou. Near the boat pier."

Feeling as if she were moving through shifting sand, Molly went to the living room window facing the bayou and looked out. Off in the distance she saw a van and several figures milling around the edge of the water. "What happened?" She turned back to face him, but the light was at her back and she couldn't see him clearly even though he removed his sunglasses and hooked them into his pocket, but she had an impression of grim eyes, golden brown, watching her.

"Someone was murdered last night on your bayou."

Murdered. "Are you sure? Murdered?" The word tolled through her, over and over, like the deep-toned bells of the First Presbyterian Church in town. *Murder.* Irrevocable.

"Oh, yes, we're sure." His thin mouth lifted. "No question. Two fishermen passing by early this morning saw the body and called us. Yes, we're sure." His long fingers curled around his notebook. "You know anything that could help us?"

"I told you. I was asleep."

"Yes. So you did." Threat, implicit. Explicit in the dark velvet of his voice, in the hidden gaze.

At some level, ever since she'd woken up on the kitchen floor, she'd been envisioning news like this. But it still short-circuited her brain and left her struggling for an answer while John Harlan's golden brown eyes followed her every twitch and movement.

"Who?" Her heart pounding like a captured bird, she couldn't hold his relentless gaze.

CHAPTER TWO

"Why don't you put on your shoes, and we'll go down to the bayou together? We believe you could save us some time if you can identify the body." The detective's mild voice coaxed her, his tone soothing. She didn't trust him for a minute. He'd reached for her hand again and his thumb rested lightly, so lightly against the wound in her palm that she felt as if he'd manacled her to him. "Can you do that, Ms. Harris?" He released her wrist with an unreadable expression.

She shivered as his fingers brushed the edges of hers.

"Will you come down to the bayou, please, and take a look at her?" Relentless, his mild voice, deceptive in its honeyed assault that hid the sting.

"Her?" Needing breath, Molly tugged at the neck of her sweatshirt. Nightmare visions, bloodred, danced in her brain.

John Harlan's gaze watched the nervous pulling of her fingers against the often-washed cotton. "Ah, I've distressed you." His words were oddly old-fashioned. No sympathy in his deep voice, though, despite his polite words. He shifted, one hip slanting forward, the expensive fabric of his slacks flowing and tightening with the casual movement. "Something bothering you, Ms. Harris?"

"You said someone has been murdered. Murder bothers me," she breathed through chalk-dry lips.

"I'm sure it does," he said, stepping so close that the power in his looming form and wide shoulders made her claustrophobic. "Well, that makes at least two of us then. I don't like murder, either." His courteous expression, at odds with his tough face, never altered as his voice dropped so deep that Molly felt its vibration down to her toes. "Or murderers."

Molly retreated. She couldn't help her backward step. Not for the life of her could she have stayed unmoving in the face of his inexorable advance.

"Shoes?" he reminded her gently, his hands resting easily on his narrow hips, not touching her. Yet she felt the press of his broad palm hot at the base of her spine.

She bolted for the kitchen.

As fast as she moved, he followed right on her heels through the living room into the kitchen.

She'd left the knife in the middle of the floor. She saw it as soon as she stepped into the room. How could she have forgotten it? She jerked to a stop. Then, moving in slow motion, her brain disconnected from her body, she reached down, picked the knife up by the wooden handle and turned to face John Harlan, the knife extended toward him.

Arms folded across his chest, he rested against the arch of the door between the kitchen and the living-room hall. Satisfaction moved across his austere face like a faint cloud as he remarked, "A mite large for peeling vegetables, I'd think."

"Yes," Molly answered, her words mechanical as she felt the knife tremble in her outstretched grasp.

He smiled, the edges of his thin, beautifully shaped lips curling up. His smile didn't begin to reach to the depths of his golden brown, watchful eyes. "Interesting decorating idea. You often store your kitchen utensils on the floor?"

"I dropped it. When I heard the doorbell." Stiff-legged, holding the knife out from her as far as she could, Molly walked to the sink and let the damned thing fall into it. Sagging over the basin, she drew shallow breaths as she stared at the dried water spots on the stainless steel. Numb, she wanted to pray, but found no words as the walls closed in on her.

No way out.

Crackle and static as the detective spoke into his handset. "Yeah, Ross. In the sink. Yeah, when you finish down there. No hurry." And then again he was close behind her, the heat from his body radiating against hers. "Your knife, Ms. Harris?" On the surface nothing more than mild interest, but underneath, oh, underneath where it counted, she heard the quiet threat in his deep voice. Lifting the knife from the sink by its sharp point, he repeated, "Yours?"

She nodded. Of course it was. She'd already admitted as much. Everything in the house was hers. Had been hers since her parents had been killed a year ago. Home invasion. Burglary gone out of control, the police had decided.

Murdered. Their blood on the floor, the walls.

The police had never caught the killer. Or killers.

Molly tugged once more at the neck of her sweatshirt. Air. She needed air. Running to the door to the porch gallery, she flung it open and stood shivering in the morning air, gasping.

The rain had become a silvery drizzle in the gray light, the soundless shapes down at the bayou emerging from the mist and disappearing back into it. The murky coil of water drifted by them.

Even chilled, she found the wet air hard to breathe, and she couldn't stand the rasping sounds she made. Weakness to let Detective John Harlan see her fear.

When he closed his palm over her shoulder, she jumped.

"Might be a virus after all," he murmured as her breath rattled in her throat. He raised his eyebrow, an elegant arch of black against his night-pale skin.

His grasp of her shoulder seemed heavy, but she knew the force was all in her own mind, not in the actual weight of his fingers curving over her. "Maybe you're right," she whispered, the air cool and damp against her face. Her pulse pitter-patted at the base of her throat. "Maybe I am coming down with a cold."

"Or something. But we'll see, won't we?"

She nodded.

He slanted his head toward the bayou. "In the meantime, to help you stay healthy, shoes?" His words once again seemed to carry another message, but Molly couldn't decipher it or his slow, appraising glance, which began at her feet, moved leisurely over her and ended at her fingers clenched in the neckline of her shirt.

"All right." Molly looked at the sinuous bayou. Down there. Someone had been murdered during the night.

"I think you might even know the victim." He turned her back into the kitchen with almost no effort.

"What?" Her knees gave way and she lurched against him before she regained her balance. She couldn't have resisted the strength in those thin fingers if she'd had to. She felt the implied power and yielded. "All right. I don't think I'll be able to help you, though. I'm sure I don't know her," she said through stiff lips.

"Won't know if we don't go look, will we?" He scratched the center of his broad back against the wall and watched as she pulled on her sneakers and tied them. "Ready?" And there he was, his hand clamped around her elbow. Despite his impression of lazy strength, he moved too fast for her.

Pulling free, she stopped. "Why do I have to identify whoever that is?" Wildly she pointed to the bayou but didn't, couldn't, look again in the direction of the sullen water drifting past her property. "Was?"

"You don't *have* to." His hand returned firmly to her elbow. "It will probably be unpleasant." He walked her to the gallery. "I'm sure you want to cooperate with us, don't you, Ms. Harris?" Silky smooth with warning, his voice vibrated through her. "There's no reason not to help us unless you have something to hide. You don't, do you, Ms. Harris? Have anything to hide?"

He'd moved her to the stairs leading from the gallery to the lawn and onto the grass before she could speak. Raindrops splatted her face as she looked at his fingers gripping her arm.

"Of course not." Glancing at him, she said, "And I don't need your help walking across my own yard. You can turn me loose." She shot him a glance filled with all the frustrated anger and fear and hostility boiling in her. "Unless you're arresting me?" Saying the words out loud diminished her fear and gave her strength. She shrugged herself out of his grasp, surprised by the ease with which she freed herself.

"Arresting you? Now why would you think I'd arrest you, Ms. Harris?" The amusement glinting in his golden brown eyes disabused her of the notion that she'd had anything to do with the fact that she was now walking unaided down the sloping, rough terrain leading to the bayou.

Detective Harlan was playing games with her. Watching her reactions, he was enjoying toying with her.

But then he had nothing to lose.

She did.

Her freedom.

Her sanity.

"As I said, why would you think I'm arresting you?" His voice intruded on her chaotic thoughts.

Letting her antagonism snake between them, Molly slipped her cold hands into her jeans pockets. "Doesn't it make sense that I would think you were trying to see if I had stabbed that woman, whoever she is?"

"Ah, well, Ms. Harris, I don't remember saying she'd been stabbed." Though his heavy eyebrows drew together in puzzlement, his voice mocked her.

"You told the other detectives to pick up my knife for evidence. I assumed—"

"Assumptions are dangerous, Ms. Harris. Especially where murder's concerned. I'm a cop. I don't assume anything. I just, well, I just look at what I find. Evidence. You know." He was so close to her that his thigh brushed against hers, a solid flex of muscle.

Avoiding him, Molly stepped sideways. She couldn't look at the black plastic bag on the ground at the water's edge. She'd seen the body bag in that quick glance through her living-room window and hadn't been able to look at it since then. She lengthened her stride, trying to put distance between herself and Detective Harlan. With his air of casual menace, he made her uneasy, made her skin itchy. "I knew because you told the other detectives to collect the knife," she insisted dully.

"Of course I did. Such an *interesting* place to find a knife, wouldn't you agree?" His long legs kept effortless pace with her shorter, hurried strides. His warm hand on the inside of her arm stopped her before she could break into a run. "Are you a murderer, Ms. Harris?" he asked politely, his low voice skimming over her skin, frightening in its indifference.

Molly saw the dead woman's face framed by the partially zippered plastic bag. She swayed, his hands slid to her waist, and with John Harlan's imprisoning arms around her, Molly felt the world go cold and dark.

She came to sitting on the wet grass, Harlan's hand pressing her head between her knees. Nothing had changed.

Everything had changed.

"Ah, you did know her then?" His fingers were firm around the column of her neck.

"Yes." Letting her head rest on her knee, Molly wiped the tears, the rain, whatever, away from her face. "She was my friend. My maid. Had been my maid for two years. I fired her three months ago.'' She pressed her face against the frayed denim at her knees, drying the hot tears burning her eyes, her mouth, her soul.

''I see.'' He hunkered at her side, the fabric of his slacks tight against his muscular thighs.

''No! You don't!'' With Camina lying on the ground in front of her, her frizzy blond hair splashed against the black plastic, Molly was suddenly filled with explosive rage. Using John Harlan's arm, she pulled herself upright, and he rose with her in a graceful unwinding of muscle. ''Someone killed my friend!''

''Simple cops that we are, we were able to figure that much out, Ms. Harris. I know our reputation is occasionally less than what we'd like, but, trust me, we had no trouble identifying this as murder.'' His laugh was rough-edged. He stepped close to her, but he didn't let his wide shoulders block her view of Camina.

He was standing knee-to-knee with her, his palms flat and hot at her waist. Such heat in his broad hands. Rain glittered in his hair, spotted his black jacket, the gleam of his black shirt. She could smell the heat of him rising to her in the rain, clean, fresh. This close to him, she realized for the first time that he wasn't as tall as she'd thought. He'd seemed enormous, terrifying, as he'd stood on her front porch. In fact, he was under six feet.

Only a man.

Then Molly looked into his face and realized that John Harlan was every bit as terrifying as she'd believed.

Nothing merciful in his golden brown eyes, no amusement in the mouth curling in a smile, nothing but steel in the grip of his hands. Implacable.

And he was hunting her.

Acknowledging the understanding between them, he tipped his head. ''There's something else I want you to take a look at.'' Marching her in front of him like a captive, he kept his hands tight around her waist. The toe of his shoe bumped the bag. He nodded to one of the technicians, who unzipped the plastic farther down.

"I can't. I can't." Sobs bent Molly in two. She saw the dark, rain-wet blood on Camina's blouse. That was enough. Covering her mouth, she pleaded, "No more, please. I want to go home."

"In a minute." Harlan was impatient as he stepped around Camina, leading Molly to the dock. "She was found there." He indicated the body on the ground and then pointed to a trail of blood leading from it to the pier. "But she was killed *here*. On the dock. Why was your maid— your friend, I think you said—waiting on your boat dock last night, Ms. Harris? Who was she waiting for?"

There were muddy footprints at the edge of the dock. A smudged pattern danced from one end of the dock to the other, the outline of Camina's footprints washing away with the drizzle.

And then, of course, the blood. Couldn't forget that. There was always the blood.

"Why was your maid on this dock last night, Ms. Harris?" Harlan's voice was relentless. "Tell me. I know you're hiding something, Ms. Harris. I just haven't figured out what. But I will, you know. Sooner or later, I'll find out. I always do." Like water plinking into a sink, driving a person crazy, his words fell around her. "You know you want to get out from under the burden of what you're keeping to yourself, whatever you're hiding behind that cool little mask." He touched her face. "Think what a relief it will be to tell me everything, Ms. Harris, to get rid of all those secrets you're guarding so earnestly." He paused and lifted her hand, traced the wound.

"I don't have anything to say. I'm not hiding anything." Molly looked him straight in the face.

"No secrets? Ah." He paused. "Well, we all have them,

you know. Believe me—'' he curled her fingers over the gash in her palm ''—there's nothing you can say that I haven't heard before, Ms. Harris. There's nothing you can't say to me.''

His voice caressed her, seducing her with its false gentleness, until Molly wanted to tell him everything. But she couldn't. She anchored herself with that knowledge even as his words continued to curl around her.

''Tell me, Ms. Harris. It won't be hard. And you'll be glad when you don't have to hide anymore. You won't have to lie. Won't have to worry about what you've said or not said. Everything finally out in the open. Secrets will destroy you, you know. Why don't you tell me? Everything. And then you can sleep.'' And, though he wasn't touching her, his hand seemed to brush over her cold face, warming it. ''You haven't been sleeping, have you? And you're tired.''

Even though she'd insisted that she'd slept all through the night, he'd known somehow she hadn't.

Tender, filled with understanding, the flow of his voice surrounded her. ''I know you're hiding something, Ms. Harris. And I want to help you.'' He brushed her hair away from her face. The wet ends clung to her cheek, and he lifted them free. ''Let me help you. You *need* to tell me. And you will—like I said, sooner or later. So why not now?''

Weaving a seductive pattern around her, into her weary, frightened mind, John Harlan's hypnotic voice went on and on, and she fought it, fought with every ounce of energy left in her.

But oh, yes, she wanted to tell him. She was so tired of being alone. And she wanted to sleep with no shadows hovering at the edge of her mind. To sleep...

The thought stirred in her sludge-thick mind and wouldn't go away.

His was the voice of her demon lover, cajoling her, and

she wanted to surrender to the velvety ease he promised. She could sleep if she were in jail, if she were safe behind metal bars hard as the steel she sensed in John Harlan. To yield to sleep, to let his cape wrap around her and to forget, if only for one night.... To sleep.

"I..." She shook her head. Raindrops scattered onto him from her swinging hair.

"Yes?" he encouraged. "Go ahead." He led her closer to the disappearing trail of Camina's footprints. "What happened, Ms. Harris? Did she come here last night to ask for her job back? Is that how it started?" He waited, his warmth in front of her, the rain cold on her back. "Did she come to tell you that you shouldn't have fired her? Did you argue? And strike out? Not meaning to, I know," he said reassuringly, betrayal lurking in the darkness of his voice.

For a long time Molly stood, head down, watching the bloodstains grow dimmer in the increasing rain while John Harlan's voice drummed against her.

"What happened?" Endless patience now in the way he never moved, endless understanding in his low voice.

And none of it real.

"Did you come out here, Ms. Harris? Did you see Camina Milar standing here in the rain last night?" He pointed to the dock. "You could have seen her from upstairs in your house. From your living room. From any room with a view of the bayou." He shrugged. "She was outside here...for a long time." He pointed to a pile of lipstick-marked cigarette butts. "Think about her, all alone out here in the rain, waiting, hour after hour. What happened, Ms. Harris?"

She would tell him everything. She opened her mouth.

Something flickered in the grass at the edge of her vision, a motion of the tall grass as though a creature stole through it. Distracted, Molly was released from the spell of Harlan's voice, and she lifted her head and looked at him.

"Nothing!" Moving very carefully—she had no wish to

stir the power hiding inside him—she pulled his hands away from her waist and turned toward her house. Over her shoulder she threw back at him, "Aren't you supposed to Mirandize me or something if I'm a suspect? Read me my rights?"

She was freezing—shock setting in. Too much had happened. She had to go inside. She would be safe there. Later, she would think about the vision he'd created of Camina standing outside, cupping her hands around her lit cigarette and smoking steadily while the rain fell around her in the dark.

And then she had died.

Stabbed.

That was how it had been.

Must have been.

Screams building inside her, Molly ran to the house, across the gallery and into her kitchen. Huddling in the corner, she sank once more to the floor and jammed her fist into her mouth to stop the screams.

If she started, she might not stop.

Ever again.

Harlan watched the slim, fragile figure of Molly Harris vanish into rain as silvery gray as her wide, innocent eyes. He'd seen eyes that innocent before, eyes that stared at him with all the innocence anyone could ever ask for. But those innocent eyes had been lying, lying all the way to the electric chair. Years ago that had been, but he'd never forgotten his brother's innocent eyes pleading with him, his brother lying with his last breath.

And why should he forget? After all, his brother had been arrested with a gun in his hand, his bloodstained shirt casually tossed into the back seat of his convertible. A lovers' quarrel. People lied all the time and looked back at you with shiny-eyed innocence.

Molly's eyes had been circled with exhaustion. He'd known she was lying about having slept through the night. She hadn't slept well for a long time, and the strain showed in the fine lines around her eyes, in the faint tremble of her soft mouth, in the constant quivers he'd felt every time he touched her. Nothing sexual in those shivers. Something else.

He'd liked the feel of her slim waist between his hands, though, he thought regretfully; had liked the feel of those shivers rippling against his fingers. Had thought about sex. Hard not to with her staring dazed at him, trembling, the rain misting in her pale brown hair.

Hot, wild sex, her tea-colored hair sliding across his chest, her eyes blurred with pleasure as she moved with him. Yeah. He'd thought about sex even as he'd looked into Molly Harris's innocent face and wondered if she had, as he suspected, stabbed Camina Milar.

Harlan raked his hands through his own hair, dismissing the feel of Molly lingering still against his palms. He thought instead about the strain he recognized in her.

That strain showed in the way she started at every sound. Guilt? Fear? They were flip sides of each other sometimes. Fear of being caught? Fear of what she'd done when she'd stepped outside the boundaries of normal behavior? Possibly.

Watching her run recklessly to the safety of her house, he slicked back his wet hair and brushed off the knees of his grimy trousers. Looking at the mud stains and God only knew what else, he frowned. Hundred-and-fifty-dollar pants, and he'd be lucky if the cleaners ever got them clean. Well, hell, nobody'd ever promised him that a detective's lot was an easy one. He slapped at an oily smear along the calf.

At the sharp crack of the screen door, he snapped his head in the direction of the house, staring at the door that had slammed behind Molly Harris as she fled into her curiously colorless house.

Her newly decorated house.

Rain ran in rivulets down the back of his neck as he regarded the graceful lines of the house. From the crushed-shell driveway leading up to the porte cochere and tall columns at the front entrance, to the long, low windows opening onto the gallery, the house was a superb example of old county architecture.

He'd recognized the address as soon as he'd seen it on the crime report. Before collecting his partner, Ross, and heading to the crime scene, on an impulse and out of curiosity, Harlan had pulled the files on the last murders at this lovely, idyllic house. While Ross drove the car, Harlan had skimmed the reports, reading for highlights while he refreshed his recollections of one of the most horrifying crimes in Palmasola County in the past fifty years.

With the prominence of the family involved and all that beautiful, beautiful money, the case had had all the earmarks, except sex, of a grocery-store scandal rag. Because of the money involved, the detectives on the case had followed the principle of *cui bono,* but the lovely daughter and charming son had had ironclad alibis. So did the lovely daughter's ex-husband. Random home invasion. Murder as a result. And the homicide division had never solved the case. Reading over the files as Ross throttled the car down to a sedate fifty-five, Harlan wished he'd been one of the investigating detectives. The case had the feel of something pulpy and rotten at the core. His favorite kind.

Now, thoughtfully eyeing the lines of the gracious old mansion, he tilted his head. Too easy to know why Molly Harris had redone her kitchen and living room. Would have taken an idiot not to understand.

Her parents had been killed there. She'd found them shortly after midnight.

Molly Harris was edging along a mighty thin wire, and something had put her out there, something in addition to the unsolved year-old murder of her parents.

He'd give a good damn to know what was stringing her so tight right now. The more he thought about Molly Harris, the more he wished he'd been on that original case.

And wished he could have been one of the first officers to question her, because the scent of something rancid about the murders called to him in the darkest part of his soul. His mouth tight in derision, he smiled to himself. An alibi was only an alibi until it fell apart.

If Molly Harris with her innocent eyes had had secrets a year ago, he would have broken her. He clasped his hands and raised them skyward, stretching out the kinks. He'd have broken sweet Ms. Molly, broken her with immense pleasure.

Either way, though, she was hiding something now. He'd known that even before she answered her front door. Her voice quavering all over creation had been the first give-away. He'd almost found out what she was protecting so fiercely, too. But he'd screwed up somehow this time. Next time he wouldn't. He'd crack her like a sweet almond.

Tasting the rain on the edge of his mouth, he smiled. Before Ms. Harris saw the last of him, he'd know all her secrets, one way or the other.

He hadn't Mirandized her. Hadn't really thought he should yet. But if she'd blurted out a confession, Thomas would have been royally pissed off, and rightly so.

It would have been his final foul-up with the chief. If Molly Harris had confessed to him, Harlan would have been lucky if Thomas had kicked his rear to Mount Vesuvius and let it fry there.

That would have been the best-case scenario.

He didn't want to think about the worst-case one.

Shrugging as he kicked at the tough saw grass and sandy

clumps near the pilings of the pier, Harlan frowned. In the grainy light, something glinted underneath the dock, caught between the rough slats.

Stepping carefully onto the mucky, spongy ground, he looked up at the bottom of the pier. There. He could see it glittering. Gold.

Holding on to the top of the pier with one hand and straining with the other, he swung one-handed out over the dark water and reached, grabbed and swung back to the shore again, the thin gold bracelet dangling from his fingers.

A prize. The catch was broken, snapped off. Only luck he'd seen the thing. He smiled. Luck.

"Hey, Ross?" Harlan beckoned the tall, red-haired, crime-scene technician over. "Look what I have." Holding the shiny chain up, he continued, "Tell Tanner I'll be through with Ms. Harris in about twenty minutes and we'll head back to town. I'm goin' to stroll up to the big house and ask one or two more questions," he said, mockingly swinging the bracelet in front of Ross's face. "Maybe I can hypnotize her into confessing, and we can all go home."

"Sure, boss, but the guys aren't anywhere near through down here. We baggied the victim's hands, collected some evidence off the pier, but a lot of stuff has washed away with the rain. I don't think we'll find the murder weapon unless a blood match shows up on that knife you wanted us to get. We're waiting on the search warrant on that. Should be here soon."

"Good." Harlan strode to the large white house glimmering ghostly in the rain and mist. In spite of everything that had happened, Molly Harris had chosen to stay in the family home. Interesting.

She was at the kitchen sink staring out at him as he approached. He heard the water running from the faucet, and thought of Lady Macbeth futilely washing her hands over and over again after the murder of the king.

Tapping on the screen door, he opened it without waiting for her invitation. "Ms. Harris?"

"Yes?" She cleared her throat.

A lovely throat it was, too, long and curving into her washed-out, winter-white sweatshirt with its gaping neckline. White was her color, all right. She looked like a pale nun, a streak of winter rain... He curbed his thoughts.

"I have three additional questions I need to ask you." Stepping into the white-and-black kitchen, Harlan watched her nervous step back, forward. He liked the fact that she was nervous. She should be. Keeping her nervous suited him. "If you don't mind?"

"Would it matter if I did? Should I call my lawyer?" That edgy animosity he'd caught earlier surfaced through her cool, husky voice. She was dragging herself together with an incredible effort, questions she should have asked him earlier now obviously coming to mind. Or maybe she'd decided how to play her role.

Either way, her struggle for control interested him. Under other circumstances, Molly Harris would be a woman with a certain sass and vinegar to her.

Sticking her hands under the water, never letting her gaze drift from his, she added, "I can, you know. I have a lawyer, and he can be here in thirty minutes. And I would still be considered a *cooperative* witness."

He'd been right. Ms. Harris had a dash of cayenne under all that fragile sweetness. Well, it was going to be fascinating to find out what else she had hidden. He was beginning to like the idea of discovering Molly Harris's secrets.

Coming closer, walking right up to the sink, he decided he liked, too, the way the washed-thin, rain-soaked sweatshirt clung to her small curves, skimming down her shoulders to mold her delicate breasts and outline their rain-chilled peaks. Where the sweatshirt rode up to her waist, caught there by the waistband, he could see the soaked and sandy rear end of her jeans, the ridged outline of her panties showing against the butter-soft denim.

He reached past her.

She shuddered but didn't step away.

Ms. Harris had courage, too.

Pushing down the faucet lever, he turned off the relentless gush of water. "Conservation, Ms. Harris," he murmured into her ear.

She leapt back, the toes of one bare foot tripping against the heel of the other. "What were your questions, Detective? I'll decide if I should call my lawyer. Ask your damned questions and then," she said, false civility riming her words, "please, get out of my house. Since you don't have a search warrant." One hand with its chewed nails crept toward her neckline until she realized what she was doing and jammed both hands into her pockets.

"Certainly," he said, matching her politeness. "And no, we don't have a search warrant. But it should arrive any minute."

She flinched, the wings of her shoulders drawing together as if he'd struck her.

"My questions are simple, really—should be no trouble for you to answer." He strolled around the room, looking, touching, knowing she was watching his every nonchalant move. He toed the dish of food on the floor. "You have a cat, hmm?"

"Is that one of the three questions?" The triangle of her face tightened, the skin around her full lips pinched with effort. Her wet hands dripped onto the black-and-white tiles.

Harlan moved.

She jumped.

Handing her a paper towel he'd torn off from the rack in back of her, he nodded. "Fair enough. All right. That's question number one."

Looking for a trick, she studied him. Her eyes changed

to a clear no-color, only that lovely, translucent shimmer of innocence shining in them. "No. I don't have a cat. I fed a stray this morning before you came."

"Did you now?" Indifferent once he'd learned what he wanted to know—the look of her when she was telling the truth—he turned his back to her. He glanced down the hall off the kitchen, but in the glass of the door he watched her reflection as he flicked the light switch. There was a very small, almost-imperceptible fleck of blood at the edge of the tab. But he saw it. Smelled the faint fetor of blood.

"Question number two?" She had wadded up the paper towel and clutched it between the small mounds of her breasts. Her hands were shaking again and her breasts trembled with the deep-down quaking he'd seen earlier.

"Ah, well, that's an easy one, number two is." Keeping his back turned, he reached into the pocket of his slacks.

Her shoulders hunched and her hands dropped to her sides, her suddenly relaxed fingers letting the wadded paper fall to her feet. She stooped to pick it up and he pivoted and moved in one step, trapping her while she was kneeling on the floor looking up at him.

"Do you know whose bracelet this is, Ms. Harris?" He held the gold chain in front of her.

She did. The dilation of her pupils gave her away. As he watched the blood drain from her face, he wondered distantly if she would lie.

Slowly, as if she'd aged thirty years in an instant, she rose to her feet and reached out to the shiny trinket. "Yes. It was my mother's. And then mine. Where did you find it? I wear it all the time."

She stopped, clamping her hands over her mouth, realization smacking her in the face.

"Well, Ms. Harris," he said, swinging the bracelet back and forth, "therein lies a tale." Pulling out a kitchen chair, he motioned for her to sit. "And since you've asked me a question, I'll answer it and add one more of my own. Sit down, Ms. Harris.'' He pushed her unresisting body into the chair.

Bonelessly she molded to the contours of the chair, in much the same fashion as her sweatshirt had shaped itself to her. "Go ahead." Her hands were clasped in front of her, so tightly Harlan had the impression that if she ever let go, she would shake apart, all control lost.

He was tempted for that instant to force her hands apart and see what happened. The craving to see Ms. Molly spinning out of control was becoming increasingly strong in him. Too strong. It would warp his judgment.

He placed the strip of gold on the table.

She didn't touch the bracelet.

"Before I tell you where we found this—" he traced it with his index finger and watched the muscles of her throat convulse once as she swallowed "—you tell me when you last wore it. Not a question, merely quid pro quo, as the man said.''

"You know I must have lost it yesterday." Defeat shivered in her murmured answer.

"Possibly. Or last night?"

He waited, but she didn't respond.

"Ah. Well, here's your answer, Ms. Harris. It was hanging underneath the boards of your dock. Caught there. Right below where the first of the bloodstains appear. Interesting, isn't it? But that's a rhetorical question, Ms. Harris, not one of my final two.''

Nodding, she didn't reply. He heard the click of her teeth, saw the narrow muscle along her jawline bunch into a small knot. She kept nodding.

"Question number three. Why did you fire your maid, who was also your friend?''

Still fisted, her small hands banged onto the table. The

thin circlet bounced. "I don't have to answer that." The nails were chewed right into the cuticle.

Stress. Fear.

Guilt.

He stroked her narrow index finger, touching the ragged cuticle and staring into her eyes as he asked his last question. Very gently, so gently that he knew he surprised her, he said, "Question number four. If you wear that bracelet all the time, Ms. Harris, and you were inside sleeping the entire night, how did this bracelet get from your wrist—" he held up her right wrist, the bones as thin as the wishbone of a chicken, that easily snapped "—to the dock underneath Camina Milar while she was being murdered?"

CHAPTER THREE

Back and forth, the gold chain swung from Detective Harlan's fingers.

Needing it as a reminder of all that she'd lost, she'd never taken the bracelet off, not even when she showered. She'd grown so accustomed to the feel of the metal on her skin that she no longer paid attention to it unless it snagged against her clothes. With her wrist cuffed in John Harlan's strong fingers, Molly wondered why she hadn't missed the bracelet this morning. Surely she should have noticed its absence from around her wrist.

But she hadn't noticed much of anything, apparently. Hadn't noticed herself strolling downstairs and picking up the butcher knife and—what?

She knew one fact that the harsh-faced man in front of her didn't. The bracelet had been around her wrist when she'd gone to bed.

"Detective Harlan," she began, fighting the cold numbness spreading through her, "are you arresting me?" She no longer had the will or the ability to fight him, not with the bracelet swaying in front of her, slipping around and around the detective's long finger as he idly swung the gleaming strand and watched her with those opaque, gold eyes.

In that instant as he studied her with that unnerving, silent assessment, Molly had the oddest fancy that his eyes would glow in the dark.

She shook her head.

At some point in the last year she'd gone mad. There was no other explanation.

In the loneliness of the long days and nights since violence had ripped through her home, she'd lost whole chunks of her life. She no longer understood herself or her behavior. Her competent, organized existence had vanished the night she'd walked in and found her parents lying in the blood-spattered kitchen. Since that night, nothing about her life had been normal.

She understood nothing, felt nothing except the panic of an ever-tightening noose around her neck.

With her free hand she grabbed the neckline of her sweatshirt. It was so tight. "Are you arresting me?"

"I haven't decided yet, Ms. Harris." His smile taunted her. Still capturing her wrist in his warm fingers, he returned the piece of jewelry to the table, staring at it as it snaked across the bleached pine. Tipping his head toward the chain but not looking at her, he asked, "How much does a bauble like this cost, Ms. Harris? Two thousand?"

"I don't know. My father gave it to my mother for their twenty-fifth anniversary." Wearily she answered his question, understanding that he was listening for nuances of tone, looking for motives. Motives strong enough to send her out in the night to murder her friend. "I never asked."

"Really? How very *un*curious of you, Ms. Harris." And now he looked down at her and smiled, a cold, calculating smile. "Three thousand, maybe?" His smile let her know he knew almost to the penny how much the bracelet had probably cost.

"I don't know," Molly insisted. She'd been right. Detective Harlan was playing games with her. She was out of her league. She tried to separate their joined hands but lacked even the strength to do that. She found a disturbing comfort in the chain of his fingers around her wrist. It was, after all, a human touch, the beat of his pulse hard and fast against her own racing beat, their two pulses joined in a momentary mating that thundered in her ears.

That was *real*—the sound of her own heart pounding to the beat of his, male to female in her sterile, clean kitchen, the sound of her blood dancing to the rhythm of his.

She'd been wandering for so long in a land where she no longer knew what was real, what was illusory, that Harlan's hard grip around her wrist gave her a peculiar solace. She could understand for the first time the way captives began to turn to their captors, sunflower to the slow-moving sun overhead.

As the thought flashed through her mind, he pivoted and stared at her, his golden brown eyes fixed unblinking on her face. She was lost in the swirling depths of their changing color, the deepening, darkening pupils, and she sighed, willing for the moment to surrender to the darkness pulling at her.

So much easier. He'd told her it would be. Told her in his low voice that once she told him everything, she could sleep, rest. And she wanted to, needed to. He'd known the need driving her and spoken to it, seduced her with that promise, seduced her with the gleam in his gold eyes. Her head was falling forward; she was tumbling into that golden darkness, falling willingly, knowing she would finally find peace once she gave up her struggle.

She'd resisted that seduction earlier, summoned the last of her waning strength and will, but now... He'd promised her she could sleep. He'd promised her everything would be easier if she told him her secrets. Caught in the glow of his eyes, mesmerized by the pulse beat drumming loudly in her ears, Molly opened her mouth to tell him—tell him *everything*.

But the pounding, it turned out, was only the red-haired man she'd seen earlier at the bayou banging on her screen door. An illusion, after all.

Letting her wrist drop to the table, Harlan turned to the man, annoyance thick in his soft tones. "Well, damn you to hell, Ross. Your timing is…'' He stopped and fingered the bracelet before he continued in a milder voice. ''I hope to hell you have the damn search warrant.''

Drawing a shaky breath, Molly stood up. She glanced from the intruder to Harlan and back. It would be more comfortable to talk with the second man. There was nothing intense, nothing threatening in his open face. ''You're going to search my house?''

''Yes, ma'am.'' Ross looked sheepish. ''John was waiting for the warrant. It's here.''

Pressing her clenched fists into her eyes, Molly waited. Footsteps clattered on her kitchen tiles, moved through her halls.

She'd been here when the police had searched the house after the murder of her parents. Today the familiar sounds were worse. She knew they wouldn't find anything. She had done *nothing*, nothing. She sank into a chair and covered her face.

Suspended in an emotional limbo, she drifted, not marking time, barely aware of the sounds and people around her. Except once, when the hairs on her arm rose as someone strode past her. Without looking up, she knew it was John Harlan. He'd stamped her with awareness of him. She'd know him in the dark of a moonless night. He went into the hall, and she sank back into the stupor that had enveloped her when he'd held up the bracelet. At some level she knew she couldn't stay like this forever, but for the moment, while the intruders tramped through her home, violating it in their own ways, she was protected by the heavy numbness muffling her.

Voices from a distance, faint.

More time passed.

''You got the Luminol, Ross?''

''Hell, no. Scott's got it.''

The hiss of an aerosol sprayer.

"Looky here, boys. No, not there. The pinpoints don't mean squat. Over here, this big area. Ain't it purty?"

She recognized the long, thin fingers pulling her hands away from her eyes.

"Ms. Harris, you need to call your lawyer." Detective John Harlan was staring at her with a curious, satisfied gleam in his eyes.

Morning had become afternoon. Afternoon, evening. And in the gloom of the rainy day and the evening darkness, all around her in the kitchen, areas of light glowed eerily. On the floor, on the wall, on the light switch.

"Blood, Ms. Harris. Traces show up with Luminol even when things have been washed down." Harlan held up the butcher knife. It glowed around the crevice where the metal joined the wood.

Light blinded her as one of the technicians flipped the lights on.

"I told you I cut my hand." She held up her clenched hands.

"Yes. I know you said that." He was so gentle with her that she wanted to lean against his wide shoulder and weep. She'd been alone so long in unending twilight.

She actually swayed toward him. "Can I trust you?" she whispered, touching his broad chest. The thump of his heart against her hand was important to her in all the illusion. Underneath his black silk shirt, he was warm, safe. She wanted to laugh at that idea, but the reality of his heat against the palm of her hand drew her anyway. "If I tell you everything, will you help me? Can I trust you?" she repeated from the depths of her confusion and despair, wanting to tell him she was afraid she was losing her mind.

"If you're smart, you won't. You should trust your lawyer, not me. I'm not here to help you, Ms. Harris. That's not what I want." His eyes held hers, warning her. "You know, you never answered my last question, Ms. Harris," he said in his deep voice. "How did the bracelet you say you always wear wind up underneath the exact spot where Ms. Milar was killed?"

"I don't know, I don't know," Molly whispered, shoving away the memories and anchoring herself to the beat of his heart.

"Call your lawyer, Ms. Harris." He looked at her with a chilly pity. "You need him. The sooner the better. Because I'm going to find out the answer to that last question. And when I do, I'll send you to prison. For life. Or to the electric chair." The pity turned his eyes dark gold. "Call your lawyer."

A sudden sizzle between them, as if a current had suddenly been turned on. "Yes. All right." She stumbled toward the phone, but she couldn't remember where it was.

His hands firm and strong, he turned her toward the wall. "I told you I don't like murderers. And, Ms. Harris," he said, his voice once more oddly formal, "I think behind your pretty face you're a stone-cold killer."

"A murderer?"

"Yeah." The rigid planes of his face as cruel as those of any Inquisition judge, he motioned to the phone.

She could see the phone moving on the wall, toward her, away from her, shrinking, disappearing into the darkness that swooped over her and carried her at last into the peace she'd been seeking.

"Hell, John. Look what you've done."

Harlan looked at the woman he held in his arms. He'd caught her as she sagged quietly to the floor, her silvery eyes locked on his blinking ones and then shutting as she took one step forward and collapsed into his arms like sea foam blown across the waves.

"What are you going to do with her?" Ross scratched his head and the red tufts sprang up. "She didn't call her lawyer."

"I know." He looked at the fine tracery of blue veins in her eyelids, at the heavy smudges under her eyes. "I guess I'd look silly as hell carrying her into the station slung over my shoulder, wouldn't I?" She scarcely weighed anything. He could feel her rib cage against his hands, her breath moving through her erratically.

"*Po*lice harassment, John, that's what it would look like. 'Course, she has enough money to hire a tag team of lawyers to sue the department, too, my man. And you're on the chief's list of people he'd most like to roast over an open fire and carve up afterward."

"Yeah, there's that, too. So, Ross, you think she murdered that woman?" Harlan stood for a moment not quite sure where to head with his insubstantial burden. Her rapid, shallow breathing sent puffs of air against his chin. Achingly sweet, her breath.

Ross was right. There were layers of issues to be considered here.

"Oh, I'd guess she did. Who else? Her bracelet down at the crime scene, her fingerprints for sure all over the knife. All the evidence seems to point right at her, straight as an arrow."

Struck by Ross's comment, Harlan paused. "It does, doesn't it? Very clearly. We'd have to be stupid to miss all the clues, wouldn't we?"

"What're you saying, boss?" More tufts of red sprang loose from the rain-flattened curls as Ross attacked his hair in bewilderment.

"I don't know. I need to think about this some more." He could smell the sweetness of her shampoo rising up from her hair. Or maybe it was the sweetness of her skin. Her lower lip trembled, its soft fullness oddly vulnerable to him as he watched her with her guard down.

"The fingerprints aren't really important, John. Leastwise, I don't think so. You said she even picked it up when y'all walked into the kitchen, so fingerprints won't mean much, not with a good lawyer, I reckon. 'Course, our guy'll insist she was smart enough to pick it up and give a reason for her prints. But, hell, John, I don't know.''

Harlan carried Molly into the living room and settled her on the cream-colored cotton sofa. "Go upstairs and get a blanket, Ross. There's not a damned thing down here to cover her up with." He brushed her face. "She's like ice. That's all we need—having her go into shock on us while we're questioning her. Hell, this is a fouled-up mess."

Her mouth parted in a sigh as his thumb lingered against the deep curve of her lower lip. He lifted his hand away. Not smart to touch her, he knew that. He didn't want to touch her delicate face, and scarcely comprehended the impulse that drove him as he brushed a strand of light brown hair away from her pointed chin.

Carrying a brilliant red-and-pink comforter, Ross returned. "You really think she's guilty, boss? She's awfully pretty." Glancing down at Molly, Ross handed the quilt to Harlan.

"Hell, Ross, you know better than that. What she looks like means diddly except to a jury. Looking like an angel at the left hand of God will sure help her if this goes to trial." He watched the flutter of her eyelashes, those spiky, thick frames for her remarkable eyes. He wanted her awake, awake so the false innocence in her gray-blue eyes would remind him not to let his guard down.

Harlan wrapped Molly up in the bright quilt, its brilliance bleaching her already drained face of any remaining color.

Ross shook his head regretfully as he looked at the small bump that was Molly Harris under the quilt. "You believe she's our killer, huh? That teeny girl?"

Smoothing her hair back from her face once more, Harlan nodded. "Yeah. Actually, I do. But I don't like the fact that the evidence is being handed to us on a silver platter."

"Most victims know their killers."

Irritated somehow by the oft-repeated cop fact, Harlan raked his hands through his hair. "I know. But it makes me uncomfortable when a case looks this simple." And something about her alibi for her parents' murder needled his intuition and irritated him. Well, it would come to him.

Harlan tucked the comforter around her narrow, bare feet. A few grains of sand sprinkled into his hands as he moved her toes.

Dried sand, caught between her toes. He brushed her feet carefully, and more grains drifted into his hands. The bottoms of her feet were scratched. Several small cuts crisscrossed the smooth soles. Shell cuts. Weed abrasions.

Possibly from the shells dotting the shore of the bayou.

"Damn, boss." Ross shifted uneasily. "This doesn't look good. I wish to hell she'd called her lawyer before she keeled over."

"Me, too." Harlan stretched, arching his back as he fought the contradictory urges to shake Ms. Molly Harris awake and to wrap her tighter in the warmth of her cheerful quilt until its brightness bled into her wan face.

A whimper, faint but audible, escaped her. Her mouth moved as if she were trying to say something, but no words came out. Harlan had the strangest feeling she was screaming, but he frowned, troubled by the idea of Molly Harris silently screaming somewhere in the darkness.

He considered the idea. If she'd done what he thought she had, she should be screaming. And if she hadn't...

Reaching a decision, he rose. "I'll be damned if I like this case one little bit. It stinks to high heaven. I mean, I love messy cases, but not where I get the real strong sense that somebody's doing my work for me. Let's give the crime-lab boys a chance to do their thing, pin down time of death, do the blood typing, and then we'll visit Ms. Harris again. We don't have to arrest her today. She's not going

anywhere." Harlan watched the rapid lift and fall of the
quilt over Molly's breasts, the shuddering movement touching him in spite of the Luminol glowing in the kitchen, the
evidence proclaiming the innocence in her eyes a sham.

Blood had been spilled here. Spilled and washed down.
Old blood. Fresh blood.

More blood than a bad cut would produce.

He glanced at her small hand, where the line of the wound
was obscene against the smoothness of her skin. It was a
nasty cut. Lifting her palm, he studied the cut again.

There was something odd about the way the wound came
around the base of her thumb, but he couldn't figure out
what.

He wanted to take her into the station for questioning,
photograph the wound and see if the samples of the blood
from the wooden handle matched hers or Camina Milar's.

She whimpered again, her mouth opening in that silent
scream. Smoothing his rumpled hair, Harlan dismissed the
feeling that somewhere, locked in the darkness of her unconscious, Molly Harris was screaming for help. Too fan-
ciful. He wanted to leave her soft mouth with its maybe
screams behind him. Wanted to get back to work. Knowing
he was stupid for doing so, he touched her mouth briefly,
his finger pressing lightly into the defenseless contours.

"So, what's the plan, boss?"

Harlan looked away from Molly Harris and the spread of
her shiny hair against her couch and reached his decision.
"I'm going back to the station. You catch a ride with Tanner, but I want one of you to stay with Ms. Harris until she
comes to. You, preferably. If you can?"

"Sure. I'll work something out. No problem." Ross
grinned. "Hell, this is the closest I've come to having a date
in a month of Sundays. I reckon I can hang around here
awhile."

"Good." Harlan heard the tiny whimper again, and it

disturbed him. Molly Harris was getting under his skin, when all he wanted was to see her in jail, where he figured she belonged. "Call the medic and have him hang around, too, Ross, okay?"

Ross nodded and reached for his walkie-talkie.

As he studied Molly Harris's unconscious form, the pain moving over her face like shadows slipping across the moon, Harlan's uneasiness deepened. He couldn't escape the impression that he was missing something important about her. And he damn sure didn't like the feeling that he wanted to stay with her.

He wanted to banish Molly Harris from his thoughts, wanted to roar down her driveway and leave her behind, never giving her another thought. And yet he wanted to keep touching her cool, satiny skin until it warmed, wanted to see her face soft and gazing up at him—

The latter instinct was so strong that he had to restrain himself from heading for the door in two long strides. He rubbed the last of the clinging grains of sand from his hands. Ms. Harris had been walking barefoot in sand and brush, that much was for sure. He sighed.

"The medic's on his way up from the bayou."

Harlan shrugged, his still-damp jacket sticking to his slacks. "From the looks of her, Ross, I figure she's suffering from stress and exhaustion, but have him check her out. Then you stay out of the way until she's awake. If the medic thinks she's having any problems, get her to the hospital ASAP, got it? I don't want any complaints about this case. Understand?" He frowned, that odd reluctance to leave keeping him where he stood despite his better judgment.

"Got it in one, boss." Waggling a skinny arm, Ross waved him on his way. "Go on along, lil' dogie."

Harlan laughed. "You been hanging around the cowboy crew again, Ross?" From the corner of his eye, he caught the shiver of Molly Harris's hair, tea against the cream of the couch.

"Yup." Ross tipped back an imaginary hat. "You'd be surprised what you can learn from that bunch of ramblers, boss."

"Yeah? Watch it. Those dudes can get you in trouble." Harlan glanced around Molly's living room once more. It had a surprising familiarity. The pictures in the file had frozen the room's dimensions in his mind, but even the white on white of its furniture resonated inside him, like a faraway chime on a still afternoon. "Well." He shrugged. "I'm gone, Ross. Check in with me after you finish here."

Once more the kitchen was dark. Walking through the room's eerie Luminol glow, Harlan stared at the dirty cat-food plate. It was the only messy thing in Molly Harris's kitchen. He reached down and picked up the plate, carrying it to the sink, where he rinsed it. He opened the dishwasher and slid the plate between two rubber-coated prongs.

A glass. Two cups. One plate. In a rinsed-out pan, a fragment of milk scum clung like cobwebs to the edge.

Ms. Harris had made herself hot milk sometime last night.

He glanced around at the well-equipped kitchen. New appliances. Refrigerator. Stove. Pausing, he frowned. Why hadn't she heated her milk in the microwave?

Harlan took the pan out of the dishwasher and carried it to the stove. Placing it on the grate above the gas burner, he thought for a moment.

She would have been in the kitchen, heating her milk. Sleepless, wanting hot milk so she could fall asleep at some point during the long night.

As if he could see her, a small, solitary form in the night moving slowly about her kitchen, he knew that.

At the stove, he looked up and straight out toward the dock.

In the gray half-light of the rainy winter evening, he could see the dark band of the bayou, the wooden finger of the rickety pier jutting into the water.

At night, what would she have seen?

The glow of Camina's cigarette. Molly would have seen that bit of light. If she'd been up, wandering through her house, she would have seen the red glow of Camina's cigarettes.

Turning away from the window overlooking the sink and the bayou, Harlan faced the microwave. His back was to the bayou and the long, empty expanse of lawn.

In the glass door of the microwave, shadows moved behind him, reflections like ghosts shimmering in back of him, watching him.

No, she wouldn't have used the microwave at night. She wouldn't have wanted to turn her back on all that darkness.

He knew that about her. He didn't know how he knew, but he did.

That ability to leap from *A* to *Z* was part of his luck. One of the things that made him a good cop. One of the things that made the chief crazy, because Harlan couldn't explain it.

He didn't know where the knowledge came from. He'd always had it. Not being given to flights of fancy, he tried not to examine the source of his knowing. He didn't believe in psychic mumbo jumbo, but even so, some things were better left unexplained, even for a cop whose intuition had always given him an edge.

He didn't like mysteries, though—especially when they were his own. So intuition was as good an explanation as any.

Glancing around the kitchen one last time, he knew Molly Harris had roamed through her kitchen last night, had her cup of milk and had gone outside. The knowledge was just there, inside him.

Stepping out onto the gallery, he looked down the rain-swept lawn toward the driveway and saw Tanner waiting beside the car. Walking toward him, Harlan turned once and stared back at the house encircled by moss-heavy oak trees, the moss hanging wet and gray in long loops.

The first-floor gallery, unscreened, wrapped the lower portion of the house. Off the rooms upstairs, a second gallery ran from the sides of the house all around to the back. With no outside staircases, that gallery was accessible only from the inside rooms opening onto it. On the tall, floor-to-ceiling windows at the front of the house, the drapes and shades were drawn back. He saw the light shining on the table next to the sofa, saw Molly Harris's red-and-pink quilt, imagined the thin line of her arm hanging down to the wooden floor. Imagined her soft mouth open in silent pleading.

The house had been closed off from outside eyes when he and Ross had first driven up. He'd thought it secretive as they drove up the winding driveway hedged by enormous double yellow hibiscus bushes. Climbing into his car and nodding to Tanner, who wandered back down toward the bayou, where bright searchlights sliced the dark, Harlan decided that Molly must have opened the shutters and pulled back the drapes when she'd fled back to the house after his earlier questioning.

He'd fought the urge to pursue her to the house.

Just as he now disregarded the sense that he should turn around and go back to her house.

Stay with her.

She'd been defenseless in his arms as he'd carried her past the open gallery into the huge, empty house.

Trying to ease the tightness between his shoulder blades, Harlan rolled his shoulders.

Firing up the engine, he let it idle for a long time as he continued to stare at the house, at the image of Molly in the long window facing him, the light shining down on her, while outside, night crept silently closer. Finally, he shifted into first and drove away, the rain blurring the windshield.

Stay with her.

The shoulder harness pulling against his chest, he turned and saw the house disappear behind him into the sheeting rain. Just before he looked back at the driveway, he frowned.

He thought he'd seen a shape move at the corner of the house.

Molly woke up abruptly, her heart pounding sickeningly.

The gleam of the lamp on the table turned the man's hair carroty.

Her pulse slowed as she recognized him. He'd been here with Detective Harlan. She turned her head.

No one else was in the room.

Her mouth was dry—sleepy dry, not the cotton dry of fear. She wet her lips. They were cracked.

She yawned. She'd slept the afternoon through. Unbelievable. Perhaps she ought to see if the man wanted to Molly-sit in the evenings.

"Hey there, Ms. Harris."

Struggling to rise, Molly found she was cocooned in her quilt, the wild hues splashing the somber, clean whiteness of her living room with streaks of reddish color.

Pushing the quilt away, she gagged, remembering the dark stains against Camina's blouse, remembering other stains. "Where is everyone?"

"All gone. Harlan told me to stay until you woke up. The doc checked you out. You keeled over like a chopped tree and went right to sleep. Doc said to let you sleep, that you'd wake up in your own good time."

"I was asleep?" She wanted verification. "Did I..." How could she ask him if she'd gotten up, draped in her comforter, and roamed her house, eyes open wide but her mind asleep, off guard?

"Relax. You never said a word." His grin was wide and uncomplicated.

She'd been right. Nothing hidden in this man, unlike John Harlan with his enigmatic flashes of irony, his comments that implied more than they said. She shivered and pulled the comforter over her shoulders. She was glad the redhead had stayed with her. She didn't like the idea of waking up and knowing that the detective had watched her in her sleep, watched her while she was vulnerable. She shivered again.

"I just...slept?" Molly huddled into the quilt, relieved.

"Oh, you squeaked a few times, like you were trying to say something. That's all." He stood up and stretched his long arms toward the ceiling. "John said to check in with him when you came to. I'm supposed to tell you not to take any out-of-town trips." He shifted uncomfortably. "I'm supposed to tell you also that John will be back tomorrow. You'll need to have your lawyer with you. If you want, you can come into the station instead, though." He wrinkled his face, too young and embarrassed to be comfortable confronting her with their suspicions.

"Yes. Of course." Molly cleared her throat. "Why didn't Detective Harlan arrest me today?"

"Well, you'll have to ask him, ma'am. Tomorrow," the redhead said reassuringly. "I don't think he was afraid you'd run off, though. You aren't going to, are you?" Worry creased his freckle-splotched face. "Because Harlan would kill me if he thought I hadn't made it clear that you were only being questioned, ma'am, not arrested. No cause to do anything foolish, ma'am."

"Not yet, anyway?" Molly managed a laugh. It wouldn't have fooled John Harlan, its high pitch patently false even to her own ears, but the young technician smiled back in relief.

"Well, good night then, ma'am. You want to lock up behind me?"

Wrapped in her quilt, Molly still felt shivers edging bump by bump up her spinal column. "Oh, yes. I'll see you out through the kitchen." Rising too quickly to her feet, she was momentarily dizzy, but she steadied herself on the arm of the couch. "Do you mind waiting with me here while I close the drapes and lock up?" She shot him an easygoing smile, not letting on how desperately she wanted him to stay in her house all night while she slept. This young man. But not John Harlan. She wouldn't have slept had he remained behind.

"Nope, I don't mind. You want some help?" He walked toward the front door.

"No. Thanks, anyway. It will only take me a second more down here." She had to check the locks herself. She didn't trust anyone else, not even this blue-eyed young cop.

While Ross Whittaker—he'd told her his name—waited, Molly went through her nightly routine. With him by her side, she felt safe from the fear that she was whirling off into some world she'd never escape from.

Ross Whittaker was so normal that he made her believe during these moments that she'd imagined everything that had happened to her in the last months.

Made her forget until she saw him out the kitchen door and bolted it behind him.

In the windows over the sink, the darkness edged close to the house, pushing at the walls, seeking entrance.

Moments earlier, with Whittaker here, she'd forgotten the way the moss in the trees nearest the gallery moved with the breeze, shadows on shadows in the darkness.

Quickly she checked the window over the sink and closed the shutters against the night. She shuddered.

She was afraid to go up the stairs to bed. She'd checked

the upstairs with Whittaker, but now she couldn't make herself go back up the dark hallway.

She should have left a light on. Why hadn't she? She'd been trying too hard to be normal, the way she'd been before, afraid of nothing, ready for any new experience.

Standing in the kitchen, staring at the back staircase, Molly fingered the satin binding of the quilt. Could she make herself climb up into that thick darkness, darkness pressing with a palpable weight down the long tunnel of the stairs?

Prowling through the rain-wet grass, he eased his way to the house.

She was awake.

He'd watched her for so long now that he knew her, knew her with an age-old knowing that went bone deep. He knew her. From the beginning, he'd recognized her. She was the one he'd been waiting for all this time.

He knew that she wouldn't sleep tonight. He circled the gallery silently, avoiding the flowerpots lining the edge of the gallery, skirting the board that creaked with his weight. Circled, coming closer to her.

He could see her now, the gilt brown of her hair. Could smell her fragrance, the light, familiar scent drifting to him in the rainy night.

The scent had clung to her hair. Familiar, that fragrance, drawing him closer to her.

Molly heard the sound.

The bump against the house raised gooseflesh along her arms and she couldn't move. This time she couldn't open the door, even though she told herself that the noise was nothing. The stray cat, probably. A raccoon. Nothing more than that.

But she couldn't move. And she was wide awake—she

knew she was. She wasn't sleepwalking. She wasn't imagining that slow, muffled sound against the walls of her house.

God help her, the sound was real. Something wanting in.

If she could move, she could reach for the phone. She would call…someone.

Then there was silence.

Heavy. Expectant.

She screamed as the huge shadow leapt from behind her, darkness flowing past her and onto the counter.

Clutching the quilt to her shoulders, Molly couldn't stop the screams ripping through her even as his head butted her chin and he stretched on his back legs, curling a smooth front paw against her cheek.

Even when the big cat rubbed against the goose bumps on her arm, his solid body vibrating to soundless rumbles, even while she clung to him and buried her face against the powerful muscles of his sides, she couldn't stop screaming.

CHAPTER FOUR

His eyes snapped open.

She had been screaming.

Against the ceiling of Harlan's room, the shadows of palm fronds swayed and lifted restlessly.

The overhead fan stirred the fringes of his Guatemalan wall hangings, puffed the fabric. Muted in the dark, the jungle figures became alive with the currents of air.

Sweat beaded down the length of his chest, pooled in his navel as he lay naked under the drifting shadows and watched them move. Never turning his head, he studied the palm-tree silhouettes, their gray, two-dimensional forms on the video of his ceiling.

She had been screaming.

As he watched, time trembled, hung suspended, and there was nothing but utter silence outside his open window.

Then, with a downward whoosh, sound filled the void. The slam of a car door two streets over. A rustling in the grass. The slip of his sweat sliding against his skin. He ran his palms over his chest, down his thighs and let his arms fall shoulder height out to the side, his feet crossed at the ankles. A crucified figure from Roman times, he lay on the sweat-damp sheet, thinking. Impressions moved in and out of his mind. He slicked his hands down his chest and recalled her hands moving over him. Dreams. Her small palms stroking him. Reality.

Things were happening, rushing out of control. He sensed that.

And evil slipped through the darkness. Face averted, it hesitated, and moved on. But it was there. It would return.

She had been screaming.

His abdominal muscles contracted, lengthened, as he sat up on the wide rosewood bed and swung his legs to the floor. With one step he was at the bare window, looking down into the courtyard of his apartment building.

The rain had stopped. Clouds scudded across the moon, hiding it, and in the fitful light, the underwater globes of the empty pool backlit leaves floating on the surface. Empty deck chairs humped in four-foot stacks against the wooden fence draped with flame vine. In the daytime, the bright orange flowers would glow. Now, in the uneasy gloom, they were shapes against the fence, bleached of color by the night.

He remembered the vague sense of something moving stealthily at the corner of Molly's house as he pulled away.

His skin prickled.

He should have stayed with Molly Harris.

Punching in numbers on the phone, he shifted the receiver from one ear to the other as he paced around the room. He rubbed his belly and waited for Ross to answer. His gut was twisting in knots.

"Yeah, it's me." Harlan shifted the receiver back to his right ear. "So you can go back to sleep after you hang up. You're young. You won't miss five minutes of sleep. You'll get no sympathy from me." Grabbing a pair of jeans from a ladder-back chair, he shrugged into them. The zipper was cold against his skin as he bent over and rummaged for his boots under the bed. "So how long did you stay at Ms. Harris's lovely abode? Yeah? Anything happen after you left? Any phone calls? No? Well, I'll be damned." Thick socks on, he eased his feet into boots, balancing easily on one foot at a time. "No, no problem. Go back to sleep, Ross. Thinking about it, I reckon you do need your beauty rest. I'll catch you up later." Harlan plunked the receiver back onto the phone base.

In seconds he'd thrust his head and arms through a black T-shirt and had reached for his wallet and shoulder holster. Hooking a thin, black leather bomber jacket with one finger, he turned to look back at the bed.

Twisting and turning in his sheets, he'd thought of Molly Harris with him there, the softness of her breasts against his hungry mouth, her skin hot against him, her fragrance rising to him....

It had been a long time since he'd allowed himself to want a woman.

But he wanted her.

Remembering, he twisted the doorknob with his fingers, their tensile strength hard against the cool metal.

Yeah. He wanted sweet, murderous Molly Harris.

The door rattled in its frame even though he shut it gently. Moving in the shadows down to the parking lot, he looked around before getting into his car. Nothing.

He left the top up and opened up the V-8 engine full throttle down the dark, untraveled back roads leading to her house, hanging curves, riding the power as the car vibrated under him.

Turning off the engine at the bottom of her drive, he coasted, lights out, until the sports car rolled quietly to a stop under a large magnolia tree. The shadows of its leaves dappled the long hood of the car as the moon moved between cloud banks. Harlan shut off the interior light and stepped out of the car, snicking the door closed behind him.

Ahead of him, lights blazed in wild abandon from Molly Harris's home. With country silence all around him, those lights shouted discordantly.

Harlan cocked his head.

The tick of the cooling engine in back of him.

He waited, listening.

A gust of wind turning the leaves. Rain dripping onto her gallery. The slap of the bayou against the dock pilings.

Way off, the susurrus of water on sand.

And then he heard her, heard her slow breathing. From her kitchen.

Slipping silently through the grass, moving up to the gallery at the back of her house, Harlan tracked the sound. He stopped below the gallery and vaulted soundlessly to the far end of the gallery and stooped there in the corner, observing her through the gap between the shutters and the edge of the window.

Shards of glass sparkled on the floor. Flung from one end of the room to the other, pans tilted crazily, lay upside down. One pot careened on a stove burner. Cupboard doors hung open, and a pile of sugar rose on the counter. In the middle of the chaos, Molly stood, curiously stationary, her chest rising and falling in a slow, regular rhythm. In one hand she held a broom, in the other a dustpan.

It was her face that fascinated him.

Serene, it was as empty as the tide-washed sand at early morning. And despite the upheaval, that slow breathing... Disturbing, that subtle movement of her breasts under her pajama top.

She let the dustpan and broom fall from her hands. They clattered to her feet and she looked down at them absently, her unchanging expression blank and empty. Her hands dangling at her side, she approached the kitchen door.

Two clicks. First one bolt, then the other.

One hand on the gallery ledge, Harlan rolled to the ground below, disappearing from the corner as the door opened and Molly stepped out. Barefoot, not looking around her, she walked in a straight line away from the house, away from the bright lights and the wide-open kitchen door behind her.

Trailing her, Harlan stepped where she had stepped, moved when she did. A cloud drifted over the moon and he moved closer to her in the darkness. Her gaze fixed on the winding ribbon of the bayou, she never looked down at the scratchy shells, the muddy edge of the sand, never looked around to see him, stalking her.

And the rhythm of her breathing never altered until she stopped at the water's edge, where Camina Milar's body had been found. Bending smoothly under the rippling yellow tape that marked off the murder scene, she walked to the dock where Camina had been killed.

A wraith under the fitful moon, Molly Harris seemed to float onto the pier as Harlan watched. Clouds dropped lower, darker. Lifting his head, slanting it, Harlan smelled the approaching rain. Before morning it would come streaking out of the sky again.

Grass parted over the toes of his boots as he edged toward the dock. A slim, pale figure, motionless, she faced out to the water, which moved darkly past. Her scent drifted downwind to him as he slipped closer, the hunt pulling him forward.

He wondered for an instant when he stepped out of the shadows below her whether he'd startled her or if she'd known all along that he was pursuing her. Almost as if she expected him, Molly Harris turned slowly to him, the hems of her white pajama bottoms drooping over the narrow, high arches of her feet, bunching and catching under her bare heels.

Stopping twenty feet away, head angled toward her, Harlan watched her hair lift as she pivoted, the dark strands sliding back to her cheeks in slow motion.

She hadn't seen him.

Her hands outstretched, she looked down at them, frowned, and turned back to the water, stepping closer to the edge of the dock. She swayed forward.

Pausing in the wet grass at the side of the pier, Harlan wondered if she were going to jump in. He didn't move. If

he had to, he could reach her, and so curiosity kept him
motionless, observing her.

The rising wind molded the pajama top against her, flipping the triangular point of the collar flat against her long
neck. Stroking her as his hands had in his dreams, the wind
shaped the baggy top into the dip of her waist and pressed
it to the outline of her small breasts. She swayed once more.

In that moment, adrenaline quickened his pulse, sent it
slamming into his throat. Adrenaline and desire commin-
gled, a twisting violence in his gut. He swallowed and slid
closer, near enough to grasp the splintered boards.

With one hand on the worn planks of the old dock, Harlan
boosted himself up, crouched at the foot of the dock and
waited to see what Molly Harris would do.

Her right hand rose, fell, and she looked around, an air
of bewilderment in the futile wave of her hand. She shook
her head and her hair swept out from her pointed chin as
she tilted toward the edge of the dock, her pale toes curling
over the end.

She didn't jump when he wrapped his arm around her
narrow waist, didn't struggle, barely reacted. Instead,
against all his expectations of what she might have done,
she turned slowly, so slowly, that her hip slid under his
fingers, the jutting point sharp and fragile against his spread
palm. Under the wing of her eyebrows, her empty eyes
gazed at him. "Hello." She reached out, touched him. Her
fingers were cool against his heated skin. For a moment,
something shifted in the blankness of her face. "Detective
Harlan?"

"Yes, Ms. Harris?" He angled his chin to the touch of
her slim hand.

She frowned, the smooth blankness crumpling for a moment as she struggled for words. "You're here."

"As you see." He spread her hand flat against his face.
The base of her thumb lay against his mouth and he cupped

her palm to his lips. He couldn't resist. In his dreams, she'd touched him like this. And more—those cool fingers running over his shoulders, his thighs, touching him everywhere until his heart had thundered, leaping out of his skin. "Yeah, I'm here. Like you, returning to the scene of the crime."

"Why?" Her words were clear, the low tone husky and torpid, a tape drawing tight in the sprockets of a recorder, slowing to a halt, distorted.

"I'm here. Sworn to serve and protect." He surprised himself.

"To protect?" Bewildered, she looked around her, glancing at the bare boards under her feet in confusion. Her head lifted as though against an enormous weight. "Detective Harlan?" she said again, and traced his mouth, his cheekbones, her fingers reading his face as if she were blind. "You're going to protect me?"

"Ah, so many questions, sweet Molly. Perhaps I should ask you what you're doing out here."

She didn't respond. The tips of her fingers stroked his eyebrows, down the hump of his broken nose.

Harlan shivered under her light touch. Not even in his dreams had he shivered like this, her delicate touch spearing hot to his groin. His arm, which had never left her narrow waist, clasped tighter against her inadvertent step backward off the dock as he moved forward, unable to stop himself. That curiosity that had held him motionless now urged him on, his hips bumping hers, his sex hard against her softness under the pajama bottoms.

He'd been so sure she'd step back.

She didn't.

And none of it made sense. Not her actions; certainly not his. Curiosity. Anger. Lust. All three, and pity—there was that, too. Pity for her lovely fragility, which would be broken. By him. By prison.

But still, careless to touch her like this under the dark sky when his defenses were lowered. Stupid. But she hadn't moved. She could have, oh, she could have. He would have turned her loose if she'd moved away from him. He could have turned her loose. Not easily, no—he recognized that even in the need flooding him. But he could have stepped aside. And would have, if she hadn't stayed so motionless, her empty silver eyes fixed on his as she outlined his mouth.

Hungry for the taste of her, cursing himself silently, even so he took her mouth, her fingers trapped between his lips, hers, sliding down his neck to catch in the collar of his jacket. He curled his free hand under her hair and clasped her neck, slipping his hand up to cup her head. Spreading his legs, he brought her closer into the cradle of his hips as he opened his mouth over hers. He touched the tip of his tongue to the corners of her lips, their cool taste water to the heat blazing through him. The taste of her was everything he'd dreamed, more. "Damn you," he muttered, swearing at himself, at her, furious with his own weakness. "Damn you to hell, sweet Molly."

"Oh, yes, I am. Damned. Cursed." Her whispered words vibrated against his mouth and he heard them, and like everything else tonight, they made no sense to him.

"Then so am I." With her whisper, her lips parted and he entered, taking the kiss deeper as she inhaled.

"Truly mad, after all," she murmured, swallowing, and he tightened like an arrow shot into the darkness of her being as she drew his tongue deeper. "Lost in darkness and mad, mad."

"Yes. But the sweetest madness." He groaned, echoing her words, scarcely attending them, knowing only that here, here in the touch of her against him, was what he'd been craving for longer than he could remember. From her waist, he curved his hand over her slender breast and stroked the delicate softness of her nipple. Swelling to him, that tiny pebble of her flesh rose hard under his index finger, as hard against him as he was against her, her flesh answering the urgent demand of his. He slid his thumb under a button of her top, seeking entrance there, too. Her mouth, her breasts, everywhere. He wanted to touch, to taste, to lose himself in her.

Bending her backward over his arm, unable now to leave the seductive swelling of her breast under his palm, he used his teeth to nudge a button loose and pushed the light fabric aside with his tongue, tasting her at last, her nipple pebbling under his tongue, its woman-sweetness against his mouth rendering him deaf and blind to everything except the taste of her. "Ah, Molly, Molly," he breathed, desire and hunger crouching in the darkness of his soul, springing against the bars.

In a wide V, the half-opened top slid back over her shoulders, her pale skin shimmering for an instant as the moon broke free of cloud-darkness. A flush moved over that pale skin and she was irresistible to him in that moment of half-light, half-darkness, as she raised her arms to him, her hands clinging to his neck, the chewed edges of her cuticles scraping in slow, electric tingles against his scalp.

Smooth alabaster against the black leather of his jacket, cool to his heat.

Against all caution, all judgment, he bent his knees, ready to lower her to the planks of the dock, to take her there. One knee jarred on the dock and she settled onto his thigh, pliant, willing woman, her knee bumping him where he burned the hottest. He *would* take her.

And yet...

And yet, her mouth, tender and inviting, was passive under his. Her eyes—those innocent, lying eyes—were open in that strange blankness where neither innocence nor lies found a home.

He bit her earlobe gently, tugging even as he tugged with his fingers at the nipple lying near his own heart. "Molly?

I want you. If you don't want to do this, tell me you want to stop. Say the words. I have to hear them. But tell me now. Yes. Or no.''

He waited.

Supple, bending to him, she didn't answer.

He could take her. And still look himself in the mirror in the morning. Could still clip the handcuffs on her and march her to jail. Her body sang to him, gave its consent to the swoop of his hand over her spine and down to the gentle curve of her rear, gave consent to the pull of his arms drawing her so tight against his arousal that he felt the flimsy barrier of panties underneath her pajama bottoms.

And beneath him in the underwater gleam of moonlight and clouds, her eyes were blank and empty, the spiky eyelashes fluttering.

He could take her. His ethics were that flexible these days. Reluctantly, he'd been drawn to her from the first instant she'd opened her door. In spite of everything he believed about her, his body craved her in this moment as if she were the breath in his lungs. He couldn't remember when he'd last wanted someone as intently as he wanted Molly Harris.

Never, he decided, as he brushed his knuckle down her throat and her skin flushed beneath his touch. Primitive, his reaction to her. Instinctive, hers to him.

He would have no compunction about bending his rules this once. If she were willing, he would give them both that pleasure of the small death. He let his knuckle drift over her taut nipple and down to her belly button. Her stomach muscles clenched at his touch.

Willing, indeed. His groin tightened, and in automatic response, his pelvis rocked against her, once, twice, the rhythm pulsing to his brain, their bodies cleaving, male to female, in an urgent, ancient language of blood. Sweet heaven. A matched pair, he and Ms. Molly. Pleasure, indeed. Lost in that long-denied pleasure, he rocked once more, a groan rumbling deep in his throat at the exquisite feel of her against him.

And yet...

Surveying Molly's serene face, unmarked by the passion ratcheting through him, Harlan felt the faint stirrings of reservations. Her body, a slim, pliant wand that was responding to his every touch, spoke one language, a language whose every nuance and inflection he read clearly. But her face...

Doubts. Underneath the piercing pleasure came niggling doubts that short-circuited the electric arc of his skin touching hers.

He had the oddest sense he was all alone in the dark.

"Molly? Did you hear me? Do you want this?" He twisted his hand in her hair and tipped her face to his. "Say yes, Molly."

It took her a long time to answer. Harlan inclined his head as he watched the sleepy flicker of her eyelids, the languid turn of her head against the leather of his jacket. "Molly?"

"Detective Harlan?" Disorientation in her lethargic voice. "What do you want? What can I do for you?"

Her toneless reply told him everything, told him nothing. Told him he couldn't take her, not tonight.

Something was very wrong. He should have caught on earlier, and would have had desire not separated his brain from his—

She interrupted his thoughts. "How can I help you?" Passivity cloaked her face, dulling the edge of her words.

Molly had been wary, hostile, evasive when he'd first met her. Frightened, perhaps. Guilty of murder, most probably. Her words had been sharp when he'd pushed, as sharp as the blade of the knife on her floor. She'd been on guard. But never passive.

He should have known from the beginning. The signs had been there—the disorder in her kitchen, her oblivious walk down to the dock, the somnolent dip under the crime-scene barrier.

She was on drugs.

That none had been found in the search of her house meant only that the crime-scene investigators hadn't searched hard enough, not that drugs weren't there.

He wanted to see her eyes in bright light. Scrutinize her slim arms for evidence of drug usage. Somewhere in her house, on her person, he would find the reason for this peculiar, trancelike numbness of Molly Harris.

Rising, he lifted her off his thigh and onto her own feet. She shut her eyes for a moment, opened them, her eyelashes skimming against his chin as he rose. She echoed his movements, malleable. Hands at her sides, she stood peacefully in front of him.

Her acquiescence irritated him. That, and frustrated lust. "So, Ms. Harris, what is it? What are you on?" He gripped her shoulders. "Been popping pills? What?" Giving her a small shake, he frowned. "Damn you, answer me."

"All right. Certainly." She ignored his grip and stepped past him, heading back to her house.

Harlan scrubbed his hands through his hair. Hell. She was one cool customer. Ice water flowed in Ms. Molly's veins. Except he'd felt the beginnings of heat under her chilled skin.

From the dock, he watched as she hesitated once more at the spot where Camina's body had been found. Her forehead furrowed and he heard her sigh, smelled the sweetness of her breath on the wind. Leaping off the dock, he caught up to her and followed close behind.

Stepping unhurriedly through the wet grass, she seemed unaware of his presence at her back until she unlatched her screen door and entered her kitchen.

She halted at the touch of his hands on her shoulders. There, surrounded by the evidence of emotional turmoil,

Harlan turned her face to the blaze of lights and examined it, lifted her arms. Unresisting, she waited as he traced her blue, silky veins with a forefinger. As he followed the veins upward and back down, a tiny shiver moved over her skin, lifting the fine, light hair on her arm.

He found nothing. He'd been so sure he'd see her pupils dilated, see the evidence of needle marks on her skin. Mystified, he let her arms drop.

Oblivious to him once more, she turned, bolted the door behind them and walked through the debris of her kitchen up the stairway that led to her bedroom, her right hand trailing along the white wall that reflected the bright lights of the hallway and kitchen.

"Molly!" Harlan glossed the syllables with command. Her bare foot hovered over the last step and then lowered as she continued up to her bedroom. Her feet were whispers against the uncarpeted floor.

The sound of a sheet slipping back. A faint squeak of bedsprings. Her sigh.

Tracking her, Harlan halted at the top of the stairs. He could see her small shape, the sheet pulled smoothly up to her chin. Her eyes were wide open, watching the stairs.

"Go away now," she murmured. "Leave me alone, please."

"I can't." He stroked the slippery smooth banister and thought of the feel of her skin. "You know I can't."

"Go away. I can't take any more." With that, her eyelids shut abruptly, and she was gone, vanished somewhere behind the mask of sleep.

Harlan left the lights on as he returned to her kitchen. He would stay this time. And he would search through every inch of her house until he found what he was looking for—an explanation for Molly Harris's behavior. The techs had missed something earlier. If an answer were to be found in her house, he would know it.

But he didn't go into her bedroom.

He couldn't forget the look in her eyes as she'd watched him at the head of the stairs.

Prowling through the quiet of Molly's house, Harlan slipped from one room to another, opening drawers already searched, lifting the lid off the back of the toilet, stirring a spoon through canisters of flour. He slid his fingers lightly over the bottoms of drawers, avoiding splinters. He looked at the backs of pictures, flipped through the pages of her books. He unscrewed an apparently burned-out light bulb and shook it, looking for anything that would serve as a cache.

Her brother's bedroom took him the least time. Stripped of anything personal, the room had an institutional appearance. Its walls, too, had been painted, and an oiled-teak dresser was bare.

A current of air eddied around his ankles when Harlan folded back the shutters. Running his fingers along the tops of the windows, he clicked the brass lock on the window back and forth, observing its easy movement. Someone had jammed jimmy rods at the top of the windows in all the rooms. Like the other windows, this one, too, lifted only an inch as long as the rod was in place.

Removing it, Harlan lifted the window that opened out onto the upper gallery. Rain swept in, wet his face as he leaned forward. Unlike Molly's bedroom on the other side of the long hall, her brother's bedroom faced the bayou.

The yellow ribbon down at the dock bent under the weight of the downpour, rose and fell to the ground, a long serpent undulating across the grass with the wind.

Frowning, Harlan shut the window and replaced the jimmy bar.

Passing Molly's room, he pressed against the wall and looked in. She still lay in that face-to-the-stairwell position, her eyes open and glazed, not even seeing him as he edged across the hall and down to the end that fronted the drive-way. All the way down the hall, though, he heard the even *shush* of her breathing, the slow beat of her heart.

Like fog drifting through her house, he left no evidence of his search.

When he'd finished, he was back in her kitchen.

Leaning against the sink, he thought about what he'd found. What he hadn't. Like the techs, he'd uncovered no bloody clothes, no stained shoes, nothing to implicate Molly Harris in murder. Except the bracelet. He'd unearthed no hidden stash of drugs or tranquilizers.

The case was like an onion, layers upon layers.

Cocking his head, he sniffed, his nostrils flaring as indistinct odors rose to him. The delicate scent of Molly's skin. The acrid tang of fear, pungent. A coppery smell of blood.

The hot burn of rage.

And the reek of evil.

Harlan began his search again. This time he started in her room.

The rain beat against the windowpanes on the far side of the hall. Her room was predawn hushed and gray. Uncharacteristically hesitant to invade the privacy of her room, Harlan glanced at her as he stepped through the door and saw that her eyelids were finally closed. Relieved, he moved, meticulously, silently, through the room scented with flowers and powder, her scent a siren call in his nostrils.

On the hunt.

Molly knew he was there and recognized him before she opened her eyes. Yesterday she would have screamed.

"Good morning, Ms. Harris." Smooth and silky, that low voice was.

She looked at him. "Is it, Detective Harlan?"

His back to her, he stepped closer to her window. "No,

in fact, it isn't. The rain has settled in.'' Abruptly, he turned to her and folded his arms over his chest.

After the fire storm of the previous day, Molly lacked the energy to sit up, but she did, pulling the sheet closer around her. Evidently she'd slept. Twice in one day, after months of twilight sleep. She'd have to think about that after the detective left. Lifting her chin, she said, ''I can see that you, obviously, have settled in, Detective. Would you like to explain to me what you're doing in my room? And how you got in?'' Molly reached for the phone, and the sheet pulled uncomfortably against her ribs until she freed both arms.

His expression was unreadable, maybe slightly interested as she spoke.

''Or would you like to explain to your supervisor?'' Molly lifted the white phone and listened to the buzz in her ear as she waited for his reply. Looking at her arm holding the sheet, she lowered the phone. There were faint bruises on her arm, just above the elbow—barely noticeable and not in the same location he'd held her during the identification of Camina. Molly's gaze flew to his. ''What happened?''

''You tell me.'' He stepped to the side of her bed in one long stride and sat down, his weight pulling at the sheet, entangling her in the cloth in such a way that she couldn't move away from him. ''What do you remember after Sergeant Ross left, Ms. Harris? What do you *think* happened?'' He leaned forward, intimidating her with his presence.

Yesterday she would have been paralyzed with fear. Today, having gone beyond fear to a different plane, she felt only bone weary, empty and strangely peaceful. But she was aware of the male scent of him swirling to her from his T-shirt as he loomed over her, aware of the bristly stubble of his beard on his pale skin, his disheveled black hair. She looked down at the smudges on her arm. ''I *think* I want you off my bed.'' She held his gaze. ''Now.''

''Ah.'' He lifted her hand. ''The kitten has claws.''

Jerking away, no longer caring what he thought or suspected, Molly said, "I don't have to answer any questions unless you've brought an arrest warrant with you. I'm lodging a complaint against you for illegal entry into my house." She reached for the receiver again, hostility lending her temporary energy.

"Go ahead." Amusement flickered, sharklike, under his politely even tones. She heard the hint of knowledge he wouldn't reveal until he was ready to pounce. He tapped in the first three numbers. "Be my guest."

Even in her terror and confusion yesterday, she'd known he liked to play games, and he was taunting her now with something he knew that she didn't.

She hung up the phone.

He smiled, that slight lift at the corner of his thin, almost cruel mouth. "Ah, a wise woman, after all."

In passion, those lips would be clever, hot. Molly frowned as she stared at his mouth. "Why don't you come right out with whatever you're suggesting, Detective Harlan?" Her throat was still raw from screaming, and it tightened with tension as she spoke. "I'm not in the mood for your games."

"What are you in the mood for, Ms. Harris?" He slanted his head toward her. "Tell me. I find I'm inordinately curious about you."

In spite of herself, she leaned back.

His smile was a thing of beauty, ironic, knowing. "Ah. Not forthcoming? Suppose I start?"

"Go ahead." She curled her fingers into the sheet. He was too sure of himself.

"It wasn't illegal entry." Tracing circles on the sheet, he tilted his head. "You let me in."

"No." She was certain about this. "Absolutely not."

"Yes." The detective nodded once. "You did, you know."

She shook her head violently. "I know I didn't."

With one index finger, he stopped her grip on the sheet. "In fact, you did." He tapped her clenched fist. "Your turn, Ms. Harris. Perhaps this question is easier. Why is your kitchen like the aftermath of a hurricane?"

"I was angry." She eased her hand free. When she'd finally quit screaming, fury had flooded her—fury that she'd been weak for so long, a captive in her own home, a prisoner of the night when she'd never had a nervous bone in her body. "I had a temper tantrum." Making fun of herself, she forestalled his comment. "And, yes, I enjoyed it. You might say I found my inner child." Her smile, she discovered, was genuine. She *had* found peace in the release of her anger. Anger was better than paralyzing fear, she'd found as she threw glasses onto the floor.

"And a very destructive child it was."

"Well..." She lifted one shoulder dismissively, keeping the sheet around her. "But you haven't told me how you happen to be in my house, in my bedroom." The rejuvenating anger she'd experienced last night percolated in her.

"Oh, but I did," he mocked, walking his fingers across her knuckles. "You chose not to believe me."

Anger evaporated like drops of water sizzling on a pancake griddle. Absolute truth shone from his amber eyes.

She remembered that the cat had stayed with her until her screams had dwindled to racking sobs. She'd dreaded losing control, believing that once she did, she'd never stop screaming until they took her away in a straitjacket.

But she'd underestimated her own mettle. In those moments when the cat had leapt up behind her, she'd touched bottom. There, with no place to go but upward to the light, she'd discovered some heretofore unknown strength and kept madness at bay.

That strength, and the presence of the cat, his large, muscular body a barrier against the terrors of the night. The cat had stayed while she gibbered for mindless lengths of time. Then, as she raged through her kitchen, flinging pots and dishes with healthy anger, letting that rage supplant all the feelings of helplessness that had held her paralyzed for months, the cat had disappeared, somehow going back wherever he'd come from.

Truth in the detective's eyes, though. Molly blinked as she sorted through her memories. Crystal sharp the exhilaration of flinging dishes and pans. And after that? She rubbed her forehead. After that, what had she done?

"You don't remember going to the bayou, do you, Ms. Harris? You don't remember—" he paused, lifted one shoulder "—almost making love with me, do you?"

Molly shook her head. She hadn't left her house. "You're lying."

"No." He stood up. "You know I'm not. What happened after Ross left, Ms. Harris? Tell me." Turning suddenly, he squatted beside the bed and cupped her chin. "I know something happened, because when I came here, you walked right past me out your kitchen door, leaving it unlocked. You walked out onto the dock and let me kiss you, touch you here—" he held the tip of his finger over her breast, not touching her "—there—" he gestured lower, and she shuddered "—until I thought we would leave scorch marks on the wood."

Molly shook her head violently. "No. It's not possible that I would…" She scrubbed her wrist across her mouth, which suddenly burned. "I wouldn't have. Not with you. Never with you."

"But you did. With me." He lifted her arm scornfully. "That's why you have those marks."

She didn't want to believe what he was saying, couldn't begin to take it in. She rubbed the bruises apprehensively. "I don't believe you. You must have rules against that kind of action on your part—regulations, *something?* Ethics, maybe? Wouldn't that bother your department?''

"Probably."

"I know you think I murdered Camina! Doesn't it bother you that you came on to someone you consider a suspect?"

"I'm sure it should, but I confess," he said agreeably, "that it didn't disturb me at all last night. I discovered that my principles weren't up to the rigors of resisting the appeal of you in the moonlight." He shrugged. "I've never claimed to be perfect. I've never found any advantage in virtue for virtue's sake. Chalk it up to irresistible impulse, Ms. Harris." He paused and then added in a voice that skimmed the surface of the acid underneath, "That's what crooks claim, isn't it? Irresistible impulse? But I'm the detective, while you're—"

"Not a criminal."

"No?" His smile was caustic. "Whatever you say, Ms. Harris." He touched the sheet exactly over her nipple. Against the swift brush of his finger, her nipple peaked. He looked down at the small point under the sheet. "All right." His eyes glinted as he looked at her. "Whatever you say."

His ruthlessness chilled her. In that moment, she feared him in a way she hadn't before. This was a man who walked outside the boundaries, a man who respected only the limits he set. He was more dangerous to her than she could have imagined.

Ignoring the tremors running from her breast to the center of her being, Molly called on the remnants of anger-generated energy from the night before. "If what you say is true—and I don't believe you, not for a second, but *if* it is—I'll file a complaint so fast—"

"Go right ahead and file a complaint."

"Believe me, I will." She thumped the bed.

He lifted one dark eyebrow. "But if you check, Ms. Harris, you'll find scratch and cut marks on your feet. From walking barefoot across the lawn and down to the bayou. There's mud caked on the bottom of your pajama legs, too," he added carelessly. "Look for yourself." He lifted the sheet as he stood up. "And then tell me I'm lying."

With his negligent pull on the sheet, Detective John Harlan opened the door to the unimaginable and made it real.

She'd been wrong after all. There *was* a level of terror beyond endless screaming.

CHAPTER FIVE

Molly rubbed her hands over her arms. It was true. What she'd feared must have happened. In the watery light of the morning, though, she could face truth, no matter how frightening, and move on. It had been the not knowing that had pushed her to the edge.

And over.

At least she knew now that the events that had been happening to her weren't figments of her imagination, that no one had slipped past bolted doors and windows. She could deal with the truth, however disturbing it seemed to be. While she didn't understand what had caused her to wander down to the bayou, apparently in her sleep, she at least had a real question that would have a real answer. An odd mix of apprehension and elation bubbled within her.

Although she didn't trust Detective John Harlan on any level, he was telling her the truth. She'd known that as his gaze had held hers. Once he'd mentioned the cuts on her feet, she'd become aware of her stinging soles and had known there was no possibility that he was lying. He'd witnessed her behavior, actions she had no memory of, but needed to discover if she were to save herself.

Pacing leisurely in front of her, he stopped, leaning against her dresser. "No comment?"

"I don't know what you're talking about. You can believe me or not."

He ran his long fingers along the edge of her dresser, stroking the bleached oak, fiddling with the brass knob of the top drawer. "Perhaps I do."

"You believe me?" Molly couldn't help the skepticism in her voice. She knew he didn't.

"Oh, I wouldn't go that far." He slid the drawer open a quarter of an inch. Closed it. "Perhaps I'm willing to consider that you might not remember anything about last night. Tell me, Ms. Harris," he said, never taking his gaze from hers as he toyed with the second drawer, "what drugs are you taking?"

Molly recoiled. "Drugs?"

"Hmm. Yes. Uppers, downers, mood-altering buzzies. Junk." With his fingers under the bottom of the drawer, he edged it open all the way. The drawer, filled with her panties and bras, tilted toward the floor. He rocked the drawer gently with his forefinger as he watched her. "Yes, drugs."

"I don't do drugs, Detective." His accusation came out of left field. So unexpected and preposterous was his question that Molly relaxed. "I never have."

"Commendable." His smooth voice turned the comment into an insult. "Not on any medicines?" Once more he rocked the drawer, watching her with that look of an animal closing in on its prey.

"None that are any of your business."

"Murder's my business, so I get to indulge my curiosity. So, yes, as reluctant as you may be to—" he shoved his hands into the pockets of his faded black jeans "—tell all, everything about you, is, in fact, my business. And I have a prodigious curiosity about you, Ms. Harris, as I said."

"Well, we all know what curiosity did to the cat, don't we?" she said nastily, pulling the sheet up around her and sliding lower on the bed.

"Ah, you're threatening me?" Again that courteous tilt of his head as he steadily regarded her, unfazed by her aggression.

The air was rain chilled. No matter how tired she was, she had to remember to stay on guard with this man. The stakes were desperately high. "No, Detective, simply making an observation."

"You grow wiser by the minute, Ms. Harris." A peach-colored bra dangled from his finger, the lace cups brushing the hair on his wrist. He ran his thumb over the satin strap. "Lovely as well as wise. A dangerous combination."

Molly inhaled and tried to ignore the prickling of her skin. "I don't like the games you're playing, Detective."

"No, I don't suppose you do. But, Ms. Harris," he said, "murder's not a game with me. I take it very seriously." Returning her bra to its original spot, he flipped through a stack of folded slips, their pastels flashing in front of her eyes like an elusive rainbow.

"Fine," Molly said, hostility and weariness nibbling at her caution in spite of her efforts. "I'm relieved that my tax dollars aren't being wasted."

"And you contribute a lot of tax dollars, don't you?" He eased the drawer shut so quietly that she almost missed the sound of wood meeting wood.

"My fair share. Like everyone else."

"But more now? Right? With your inheritance after the death of your parents?"

Molly blanched. Stunned, she felt the blood draining from her face. Even weary as she was, she understood his oblique accusation. "You think I killed my parents, too?" She wadded the sheet in her hand, holding on to it. Everytime she thought she'd faced the worst, he attacked from a different direction. "Camina *and* my parents?"

"You had a motive, certainly." He held out a tray of folded nylon stockings, their smoky grays and off-whites shading into each other.

"No. Never. Not for Camina. Certainly not for my parents."

"Ah, but money's always a motive. For lots of things, but especially for murder," he said, letting the nylons slip through his long fingers, slide against his palm as he held the sheer hosiery up to the light. "I like your taste in underwear, Ms. Harris. Very elegant. And very expensive."

"You can't think for a second that I would murder my parents!" Molly stared at his angular face, at his mouth, which tightened in cynicism with her outburst. She'd scarcely borne the horror of their deaths, emptiness and desolation swamping her with the discovery of their bodies. Shortly after, her brother, Reid, had returned to the Costa Rican ranch and she'd been utterly bereft of family. Remembering, Molly fought the tears of loss. "I loved my parents."

"And Camina Milar was your friend. Yes, I remember."

"Why would I have killed Camina?" With every ounce of her energy, Molly was trying to follow the twisting threads of his suspicions.

"She worked for your parents and stayed on after their deaths. Perhaps she saw something. Knew something." He was at her bedside table, lifting the lamp, looking at its base. "Or she might have overheard something you didn't want her knowing?"

"That's preposterous. You have an evil mind, Detective." Recoiling at the sludgy depths to which he'd taken her with his suspicions, Molly closed her eyes.

"If I do, Ms. Harris, it comes from the company I keep. I've been around a fair number of folks who are wicked and frequently evil—evil from the moment of birth, something kinked in their nature. I understand human beings like that. I know how their greedy, selfish, angry little brains work. And I enjoy catching them."

Heat enveloped her. The detective was leaning over her toward the table on the far side of her bed. She understood he invaded her space on purpose in an effort to throw her off balance, recognized his ploy and still pushed against her headboard in a vain attempt to remove herself as far as possible from the heat that curled invitingly around her. That heat teased her with the possibility of letting go, drifting in its warmth like a cat on a windowsill soaking up the sunshine.

Again she closed her eyes, to shut out his sardonic face inches from hers, to diminish the impact of that heat that drew her irrationally, to draw a curtain between herself and Detective Harlan's amber eyes, which tantalized her with the possibility of surrender. Her mouth gone dry, she said, "Would you mind letting me change, and then finish your search quickly, please? Or shall I add this harassment to my list of complaints about your investigative techniques?"

The bed dipped as he supported himself with one outstretched arm on either side of her. "Are you feeling harassed, Ms. Molly?"

Her eyelids flew open. "I said I was."

He was near enough to her that her eyes crossed slightly as she saw the crescent-shaped scar at the corner of his mouth. A scent lured her, clean, warm, male. John Harlan's scent.

Bubbling up from her unconscious came a sensation of that mouth against her, his thin lips hungry, urgent.

Pleasure speared her.

And revulsion at her weakness in the face of his threat to her. She focused on the shiny horizontal dent at the bridge of his nose. "I don't like the way you're trying to intimidate me. I don't like anything about the way you're investigating Camina's murder, and I don't like you. Now let me up."

He angled closer. "You don't like me?" His breath feathered along her neck.

"No." Her throat closed.

He smiled, the side of his mouth rising infinitesimally, letting her know he saw through her defenses. "Not even a little?"

"No," she choked out.

He tilted his head and let his gaze roam over her. "Then why did you let me touch you last night, Ms. Harris?"

Her voice rising, Molly covered her face. "How many times do I have to tell you I don't remember *letting* you touch me, letting you into my house! I don't know, I don't know!"

Pulling her hands free, he stared at her, his face close to hers. Looking into his golden brown eyes, their colors shifting and changing, fascinating her, Molly once more felt as if she were spiraling forward into a tunnel filled with light. For a long time he stared at her, snaring the breath from her lips, emptying her lungs of oxygen until the air around her shimmered and glowed and she couldn't breathe at all, caught in a place where breath and air didn't matter and held there as long as he chose by his glittering eyes.

Finally, leaning back, he released her. "All right, Ms. Harris. I believe you," he said pleasantly. He walked around the foot of her bed and opened the drawer of the end table to the right.

"You do?" she whispered, still breathless. "You believe I didn't kill Camina?" Relief, rich and thick, pounded in her veins.

"Ah, but I didn't say that."

"You said you believe me!"

Head down, he explored the drawer. "I said I believe you when you insist you don't remember what happened after you left your kitchen last night."

A groan escaped her. He'd duped her twice, letting her hope for those seconds that the nightmare was over and he no longer considered her a suspect. Each time, he'd let out the leash and given her a taste of freedom before jerking her back to reality. He was playing head games, toying with her and disturbing her equilibrium in his attempts to trip her up. "I thought you meant Camina," she said. She hunched her shoulders. "That you realized I couldn't have murdered her."

"Ah, well, the jury's still out on that question, Ms. Harris."

"You're not my jury. Not my judge, Detective." Molly took a deep breath, oxygen flooding her brain.

"And lucky you are that I'm not," he said, holding up a round plastic container. "A real nineties woman, I see. Birth-control pills?" He rattled the case. "You're like the Boy Scouts? Always prepared?"

"They're…from before."

His glance was quizzical as he waited for her to elaborate, and Molly fumbled for words, loath to rip off the scab of her wounds for him, her failure still painful in odd, shameful ways.

"Yes, Ms. Harris?" he encouraged. "Before?" He knew, but he was going to make her spell it out. He was relentless.

"Before. Before my divorce."

Shaking the plastic again, he returned it to the drawer, the pills ricocheting inside the container. "From Dr. Bouler."

"Yes. Paul."

"Shortly before your parents died."

"Yes." Drawing her knees up under the sheet, Molly bent double over them, burying her head in her arms. "But you knew that without asking, didn't you?"

He was between her and her bathroom door when she raised her head. Silhouetted by the eastern light coming in from the hall, his shoulders filled the arch separating the two rooms. The backlighting obscured his expression. "I did my homework, Ms. Harris." From anyone else the note that shaded his somber voice would have passed for sympathy.

Lifting her head wearily, Molly sighed. She knew better. He played both roles with her—bad cop, good cop. She couldn't expect sympathy from this man. She'd be a fool if she did, and she'd already learned how humiliating it was to be taken for a fool. "I'm sure you researched everything about me and my family that you could get your hands on."

"I always do. Makes my job easier."

"I'm happy for you." Shrugging, Molly clapped her hands together in sarcastic applause. She hitched up the sheet, which had slipped from her shoulders. "Do you want a gold star, too?"

He shifted, the small movement suddenly threatening, but his voice was still exquisitely polite as he said, "I have a star. Silver. On my shield. That's sufficient." He pivoted and disappeared into her bathroom.

Pulling the sheet off the bed and wrapping it around her like a toga, the ends trailing on the smooth wood, Molly followed him. She didn't go into the bathroom, though. Intuitively she knew that the room, not small at all, was nevertheless too small for Detective Harlan and herself at the same time.

The flick of his fingers across her perfumes and boxes of bath powder, over the still-damp towel draped over the brass hook, down her white satin bathrobe, disturbed her in ways his examination of her lingerie hadn't.

This was more intimate. She saw, and looked away from, the curl of his fingers into the satin fabric, but she felt their rough catch against her own skin, felt their callused tips moving down her throat as he returned the robe to the hook. As he stood in the middle of the bathroom, his back to the sink with its vase of deep red mountain ebony on the white porcelain, Molly spoke, her mouth dry with something that wasn't fear. "You haven't found anything except outdated birth-control pills. Are you satisfied now?"

"Such a leading question, Ms. Harris. I find it very difficult to resist the reply." He straightened and stepped, one long stride only, toward her, but he didn't touch her. "In fact, no, Ms. Harris, I'm not at all satisfied.'' His voice was rough and grainy as he tugged the end of the robe's tie and looped it around his hand. Letting the silky fabric slither through his fingers onto her shoulder, he trailed the tie lingeringly across her neck, a taunting caress of satin on her skin. ''Here, Ms. Harris,'' he said as he unhooked the robe and handed it to her, ''perhaps you should get dressed. And let me remain unsatisfied.'' Hunger flared deep in his amber eyes. Danger.

The robe slipped from Molly's grip.

He stooped and picked it up. ''Take it. Now.''

Molly did.

The tips of his fingers grazed the pulse beating at her neck as she reached for the robe.

Behind him, the five-petaled flowers seemed to burst into flames.

He closed the bathroom door as she left. The small tick of the metal tongue into the slot shivered the length of her spine as she dropped the sheet and pulled the robe around her, knotting the tie. She *would* lodge a complaint.

Pulling the ends of the robe tighter, Molly sat down on the bed and picked up the phone. Holding it in her hands, she weighed the consequences as she twisted the receiver around and around.

The bathroom door opened. Standing in the archway, Harlan flipped a medicine vial onto the bed.

Molly put the receiver down.

''Sleeping pills, Ms. Harris? But they're not from 'before,' are they?''

Rolling the brown plastic bottle between her fingers, Molly shook her head.

''Actually,'' Harlan said as he removed the vial and extended it to her, ''this prescription goes back only three months, to September. You have three pills left. When did you take one last, Ms. Harris?''

"I don't know." Molly kept her hands safely in the folds of the robe.

"Isn't it unusual that your ex-husband prescribed them for you?" His thighs, long and heavily muscled, blocked her view of the hall.

"Maybe. We've remained friends." Molly slid her bare toes back under the bed, away from Harlan's pointed boots. "I told him—"

"That you couldn't sleep. And he helped you out." He dropped the vial into his pocket. "A little irregular, isn't it? For a dentist to prescribe sleeping pills? Does his medical license cover Class II drugs?"

"I don't know what class of drugs they are. They're mild. Only a little stronger than an over-the-counter medicine. Paul wouldn't have given them to me if they had any addictive effects. He said they would relax me. I'd been under a lot of stress. I was grateful to him, do you understand? *Grateful* that he tried to help."

Paul had assured her there were no weird side effects to this medication, had promised her they were extremely mild. They would relax her only enough so that she could go to sleep on her own.

They hadn't.

As far as she could tell, the confounded pills hadn't done anything for her.

"Did you by any chance take one night before last?"

"If I took one, I don't remember, *Detective*. I've told you that over and over! I might have, but if I had, what difference would it make? They don't even work for me. My metabolism, I guess." Molly shrugged and burrowed her hands deeper into the robe.

"I'm taking them to the lab for analysis. Perhaps they're what you say. Perhaps not. Who knows?" He rubbed the back of his neck, disturbing a strand of his thick, black hair, ruffling it. "We'll see."

Now Detective John Harlan was including Paul in his nasty insinuations. Paul, who'd done everything he could to help her, would be sucked into this nastiness that was enveloping her.

"Paul and I are friends."

"Interesting. You must not have loved him." He leaned against the wall, sliding down it until he was hunkered down, his weight balanced on his thighs.

"Of course I did," Molly insisted stubbornly, knowing she could never make this cynical man understand her relationship with her former husband. Hopeless, hopeless.

"I doubt it. Hard to be friends with someone you've been passionate with, passionate about. The psychology doesn't work that way. Unless, of course, your relationship with the accommodating doctor was never very passionate to begin with?" he said, flexing his thighs and rising to his full height. "Is that what it was like between you and Dr. Bouler? A lukewarm meeting of the minds and not a passionate meeting of bodies and souls?" He shoved his hands into his jeans pockets. "Somehow I doubt that there was much *passion* between you and your very helpful ex-husband, Ms. Harris." John Harlan's smile taunted her with the memory of the satin tie slipping across her skin.

Molly jerked to her feet, her palm swinging wildly for his mocking face.

She never had a chance.

From two feet away, leaning forward in a blur of motion, he clipped her arm uselessly to her side. "I wondered what it would take to break through your nice, ladylike behavior." His mouth curled up with pleasure. "It took longer than I expected, but now I know. Like a volcano, you bubble away and finally explode."

"I hope you're satisfied." Bitterness etched her voice. She'd been a fool. She'd fallen into his intricate trap.

"Ahh. That word again. Well, there's satisfaction—and

satisfaction.'' He gave an insistent tug on her arm, pulling her off balance. She would have landed against his chest had he not steadied her, inches away.

"Is that what all this harassment is about?'' Fury simmered in her. If he'd turned her loose, she would have tried to slap his face again. He'd pulled her strings like a puppet, manipulating her, his every gesture, every expression calculated to get a reaction from her. "You were trying to trick me?''

"I've seen your kitchen. It made me wonder how much—'' he tugged once more and again halted her fall toward him "—emotion hid behind your trembling mouth and your innocent eyes. And now I've seen you lose control. Underneath that sweet innocence, you have a real temper, don't you?'' He walked her backward until her knees bumped the edge of the bed. "Slapping people isn't *nice*, Ms. Harris,'' he chided.

"You deliberately provoked me,'' she said, trembling with fury and fear.

"Is that what happened with Camina? Did she provoke you, too? Only you had a knife in your hand that time?''

Forgetting all caution, Molly stepped right up against him, her thighs nudging his. "Detective Harlan, I intend to file a complaint about the kind of persecution you've subjected me to. No matter what you think, I didn't kill Camina, nor do I remember walking outside my house last night. Now, make of that whatever you want, but unless you have enough evidence to arrest me, get out of my house.'' She shrugged out of his grip, throwing his arms aside as she stormed toward the stairs, propelled by the sheer force of her anger at his manipulation of her emotions.

Close as her shadow, he followed her to the bottom and into her wrecked kitchen. Pulling out a chair, he turned it around and sat on it, resting his arms across the back.

Once again, he'd surprised her.

Picking up the broom and dustpan, Molly faced him. "I asked you to leave, Detective. If I have to, I'll call the police to come and take you away."

"You would, too, wouldn't you?" He stretched one long leg out to the side, hooked the other on the rung of the chair.

"Yes."

His gaze as he stared at her was pensive, all heat and threat tamped down. "Good for you. That's precisely what you should do. It's what an innocent person would do." He curled his fingers over the back of the chair and rested his chin on them. Closing his eyes, he seemed to shrink, fade, his outline wavery against the muted light from the shuttered kitchen windows.

Quiet, all his predatory energy diminished, he became another creature entirely. It was as if he had switched off an internal engine, vanished and left only a tired shell of himself. His rumpled black hair showed the streaks where he'd raked it back from his forehead. She saw the circles under his eyes, the bristles of his heavy beard against his pale skin, the line of perspiration at the neck of his T-shirt even in the chill of the morning. All-male from his wide shoulders down to the elongated, powerful thigh muscles of his extended leg, he lounged at his ease in her space.

Rain drumming against the windows muffled sounds, enclosed them in the small world of her kitchen, intensified her awareness of him.

Eyes closed, his head still on his chin, he sighed. "You are beginning to convince me in spite of everything, Ms. Harris. Either you're a very good actress, or you might be exactly what you seem. Possibly you are as pure as the proverbial snow they talk about up north." He yawned, his even white teeth flashing for a second before he widened his eyes and rubbed the back of his neck. "It's been a long night. I should apologize to you for my behavior. If you want an apology, you've got it." He lifted his head and rotate his neck.

Molly heard the cartilage cracking as he turned his head from side to side. Admitting his conduct, he'd tipped her off balance again.

"I won't offer you any excuses for my behavior. Whether you're guilty as the devil or as innocent as one of God's angels, I screwed up. I stepped over the line. Period." Raising his arms, he clasped them behind his neck and pulled. The butt of his gun in its shoulder holster showed through the opening of his jacket.

"Way over," Molly whispered.

"Yeah. I know. I won't defend what I did. Like I said, if you want to register a complaint against me, go right ahead. I'll even pull the forms for you. But to tell you the truth, Ms. Harris, I don't give a rat's damn if you file a complaint or not. Personally, I think you should. It's what I would do if I were in your shoes." He glanced at her feet. A weary smile tugged at his mouth. "Don't you ever wear shoes, Ms. Harris?"

Molly shook her head, bewildered. He'd pricked the balloon of her anger, justified though it was. "Are you trying to soft-soap me? Get me to back off so that maybe you won't be fired? Is that what this hundred-and-eighty-degree turn is all about?"

"No. I don't care one way or the other about being fired, either."

"Would you be fired if I reported you?" she persisted.

"I could be." Total indifference flattened his deep tones.

Working her way through the labyrinth of her thoughts, Molly traced the molded edge of the beige dustpan. "If I complain, and you're not fired, will you be taken off this case?"

"Probably." His smile was a thin flash of white. "That should please you."

Ignoring him, Molly twirled the dustpan slowly in her hand, trying to work out what would be best for her. "If you're off the case, what happens next?"

"Someone else takes over."

"But not like you."

"No. Not like me." Narrowing his eyes, he watched her with a knowing smile. Lines radiated from the corners of his eyes, slanting up and briefly giving him the look of a sleepy tiger observing a distant antelope.

"You're a hunter, aren't you, Detective Harlan?"

"Yes." Amusement twitched one corner of his mouth. His boot heel squeaked against a tile as he shifted on the chair.

"You won't give up until you find Camina's killer, will you? You may think I killed her, but until you know for sure, you won't give up the pursuit."

"You know I won't." His eyelids half-closed, he seemed even sleepier and more indolent as he yawned widely.

"But I could make a lot of trouble for you."

"Sure. Easy as breathing."

She couldn't help it. She inhaled.

His eyes narrowed drowsily as his gaze lingered on the lift and fall of her breasts.

Her breathing erratic as he watched her, Molly discovered that the idea of annoying John Harlan was barely resistible. "It would be annoying for you if I caused difficulties."

"Oh, yeah. I'd be ticked off."

Nodding, Molly murmured, more to herself than to him, "I'll just bet you would be."

"Are you looking to get even? Is that your goal? Go ahead." The gleam of his teeth was the smile of the tiger after a meal. "It's your hand. Play 'em or fold 'em." He shrugged. "But don't forget to include that I came on to you down at the bayou, Ms. Molly. It'll make your complaint stronger, you know. Even if you don't recall our little tête-à-tête, I'll own up to it.''

He must have read her obvious discomfort in her grimace because he sat a bit straighter, mockery sparking in his extraordinary eyes as he drawled, ''Usually, of course, a gentleman doesn't kiss and tell, does he?''

Molly frowned. She wished she could remember exactly what had happened in that lost time.

''But then I'm no gentleman, am I?'' He raised an eyebrow as she remained silent. ''What? No answer? I would have thought you wouldn't let the chance to throw that into my face pass you by.''

The broom rested against her chest as she gestured, one palm up. ''You're hard on yourself, aren't you?''

He curled around the chair again as if he were double-jointed. Weariness grooved the corners of his mouth. ''Well. I've never pretended to be a gentleman. I am what I am.''

As she'd thought, he lived by his own rules, judging his conduct by some arcane code he kept to himself. No explanations, no defense, and let the chips fall where they might. By his private guidelines, he'd been wrong, and she could retaliate as she chose. He couldn't have undercut her determination any more cleanly if he'd planned it.

Maybe he had. The idea insinuated itself into her brain. Going on her previous experiences with Detective Harlan, Molly decided she couldn't put anything past him. He was devious, cunning and clever, too clever for her to keep up with. But like the truth she'd seen earlier in his eyes, she sensed a truth here, confusing though it was.

He really didn't care whether she filed a complaint. He genuinely didn't care if he lost his job. Regardless, he would stick to her like a burr on a dog until he knew who the killer was.

''So, Ms. Molly—'' he arched his back ''—*are* you going to make trouble for me?''

John Harlan was her enemy, but he was also her best hope for discovering the truth and saving herself. "I haven't made up my mind yet." But she had.

"Ah, you haven't?" His shrewd smile disturbed her as he uncoiled from the chair and stood up. She had the oddest sense that he knew exactly what she was doing.

"No, but I'll let you know what I decide," Molly said in her best lady-of-the-manor voice, wanting to maintain any power she might have.

"Fine. In the meantime, give me that damned broom you're waving around. You're going to slice your feet open on all this damned glass." He cracked another yawn. "You had yourself one hell of a temper tantrum, didn't you?"

"Yes." Molly wasn't sure she could ever admit to anyone the degree to which she'd relished the crashing of glasses and banging of pots, but the contradictions she sensed in John Harlan told her he might be the one person in the world who could understand the wild anger that had spurred her as she'd whirled, out of control, through her kitchen.

She contemplated the floor. A pot had cracked off a corner of one of the tiles. "It's worse than I remembered."

Circling her waist with both hands, John Harlan lifted her easily onto the counter. "I'll help clean up."

"I'll clean up my own messes, thank you, if you'll just leave," Molly mumbled. Embarrassed and uncomfortable, she slid off the counter, wincing as she braced her weight on her wounded hand. Before she could blink, she found herself settled back onto the counter, her hand in his.

He rubbed the wound with his thumb. "You should see your doctor about this." He raised his eyebrow. "It's deep. It could easily become infected."

The hem of the robe flapped open, snagging on the bottom of his leather jacket. Carefully, he pulled the edges together, smoothing them down over her legs. His touch remained impersonal, but his quick intake of breath betrayed him.

"You confuse me, Detective."

"Small wonder, Ms. Harris. I confuse myself at times. I reckon I'm having my own version of a mid-life crisis." He patted her knee, but there was nothing sexual, nothing provocative in the light tap. Surveying the shards of glass on the floor and the sticky cocoa spots on the stove, he said, "Who's been cleaning for you since you fired Camina?"

"Me."

"Yeah?" He looked up at the high ceilings, the hall leading to the other rooms at the front of the house, the row of long windows. "It's a big house. A lot for one person to keep up with."

"Living by myself, I don't have much clutter."

"I reckon not." He motioned to the kitchen, to her plain white robe. "No, you don't look like a clutter-making woman, that's for sure. Polished, no frills, stripped down for action like a racing machine. That's you."

Maybe he hadn't meant the words to carry a second meaning, but they did, and Molly's blood rushed to her face.

The bones in his face seemed to sharpen as he studied her, and all the banked energy and heat in his powerful body suddenly blazed forth. "I want you, you know," he said casually, his tone as nonchalant as if he'd asked her for a glass of water. "And I'm ticked off with myself because I can't forget the feel of your skin under my hands." His palms seemed to shape the air in front of him and she shuddered. "So you see, you've already created a troubling situation for me."

"What do you mean?" She whispered, afraid to disturb the delicate equilibrium of the moment, afraid to move in the face of his intensity.

"I can't forget the taste of your mouth, Ms. Molly, that's

what I mean. And one taste isn't enough, not by a long shot.''

The words hovered like early morning mist between them, just *there*. But she dropped her gaze, he swept the broom over a piece of shiny black glass that had been a soup bowl and the moment passed.

Something had changed between them, however, and she knew it.

The broom whisked a counterpoint to the rain beating against the shuttered windows. Glass tinkled as he swept it into the dust pan. He tossed his leather jacket next to her on the counter. The black leather, supple and expensive, smelled of cool air, rain and him, his elusive, masculine scent. Not cologne. *Him.*

His scent seduced her with a promise of darkness and a pleasure so intense it would border on pain. Against the spiraling tension in her abdomen, Molly drew her legs up onto the counter. She rubbed her arms where he'd held her. His scent lingered on her skin, rose to her. She knew her sheets would carry that faint scent. Like the cat that had wandered in during the night, rubbing against her legs, John Harlan had imprinted her with his scent.

Unlike the cat, though, the man would turn on her.

And the man wouldn't be satisfied with a bowl of milk.

A line of sweat glued his T-shirt to his spine. As he squatted to sweep more glass into the dustpan, his unbelted jeans tightened over his butt. Muscles along his ribs ridged and flattened with his movements, and where the harness of his holster caught the side of his shirt, Molly glimpsed the corded muscles of his stomach, taut under his sleek, smooth skin.

Suddenly, as if the languorous sweep of her eyes had touched him, he looked at her.

Rocking on his heels, he considered her for a long mo-

ment, awareness growing in his darkening eyes with each
quiet click of the clock on the microwave.

Neither of them had thought to turn on lights.

Against the windows and the side of the house, the rain
beat a steady tattoo.

CHAPTER SIX

A gust of wind rattled the shutters.

John Harlan's voice, low and rough, filled her ears. "I don't like the situation any better than you do. But there's something between us, whatever it is. We're both adults, and if you're honest, you'll admit you're as aware of me as I am of you. I'd like to think it's a result of prolonged celibacy on my part. That's what I'd like to believe, but you want to know something, Ms. Harris? Last night, out on your rickety old dock, I didn't give two hoots in hell *who* you'd killed. And that's why I have a problem. Because, like you said, I can't give up until I track down Camina's killer. It's not in my nature." He tilted his head. "If it turns out that you indeed killed her, and I haven't been able to keep my hands off you, well, unlike being fired or taken off this damned case, that situation would present me with a...problem."

She needed walls, doors, locks to give her breathing room, but she sought refuge in words, a pitiful substitute for locked doors. "You'll have to exercise a bit of self-control, then, won't you, Detective? Will you be able to manage that?"

He didn't move, but she felt as if he'd crowded close to her and there was no room to back away.

If John Harlan really wanted to get to her, locked doors wouldn't keep him out.

"I can. Can you?" He rose, his thighs bunching and flowing with his smooth movements.

Suddenly he was next to her, whipping a long strip of paper towels off the holder to her left and enclosing her in the triangle of his body. Lifting the faucet handle, he soaked the strip of paper, and his forearm, damp from the splashing water, bumped her knee.

"Of course I can."

His comment had been a straightforward acknowledgment of the humming awareness of his body for hers, hers for his, and once more she found herself wondering what had happened during those lost hours the night before.

"Good. Neither of us will have a problem then." His grim smile was a brief baring of his teeth as he turned and wiped the floor with the gray-printed paper towels. Sparkles of glass splinters shone against the paper as he wadded it up and opened the door under the sink to toss the paper into her waste basket. "You won't cut your feet now."

Molly kept her knees drawn up to her chin. She didn't want any more accidental brushes against his lean form. She'd stay safe on the counter until he left.

His sideways glance as he took the dishrag and went to the stove acknowledged her protective posture. "Very cautious. Good for you. You might want to be even more cautious for a while."

"What do you mean?"

With the burner grate in one hand, the soapy rag in the other, he faced her. "You've been so focused on convincing me that you didn't kill Camina that you've ignored one or two points."

Puzzled, Molly slid off the counter. "What?"

"It's like this. Suppose, just for a second, that I'm convinced you didn't murder her, okay?"

"All right." Molly stooped to collect the pans in the far corner of the room, stacking them in her arms as she approached the cupboard. "Then my life returns to normal, whatever that is these days," she added in an undertone that he caught.

"No. It doesn't." He stopped her with a grip on her elbow. "If you didn't kill Camina, someone else did, someone who could have walked in right behind you the same way I did last night. You didn't know I was there. Would you have known a killer was slipping along behind you? A killer who could have entered your house, stayed while you locked up behind him—or her?"

"Stop it," Molly said as fear tiptoed up her spine and breathed ice down her neck. She'd already thought about everything he was saying, but hearing her thoughts spelled out in his even, factual tone gave credibility to her fears. "You're scaring me."

"Think about it, Ms. Harris. Locks keep things out. But not if you swing the door wide open and wander off. And you've done that at least once. I saw you. I saw you lock up behind yourself and go to bed—oh, not to sleep. You didn't shut your eyes for quite a while after you lay down. But you didn't know I was here, searching through your house, did you?"

"No." Ice settled in her stomach.

"While you were—well, whatever you were, sleeping, unconscious, doped up, whatever—I could have done anything. I could have smeared blood on your walls—someone did, you know. I could have carried you downstairs and left you here on your floor. Anything could have happened last night, Ms. Harris. *Anything.*"

She fastened on the thought that had sustained her earlier. "But you're still here," she argued. "That's why all the bolts and locks are fastened. If you'd left, one of the doors—or windows—would be unlocked!"

"Think so? People have been able to lock doors behind them. In some cases." His voice had dropped so low and gone so soft that it rasped over her nerve endings like a sandy velvet glove, raising the hairs on her arms.

"I know so! People don't pass through locked doors and

windows. Not this kind of lock.'' She hugged her arms to herself. ''Not in a world that makes sense, not in a world that's rational!''

''Ah, that's the point, isn't it? What if this isn't a rational world? What if there are—'' he searched for a word, lifted one shoulder and continued ''—*things,* unlike magician's tricks, that can't be explained *rationally?* What then, Ms. Harris?''

''If I left this house the night Camina was murdered, no one came in behind me and left,'' Molly insisted stubbornly. ''No one could have. Not without leaving a door or window unlocked, not without some sign that he—or she—had been here.''

''If I accept that, Ms. Harris, and if the blood on the knife handle turns out to be Camina's, that leaves me, and you, with only one or two possible conclusions, doesn't it?'' His grip tightened on her elbows.

She knew. At some level, she'd known from the first. ''Either I killed her, or I saw who did and don't remember what I saw.''

''Excellent. You get an *A* for the quick course in crime investigation, Ms. Harris. Murderer? Or next victim? Which conclusion do *you* prefer?''

''Oh, God,'' she said, wrapping her arms tighter around herself. She'd thought she might be mad, might be a murderer, but she'd never considered the idea that she, too, might be a potential victim. ''I have to *think.* I have to figure this out! Oh, God.''

''I hope that's a prayer, Ms. Harris, because I think you're going to need all the help you can get.'' He dropped his arms. ''Lots of help. Unless you decide that maybe the world isn't so rational and that I—or someone else—can enter and leave your house at will. Do you find that you like that choice better, Ms. Harris?'' Anger scoured his face.

"Which is it—the lady or the tiger? Or the demon that walks by night?"

Hours after he'd left, his words still echoed in her mind. He'd made her go through her house, door by door, window by window, examining every possible entrance until they were both short fused and spider webs from the attic turned her pajamas gray.

Once, in the pantry off the kitchen, he'd stopped, the rigid line of his back making her uneasy as he'd stayed motionless, head tilted, looking around the small, old-fashioned room. Canned peaches and tomatoes, boxes of cereal and pasta, packages of sugar and flour, bottles of olive oil and Ovaltine neatly lined the white plastic racks on either side of the chest-high window streaked with rain. He brushed his hand across the bottles and packages, the cans, the lock with its bubbled-up layers of paint and rust. He rubbed flecks of old paint between his fingers.

"What is it?" she'd said, unnerved by his stiff movements. Like him, she stared at the homely array of supplies, the bin of onions.

"I don't know. Something. Nothing, I reckon." He took a deep breath, and the rainy light, dim in the confined space, shimmered over him, blurring him for a moment as she watched. "Has this always been a pantry? Was it ever an entry porch that was later enclosed? Perhaps remodeled?"

"No." Molly traced a line of raindrops down to the corner of the window. Lifting her finger, she concentrated on another rivulet of drops merging, slipping down the cool pane.

"Are you sure?"

In the distance, thunder rumbled, mingled with the sound of rain spattering against the window, echoed her thudding pulse. "It's always been a pantry. I put in new shelves, painted it again, that's all."

"You did the work?" He turned in a slow, deliberate 360 degrees. Air stirred around them with his movement, carried his slightly astringent scent to her.

"Reid helped. He and I painted the kitchen together, but he had to get back to the ranch before we finished this room."

"The ranch?" Harlan touched a line of raindrops next to her finger. "That's where he is now?"

"Yes." She nodded. "He stays down there. The will split the estate evenly. He got the ranch and the farm in Costa Rica. I have this house and the investments."

"How often do you see him?"

"When he can get away. Not often. He's busy."

Next to hers, his finger trailed down the window, matching her movements as the streaks of rain merged, separated, merged one last time, leaving his fingertip briefly joined to hers. Her finger burned. Heat ran up her arm, up her neck, burned in her lips.

Molly dropped her hand.

"Why didn't you sell this house instead of staying here alone?" He flattened his palm against the window as she moved away. His broad hand and long fingers covered one of the panes, darkening the room as if a figure had stepped between her and the light.

"I might. Eventually. When I'm ready."

When he left, walking out of sight and disappearing down the driveway to wherever he'd parked, Molly stayed at the door, listening to the sound of his car as the engine coughed and fired, waiting until the reverberation died away in the distance. She'd wanted to walk out the door behind him, follow him to town, seek out lights and people.

She didn't want to be by herself in the silent house. Molly twisted the tie of her robe around and around her little finger. When she let it fall, it unwound in loose spirals, like the end of the yellow crime-scene tape blowing across her yard.

With his matter-of-fact statements, John Harlan had given her a framework for her scattered thoughts. As if he'd twisted the focus knob on a microscope, everything jumped into clarity. Murderer or next victim?

Or something else entirely?

She didn't believe in demons.

She had no intention of becoming a victim.

The rain dripped steadily onto the gallery in front of her and onto the closed blossoms of the hibiscus hedge lining the driveway.

The wind had risen by the time she parked in the open lot in front of the medical building Paul shared with a group of three other dentists, a plastic surgeon, a pediatrician, a psychiatrist, an obstetrician and the group's pharmacy. Set back from the road, the medical center's discreet and very expensive sign swung on its chains.

Under the banyans and live oaks ringing the parking lot, puddles shivered like crumpled foil in the wind, their surfaces flickering with light and clouds. Each office fronted onto the wide colonnade that circled the building. Curved, brick-red tiles topped the elegant, cream-colored columns. Leaves plastered the slick roof tiles and clumped in sodden piles at the bottom of the rain gutters, where steady streams of water flowed into the parking lot. Leading from the area, a portico lined with four-feet-high clay pots holding *Ficus* trees and low planters filled with vines and geraniums offered a gracious and reassuring entrance to the colonnade.

Hurrying through the puddles, Molly tried to steady her umbrella against the wind whipping it out of her grasp. She'd always thought that the building's quiet stateliness was as good as an anesthetic for Paul's patients. The heavy plantings and careful landscaping blocked the sounds of cars and passersby. Once in the colonnade, patients were screened from view, thus assuring privacy, whatever the medical services needed.

Paul had said patients wanted security and peace. He'd added that even though the building had cost more than they'd figured, it would pay off in the long run because people were willing to pay for ambience, even in an oral surgeon's office. Patients *really* wanted ambience in a plastic surgeon's office, he'd added, laughing.

A gust bent the umbrella ribs inside out as she stepped into the colonnade and walked down the mosaic hall of muted creams and browns and rusts to the east side and the door to Paul's suite of offices. Here, no sounds intruded. The quiet was almost total, marred only by the steady pattering of rain on the roof tiles and the leaves of the plants and trees.

Despite the quiet and privacy provided by the expensive building, a drift of movement past the columns caught Molly's eye. Suddenly uneasy, she stopped, her hand resting on the doorknob. The hairs on her arms rose as she turned toward the grounds of the courtyard and tensed, listening.

The leaves of the hedges lifted in the wind, turned, settled. The tall, pale trunks of the royal palms gleamed, their branches rattling, clicking.

Shadows and shapes, nothing more.

A sheet of rain slanted in and splashed her ankles.

Detective John Harlan had made her aware of how vulnerable she was. Even after her parents' murders, Molly had never thought of herself as a potential victim.

Now, thanks to John Harlan, she did.

Molly hunched her shoulders. She had a sudden vision of an enormous target painted on her back. She didn't like the sense that someone was out there, watching her, following her.

A tree branch lifted. She turned quickly at its fluttering motion.

There was nothing out there, of course.

Flattening the umbrella back into shape on its metal frame, Molly closed it and twirled most of the water off before dropping it into the enormous porcelain vase inside the office, to the left of the heavy, carved-wood door.

Annie Doublee looked up as rain and wind blew in. "Hey there, Mizz Bouler!" she said. Her perfect teeth opened in a perfect smile, wide and generous. "Oops. Mizz Harris. Sorry. I forget. Habit." Annie wrinkled her perfect oval face. With her narrow nose scrunched up in embarrassment, her enormous and brilliant blue eyes squinting in awkwardness, Annie still looked irresistibly adorable.

Even Molly thought so. Paul certainly had, for a month or two, anyway.

The sheer impact of all that perfection stunned Molly every time she saw Annie.

Unfortunately, Annie was bright. She was also funny, winsome and nice in an age when niceness was undervalued. Worst of all, Molly liked her. "Hey, yourself, Annie. Paul in?"

"He has a patient right now." Annie rolled her eyes.

Molly couldn't help smiling. "Oh."

"*Oh* isn't the half of it." Annie rolled her eyes again, mischief shining across her translucent skin. "She's divorced, rich and her root canal needs the doctor's *immediate* attention." Annie grinned. She should have looked childish, silly, goofy. She did. She also looked stunning.

Watching Annie, Molly decided that Harlan might have been right. The universe *was* irrational. In a rational world, Annie would have been vain, mean, spiteful. Molly sighed. "Any chance I can see him for a few minutes, Annie?"

"You know you can. He always has time for you."

"Without throwing his schedule out the window, I mean."

Annie thumbed down the appointment sheet. "Sure. The wisdom tooth's not due for another forty-five minutes. If Mizz Root Canal can tear herself away, he should have half an hour free." Annie's face softened. "You know it wouldn't matter. If you needed to see him, he'd make the time, Mizz Harris. He really would."

"I know." Molly sank onto a pale blue Italian-leather chair. Paul would do almost anything for her. He'd been her friend all her life and her husband for five years. He'd seen her gap toothed and flat chested. She'd suffered with him through a squeaky voice and acne.

But they should never have gotten married. That failure still made her cringe.

"I'll buzz him." Annie swiveled to the intercom button and pushed it. When she turned back to Molly, she was smiling. "He's overjoyed. He'll be right out."

The leather creaked as Molly shifted position. It had only been a branch she'd seen. That was all. Nothing else. Only a branch, gray in the rain, moving with the wind.

The door to the inner office swung smoothly open. Paul's broad, genial face was creased with concern. "Now, you call me at home if you have any problem, hear?" He patted the root-canal on the shoulder. "Take care, now."

Molly knew his concern was genuine. So was the amiability. So, too, was the pleasure in his eyes when he saw her. "Hey, hon," he said, ambling over to her. "Come on in." He wrapped one big arm around Molly and squeezed her to him. "Where you been hidin'? I've missed you. And why didn't you call me about Camina? What a mess, hon. You okay?" His questions tumbled around her.

His patient glanced once at Molly, frowned and walked to Annie's desk, where she conversed for a few seconds with the receptionist. Courtesy of the custom-ordered acoustical design, their voices were hushed.

Leading her to his consultation room, Paul kept his arm draped over her shoulder until she sat down on the sofa. "What happened with Camina, hon? I heard about it on the late news last night." He picked up the coffeemaker from the low credenza next to the sofa. "Want some?"

"Sure." She'd forgotten to eat in her rush to leave the house. She'd made a decision, and she hadn't wanted to waste time with food. "What else do you have? Any crackers?" she said, casting him a pleading glance. "Please, please say you have crackers."

His sideways glance was teasing. "You can have anything I have, hon."

Molly shook her head. "You never change, do you?"

"Nah," he said, clearly unrepentant. "I was always hot for your bod, hon, you know that." He lifted the cover of a plastic container. "Pecan pie?"

"Lord, no. Sugar coma." Molly made strangling noises.

He lifted another cover. "Tomato bread?"

"Terrific. I'm starved." Molly broke off a piece of the bread as he handed it to her on a small china plate. "Your patients take good care of you," she said, chewing slowly. "This is wonderful."

"Not as wonderful as some other things I could name." He sat on the edge of his desk, a big, furry teddy bear of a man smiling affectionately at her, his dark brown eyes teasing and warm.

It had been a while since food had tasted this good. She held out the plate. "More? Please?" She was starving suddenly. A quick memory of an altogether different kind of hunger gleaming in John Harlan's eyes made the plate tremble in her hand.

Paul edged off the desk, sliced another piece of bread and eased it onto her plate. He settled on the arm of the sofa.

"So you're not here to throw me to the floor in a wild, passionate assault?"

Mumbling around a piece of tomato bread, Molly said, "Not this time."

"More's the pity, hon. So, what's up?" He grinned, his mustache quivering at the ends. "Besides me?"

"You're incorrigible," Molly grumbled, biting into the bread.

"I know," he said, preening. "It's my charm. It's why you married me. I could always make you laugh."

Under the teasing, Molly detected a wistful note, but that was Paul, too. Settling the plate in her lap, Molly brushed her fingers together over it, watching the crumbs fall onto the blue-and-green china. "No—" she shook her head slowly, remembering back to their impulsive decision to elope "—it was because you were my best friend and because you were the sweetest man I'd ever met."

"Hell. And I always thought it was because you couldn't keep your hands off me," he said mournfully.

His words oddly echoed Harlan's, and Molly jumped, a buzz running over her skin. The plate rocked on her knees and she handed it back to Paul. "Why did we decide to elope that night, Paul? Who brought it up first? Me? You?"

"It was that fifth glass of champagne at your cousin's wedding. Put us both in the mood, is all I remember. Seemed like a good idea. I sure thought so." He took the plate, his stubby fingers gripping the plate carefully. Despite his awkward-looking hands, he was amazingly dexterous. His patients raved about his gentle touch. "It should have worked, Molly. Why didn't it?" His amiable face creased.

Molly rested her head on the heavily upholstered back of the sofa. "You know why, Paul."

"But, honey, that's just the way I am." He was bewildered. "You knew that when we eloped."

"I did, didn't I?" Molly sat up. "But you know what, Paul? I thought you'd be faithful to me. Foolish, wasn't I?"

"I tried, Molly. Really I did. For two years." He looked sheepish. "Really." He nodded earnestly, like a small boy trying to convince himself and everyone else he hadn't thrown the ball through the window. Paul could have stolen the crown jewels, had them falling out of his pockets and still denied the theft.

"Was it so difficult to be faithful to me, Paul?" Molly held herself still. She hadn't come to see him to thrash out the breakup of their marriage, but the answer had become important to her during the last year. She'd found out about his affairs, filed for divorce, and they'd never discussed the issue. She, because she felt stupid and gullible. And Paul? Well, Paul had never liked to confront unpleasantness. They'd remained friends, but friends with a wall of history and hurt between them, that wall turning their friendship into a habit, no longer the real thing.

Had she missed the friend more than the husband? The thought sliced through her, pain following it. "Was it something I did, Paul? Didn't do? How did I fail? Tell me."

He tugged the end of his mustache. "It was me, hon. I'm just not…" He stopped, distressed.

She knew him, after all. "Just not a one-woman man," she said, amazed at the lingering power of the old pain.

He nodded, his hands dropping to his sides.

"And I'm very much a one-man woman."

"Hon, I'm a heel. I admit it." He smiled, trying to charm her, meaning it, too. He patted her hand.

"Yes, you were."

"But, hon, it's like that old snake story—you know the one."

Brushing a crumb off her skirt, Molly shook her head.

"Sure you do, hon. The lady sees the poor ol' frozen rattler and is going to pass him by, but the snake begs her and pleads with her to help him. She won't, of course, because he'll strike her, but he promises not to. So she picks him up, tucking him into her bosom so he'll stay warm, and carries him home, where she wraps him up next to her fire. After he's all thawed out and cozy, he rears up and strikes her, and she can't understand why he's done this. He replies, 'But you knew what I was when you picked me up.' That's me, Molly. I don't seem to be able to change what I am.'' He shrugged, the same concern she'd seen on his face earlier there once more. "But I tried. I swear on my momma's grave, I tried to be different for you. I was the one who failed, not you, hon." His mustache quivered.

Molly looked deep into his earnest, easygoing face. "Maybe you did, Paul."

"Of course I did, hon. I loved you. I still do."

"But you couldn't be faithful."

"No, hon, I'm a weak and sinful man," he said mournfully. "Lord love me, but I'm a lost lamb."

Molly grinned. She couldn't help it. His expression was so woebegone that she couldn't help seeing the whole absurdity of the situation. "Well, it's not my business anymore, Paul, but I hope you're a cautious, *safe* lamb, if you know what I mean. Your life-style isn't, uh—''

"The most careful?"

"Well…'' Molly shrugged, affection moving her when she'd never expected to feel any for him again.

"Hey, hon, I'm *always* careful. And very, very *safe*.'' His grin was naughty. "I have the tests to prove it.'' When she smiled, reservations unspoken, he added, his little-boy attitude gone, "I have a living to make, and, trust me, I'm damned careful."

Molly did. Paul had planned on being a millionaire by the time he was forty. He hadn't been able to stay faithful to her, but he'd never betrayed his youthful goal. Underneath all the expensive Italian leather and decorator-subtle blues and greens of his glossy office, Paul Bouler was still that young boy from the wrong side of the tracks who didn't ever intend to look back.

"You remember when I dropped that worm down your pants during eighth-grade graduation?" Molly remembered his pants had been an inch too short for his shot-up-overnight body.

"Damn sure! And I got even by dumping punch over your new perm." He chortled. "Lord, but that was the frizziest pink head of hair I ever saw, hon!"

They'd been able to forgive each other over the years. "Maybe we should have stayed friends, Paul. Maybe we weren't ever meant to be lovers. Partners."

Taking her hands between his, Paul rubbed her knuckles. "I'd like to be friends again, Molly. I've missed you."

Imitating Annie, Molly rolled her eyes.

"In my own way, hon, really," he added earnestly. "I know, I know—" he threw his hands heavenward "—I'm incorrigible. But you love me, too."

"In my own way," Molly said, understanding at last, "I guess I do."

The failure had been hers, yes, but it hadn't been a failure of character or will. She had mistaken youthful hormones and friendship for love. Not a tragedy, but it could have become one had she stayed with him as his wife. Paul was right. He wasn't a man who could stay faithful to one person. The hurts and losses of his childhood had scabbed over, and he was perfectly happy—in fact preferred—skimming cheerfully along life's surface. And he had always made her laugh, no matter what.

But she needed more than laughter. She needed someone who would cherish her because she was as important to him as breath itself.

She'd always yearned for something else. Something that went taproot deep with another person. An emotional connection that left roots and branches twined inseparably. That kind of linking would never have been possible with Paul.

With the lamps shining on Paul's oak desk and the smell of fresh coffee in the air, Molly was more at peace than she'd been in a year. She liked having Paul around, liked having his bulky body next to her, his arm draped casually across her shoulders. Most of all, she liked having her friend back.

As they sat and sipped coffee, feet close together on the round table in front of the sofa, Molly felt the tension inside her uncoiling, floating through her as smooth as the cream in her coffee. She hadn't realized how lonely she'd been. She'd dived into grief and stayed underwater so long she'd forgotten there was another world if only she'd swim toward the light. Not budging from her side, Paul seemed equally content, stealing a nibble from her plate and laughing when she slapped his hand. They'd been lovers, after a fashion. They'd been husband and wife. And now they were friends again.

He was so relaxed she would have thought he didn't have another appointment for the whole afternoon if she hadn't talked with Annie.

Nibbling on a fourth slice of bread, Molly finally plunked the remnants back onto the plate. He had a schedule to keep and she shouldn't take up any more of his office time. "I need your help, Paul."

"Sure, hon." He cuddled her closer. "Whatever you need. Does this have anything to do with Camina?"

"In a way." Molly noticed her skin didn't hum the way it had when John Harlan had merely glanced at her, his gold eyes making her edgy and frightened. She'd had enough tension during these past months to last her a lifetime. Leaning her head companionably on Paul's broad shoulder, Molly decided there was something to be said for cuddling, after all. And unlike John Harlan's edgy awareness Paul's warm brown eyes and teasing comments didn't make her feel as if she'd stepped off the edge of a riverbank with no bottom in sight. She'd vote for cuddling any day, especially with a teddy bear.

"God, I couldn't believe she was murdered. Awful." He tugged the ends of his mustache. "What happened?"

"She was stabbed with a butcher knife. One of mine from the house."

"Sh—" He gripped her shoulder. "God almighty." His fingers dug into her flesh. "What a shock for you."

She started to tell him that she was a suspect, that she'd been having strange, out-of-consciousness incidents. Started to tell him about the times she'd woken up on the floor of her kitchen. "You don't know the half of—"

"Do the police know who 'dun it'?" Paul looked at her intently, anxiety pulling his thick eyebrows together, the teddy bear cuddliness gone. Too intense.

His fingertips bore into her shoulder and she wriggled loose, momentarily uncomfortable. "No." Molly stood up, straightened her skirt, fiddled with her pearl ring. Loose, it stayed with the pearl turned in.

"Who's high on the list of suspects? They talked with you, I guess. Right? They don't think you killed Camina, do they?" He grabbed her hand and squeezed it.

The prongs holding the pearl in her ring dug into her palm where she'd cut herself, been cut—who knew which? She sure didn't.

In that instant, Molly changed her mind. She didn't want Paul knowing how terrified she'd been. He was her friend, yes, but he was also a hybrid, thanks to their divorce. He was an ex-husband, and divorced wives shouldn't lean on ex-husbands. There was a certain dignity involved. Pride. He could be her friend, but for the time being, they'd have to recement even that relationship.

"Listen, I'll tell 'em I was with you all night long. You

need someone to vouch for you, and I'm your man.'' His grin was roguish. ''I won't let 'em put you behind bars, honey.'' He was still holding her hand. ''Nobody's threatening that, I hope?''

Molly pulled her hand free and turned her ring around. Her palm was red where the prongs had pierced her skin. ''No. Of course not.'' Lying was becoming second nature to her. She didn't understand why she was reluctant to tell Paul that she was pretty high on the list of suspects.

''Really?''

She nodded emphatically.

''Good, but I'm kind of surprised. Being on the scene, so to speak, you might have been their logical target. Didn't they have a bunch of questions about why Camina left?''

''Yes, but it's not a problem.'' Molly swallowed the bitterness in her mouth.

''No?''

Her hair swung into her eyes as she shook her head. She looked down at her hands where she'd wadded her skirt.

''Great. That's terrific. They'd be crazy to think you had anything to do with her murder, no matter how things looked.''

Molly wished he wouldn't keep harping on how things looked. She knew exactly how things looked to Detective Harlan, and he wasn't crazy. Persistent. Relentless. Determined. But not crazy.

Paul's thick eyebrows were still drawn together as he continued, ''But, listen, if they bother you, you call me, okay? I'll give you an alibi, find you the best lawyer in the state, whatever. You know I'll help you. I've already told you that.''

''I do need your help, Paul.'' Molly rubbed her hands down her charcoal gray skirt. Her damp palms left their mark on the smooth, light wool. ''Here's the situation. I haven't minded living alone on the bayou until this inci-

dent,'' she lied, ''but now I'm frightened. I want one of
Dad's guns back. Unless you've sold them?'' She made her
hands stay calmly in her lap, when what she wanted was to
grab his and grip them, shake him into agreeing with her.

He jumped to his feet.

''You didn't want those guns in the house after your folks
were shot. You said you couldn't stand to look at your dad's
collection, and Reid didn't want them, either. That's the
only reason I took them.'' He was scowling at her. ''Guns
are dangerous, Molly.''

''I know, Paul. That's why I want one. There aren't any
streetlights out where I live, and it takes the police at least
twenty minutes to reach my home. If I'm able to call them.''

''Why don't you get a dog if you're scared? For damn
sure I'd be scared witless out there myself after all that's
happened. But a gun...'' He walked away from her to his
desk, then back again. ''A dog's the best idea, hon. Really.''

''Maybe. But I want Dad's 9 mm Luger.''

''You could hurt someone with a gun, Molly.''

''I know. That's the idea, Paul. I don't want anybody in
my house who doesn't belong there.''

''Damn, Molly, I never knew you had this bloodthirsty
side to you.'' He was digging in his heels. ''I can't let you
have one of the guns. That doesn't make any sense. It's a
damn fool idea, is what it is. Get a dog. They bark. They
make noise.''

''And after my dog barks like crazy, what then, Paul?
What if the intruder comes in anyway? And the telephone
doesn't work?''

He glowered, a five-year-old on the brink of pouting. ''I
still think you should get a dog.''

''Dogs can be poisoned.'' Molly didn't want to beg, but
she would. ''Listen, Paul. I'm not going home without
Dad's gun, without some kind of protection. I'll rent a room
at Sally Lou's Motel out on the highway first.''

"You're dead set on this, aren't you?" He pulled at his mustache.

"Maybe you could rephrase that?" Molly asked gently.

"What?"

"*Dead*'s not one of my favorite vocabulary choices these days." She didn't have the strength to go into that house tonight by herself, unarmed, unprotected. And she wasn't about to phone up her friendly local detective John Harlan and ask him to hold her hand while she checked through her house again.

"Come on, Molly, get a dog." He was weakening.

"I don't want some helpless animal killed because of me."

"But you'd shoot someone?"

"If I had to." A chill went down to her toes. "If someone were threatening me, I would shoot him, Paul."

"You'd be in a pickle if you did."

"I'd be dead if I didn't." The knowledge was there inside her. She had to take care of herself.

"You know I hate guns. I always have. I only went hunting with Reid and your dad because Reid was my buddy. I mean, I liked your dad, too, but hunting was their thing, not mine."

"But you hunted. You went with them, Paul. And you shot your share of ducks down at Lake Okeechobee every Thanksgiving."

"I have a better idea. Why don't you stay with me until the cops catch whoever did it?"

"What if it takes six months? A year? Never? I can't stay with you, Paul." Molly put everything she had into her last question. "Please, Paul. Be my friend and help me?"

In the end, he agreed. He seemed miserable. She was uncomfortable. He told Annie to let his next patient know he was running late. Molly waited on the couch until the room closed in around her, then went out to the reception area.

"I'm going to walk around for a few minutes, Annie. I'll be right back. I need some fresh air." She laughed at Annie's expression. "Yes, Paul put in the most expensive and technologically advanced environmental-control system he could find—did I leave anything out?"

Annie shook her head. Her glossy black hair caught the light. "Not a single thing. It's the kickiest."

"Kickiest?"

"That's what my eight-year-old says all the time."

"I won't go far. Around the colonnade, the portico. I want to smell the rain, that's all."

She stepped out into a gray day that had slid into a grayer twilight. Most of the offices were closed, because some of the doctors still took the traditional Wednesdays off. With flooding in the low-lying areas and beaches a problem after two days of a steady downpour, other doctors had obviously gone home.

Paul hadn't.

Molly walked to the west side of the building, past empty offices. Not yet four o'clock, but the lights in the parking lot had come on, their subdued glow friendly and welcoming. Outside their cones of yellow, though, darkness slid under the trees and crept toward the building.

The scrape of a shoe against the mosaic set into the brick flooring startled her. It had come from the farthest end of the west corridor. She didn't move as she tried to catch her breath. At that end the complex seemed deserted.

She backed up, step by step, placing her feet noiselessly on the tiles.

Something brushed her cheek lightly, like a lover's kiss in the dark. Cool, wet, clinging. Gulping for air with burning lungs, she turned and ran, flailing wildly at her face. The clatter of her heels clicking and slipping on the wet tiles echoed behind her.

CHAPTER SEVEN

He'd followed her on the rain-swept roads from her house to the medical center, watched as the wind buffeted her and her oyster gray umbrella. When he saw her turn into the offices on the east side of the center, he lagged behind, giving her enough of a lead so that she wouldn't hear him or see him as he trailed her on the outside of the colonnade, matching his steps to hers, moving when she moved, her shadow.

He thought he'd made a mistake when she paused with her hand on the heavy metal doorknob. As she turned, he faded backward, only a leaf moving behind him as he disappeared into the foliage. He waited patiently, rain dripping off the ends of his hair, down his neck and under his collar, and soon a thin blond woman left the office. Her collagen-plumped lips were bracketed with white parentheses and her shoulders were slumped, but as he watched, she flipped her hand under her toned hair, straightened, and by the time she'd reached the portico, she was humming.

Yawning, he leaned forward, letting the blood flow into his head. He was tired. He should have gone back to his apartment and spent the afternoon sleeping. He needed sleep. And he would, but first he wanted to find out why sweet Molly had torn out of her house like a bat out of hell and driven ten miles over the speed limit all the way into town and through it until she skidded to a stop in Dr. Paul Bouler's parking lot.

Harlan's ears popped as he yawned again. For a moment he entertained himself with the idea of curling into a ball under the hedge and sleeping. Her footsteps would wake him. He shook his head, arched his back and touched his toes. Drops of water skittered off leaves and flew with his movements. He edged forward, blended with the hedge and stilled his breathing while he waited for Molly to come back out.

The dentist, her ex, came out a side door to the suite of offices, clambered into an expensive sports car and left. Molly remained inside. Interesting, Harlan thought, running his hand under his collar and stopping the river of water running down his back, very intriguing, but he would stay on Molly's trail. Harlan knew the ex would return. The reason for his abrupt departure would become clear. Patience.

Hunting required infinite patience. To his left, a cat slunk quietly under the shelter of the hedge and settled, wet and miserable. Hunching his shoulders, Harlan waited, his ears tuned to the sounds around him. Raindrops slipping over the leaves, plopping to the ground. The electric hum of the parking lights off to his right. In the distance, the slap of tires against the road. A creaking of shoe leather.

Harlan lifted his head, angled it to the right. His nostrils flared. Lightly, lightly, over the clean smell of wind and rain, came a stench of evil.

His head swiveled as Molly came out of the office door, the wind catching it out of her hand and slamming it behind her. Her slow stroll through the deserted colonnade gave him time to slip easily behind her. Her hair swung against her shoulders, the pale brown strands catching against the gray knit sweater, swinging free as she turned her head, staring his way. The feeble light outside one of the offices turned her hair to melted caramel.

Harlan slowed his breathing. Molly frowned, took a step forward and stopped, peering ahead down the long west passage of the colonnade. Staying in the gloom of the landscaping, he focused ahead of her, his eyes dilating in the rain-induced twilight.

He could smell it stronger now, that stench of corruption, and he eased his way forward, his shape blending with the phantasms of light and shadow lurking in the dusk.

When he was three feet ahead of her, breathing in and out silently, slowing his heartbeat, Harlan sensed a presence. He suspended his motion midstep, his right foot hovering over a sodden clump of leaves, waiting.

Molly's backward step, her clattering flight away from him and her raspy breathing sent him slipping quickly after her, and the scent blew away with a whirl of wind. Looking behind him, Harlan saw a lingering aura that faded even as he stared, its reddish glow shimmering in the darkness at the corner of the building.

Gone. Nothing there. Only an awareness curling inside him of something nasty.

Harlan heard the scratch of Molly's fingernails against the metal of the doorknob, her quick inhalation as she shut the door behind her. Hovering near the solid door, he heard, too, the fabric of her skirt whisper against the wood as she leaned back, panting. Flattening his palm against the wood, Harlan felt the stuttering vibration of her small heart, banging like that of a terrified bird.

He slid his hand down the door, tracing Molly's small, slight shape on the other side.

Immobile except for the slow sweep of his gaze, Harlan surveyed the complex.

Something had been here.

Something that threatened Molly.

Interesting.

Merging back into the shadows, he stayed alert, senses vibrating.

Some time later—he'd lost track of time now—Molly left, hurrying across the colonnade. He saw the gleam of her keys as she ran across the parking lot to her car, skidding to a halt. Her purse thumped heavily against the door and back onto her hip. She shoved the key into the slot and leapt inside, slamming the door behind her.

The snap of the locks was loud.

Sounds and smells had become hyperintense, his senses honed.

Safe behind the steamy windows of her car, she slumped over the steering wheel and buried her head between her white-knuckled hands. Where her hair parted over her slender nape, the skin gleamed, pale and fragile in the dimness. Like satin sliding between his thumb and forefinger, he could feel it, could taste its sweetness on his mouth. She made him hunger for impossible things.

Of all people, Molly Harris had pierced the wall around him. He'd let down his guard briefly when he'd held her in his arms on the bayou, but he'd been lucky that all he'd done was kiss her.

Perhaps a little more than *kiss,* if he were honest with himself, and he made a point of facing the truth about himself—his nature, his weaknesses—no matter how unpalatable the truth was. If he'd made love with her—well, it wouldn't have been *love,* but something else entirely—if he'd weakened, worse things could have happened than losing his job. Disaster.

Concentrating, Harlan saw her flick open her purse, pull out a tissue and blow her nose. Her shoulders squared with determination and she turned the key, the tiny click of metal alerting him, and he slipped between the hedge and an oak tree, invisible to her as she whipped the car around in a three-point turn and passed him.

She had a gun in her purse.

She hadn't had one when she'd gone into the medical building.

As she turned onto the road, Harlan remembered what had tickled his memory about her alibi for her parents' murders. Her alibi had been her ex-husband.

Get FREE BOOKS and a FREE GIFT when you play the...

LAS VEGAS

GAME

Just scratch off the gold box with a coin. Then check below to see the gifts you get!

YES! I have scratched off the gold Box. Please send me my **2 FREE BOOKS** and **gift for which I qualify.** I understand that I am under no obligation to purchase any books as explained on the back of this card.

345 SDL DRQH   245 SDL DRQX

FIRST NAME	LAST NAME

ADDRESS

APT.#	CITY

(S-IMB-12/02)

STATE/PROV.   ZIP/POSTAL CODE

Visit us online at **www.eHarlequin.com**

7	7	7	Worth TWO FREE BOOKS plus a BONUS Mystery Gift!
🍒	🍒	🍒	Worth TWO FREE BOOKS!
🔔	🔔	♣	TRY AGAIN!

Offer limited to one per household and not valid to current Silhouette Intimate Moments® subscribers. All orders subject to approval.

If offer card is missing write to: Silhouette Reader Service, 3010 Walden Ave., P.O. Box 1867, Buffalo NY 14240-1867

BUSINESS REPLY MAIL

FIRST-CLASS MAIL   PERMIT NO. 717-003   BUFFALO, NY

POSTAGE WILL BE PAID BY ADDRESSEE

SILHOUETTE READER SERVICE
3010 WALDEN AVE
PO BOX 1867
BUFFALO NY 14240-9952

NO POSTAGE
NECESSARY
IF MAILED
IN THE
UNITED STATES

His, of course, had been innocent Molly Harris.

Her parents had been shot to death.

And now sweet Molly had a gun, one given to her by her friendly ex.

Why had her ex-husband given her a gun?

A friend was a wonderful thing to have, Harlan mused as he started the car. Letting the engine idle, he scanned the parking lot and colonnade, the dim lights showing over the office doors.

Tapping his fingers on the steering wheel, he saw again, like a flash of light in the dark, the image of Molly with her head between her hands, her fists clenched.

Who was doing who a favor?

And where had the friendly Dr. Bouler been in those seconds when Molly had bolted down the empty corridor back to his office?

Harlan slipped into first gear and followed Molly. He knew where she was going. He didn't have to hurry. She wouldn't be far ahead of him.

He sighted through the slashing rain as the windshield wipers labored to clear a view. Thoughtfully he shoved his sunglasses up through his wet, rumpled hair and settled them on his head.

Adrenaline was flooding through him with the twists and turns of the hunt.

He didn't feel like sleeping anymore.

His whistle was tuneless as he trailed Molly through the rain. Almost out of sight far ahead of him, she braked and turned, heading for the road paralleling the bayou, her red lights a blurred glow that winked and disappeared.

"Catch you later, Ms. Harris," he murmured and smiled, thinking about friends and favors.

Approaching her house in the dark, Molly slowed in the driveway. Shells crunched underneath tires as she stopped.

She was relieved that she'd left the lights on. Looking at the graceful house shining like a sanctuary in the dark, she wished she hadn't left all the shutters open, though.

From outside, anyone could follow her progression from one room to the other throughout the house—upstairs, downstairs. With the lights blazing from each room, the windows became a silent stage where the story of her life unrolled.

Seeing the rooms as separate stages, she realized abruptly how *open* her home was. Living so far from town, she hadn't concerned herself with privacy when she was growing up. None of them had. Who, after all, was there to walk casually by and peer in their windows?

The solitude of those days, idyllic and serene, mocked her with memories, taunted her with the knowledge that she would never again go into her house and leave the windows unshuttered. The sleepy rural solitude of childhood days had become a threat to her with its masking of eyes, eyes glowing in the dark, staring—

"Enough," she muttered, grabbing her purse. She'd have herself so damned goosey she'd end up sleeping in the car, or turning around and driving pell-mell back to Sally Lou's Motel after all. Although she'd agreed with every one of Paul's points about having a gun, she'd needed something more than her locks and jimmy bars. Maybe getting the gun back from Paul hadn't been the smartest idea. She was embarrassed to admit that having it reinforced her determination not to wind up screaming on her kitchen floor until she couldn't scream anymore. Never again.

Taking her foot off the brake, she rolled to a stop under the porte cochere off the left side of the house, the side opposite the kitchen and under the gallery outside her bedroom.

She held the gun loosely by her side as she locked the car doors behind her and walked across the wet veranda and around to the kitchen entrance, looking inside the bright rooms like a stranger as she passed them. Molly made herself breathe deeply and evenly. She didn't allow herself to dwell on those fearful seconds outside Paul's office.

Instead, as she walked slowly past her flowerpots and boxes, she made plans. She should see Bob Nolan tomorrow. He'd drawn up her parents' wills, hers. He could recommend a good criminal lawyer. She'd be smart to have a name handy if Detective Harlan showed up tomorrow with a warrant for her arrest.

If the police decided to arrest her, she hoped they would send someone else. She didn't think she could endure having Harlan surround her with his presence, fix those golden eyes on her and handcuff her. Molly shivered. Not Detective Harlan.

If she weren't arrested, she'd go back to work. She'd been missing too many days, and she didn't want the dentists in her territory to start ordering from someone else. She'd been doing a half-hearted job lately contacting them and checking to see if they needed new supplies or equipment. She was lucky she'd been allowed to keep the Gulf Coast area this long, but her bosses wouldn't be understanding if she had two abysmal quarters in a row. They'd made appropriately sympathetic noises for the first period—they understood her situation; of course they didn't want to imply that family wasn't important; but ultimately, was she coming back to work or not?

She'd gotten the message. She just hadn't been successful at reestablishing her former pace after the nights she spent staring down her stairwell.

She wouldn't let herself spend any more nights craving sleep and cowering in her house.

Before inserting her keys into the locks, Molly tried the kitchen door. Of course it was locked. That was how she'd left it. She'd left the ceiling paddle fans running to circulate the air when she left, and their low-pitched drone comforted her as she reentered her home.

Her relief at seeing the kitchen exactly as she'd left it was excessive.

Running up the stairs, she kept the gun beside her, laying it on her dresser while she changed into jeans and a ragged green-and-orange University of Miami T-shirt that Reid had left behind. Head poking through the neck, she paused. She would call Reid in Costa Rica tomorrow, too. She would tell him everything that had happened.

Living in the country as they had, she and Reid, fraternal twins, had been each other's only playmates until kindergarten. She'd always secretly thought that they were linked intuitively, psychically, but he'd scoffed, punched her on the arm and blown a big, rude raspberry at her when she'd suggested it. She'd never mentioned it to him again. She'd kept the feeling that they shared a special bond to herself.

Paul had tried to reassure her today, but he'd had to work at it. She didn't have to be a mind reader to hear his discomfort loud and clear. Irritably, Molly snapped the shutters of the bedroom together. Paul had dismissed too easily her lie that she wasn't a suspect, that she didn't need any alibi. She'd heard the reservations underlying his playfulness.

But Reid knew her better than anyone.

He was her twin, all she had left of family, and she found that she wanted him with her now, a barrier against the dark intimidation of John Harlan and his suspicions.

Her threadbare jeans were soft, the waistband loose enough after the weight she'd lost over the last months for her to slip the gun into the small of her back. It scratched her skin, but she liked knowing it was within reach. Leaving the lights on, she went downstairs, found the scrub bucket in the pantry and filled it with hot water and disinfectant.

She wanted nothing left in her house of the detectives and their greasy, black fingerprint powder. She wanted nothing left to remind her of those moments on the floor when she'd thought she'd gone to some endless hole of despair and desperation, where the sound of her own screaming would never leave her ears.

Putting pot holders over her knees, Molly started with the floor, suds sloshing over as she plunked the bucket down by the door and began. The water was hot even through her plastic surgical gloves, but the heat felt good.

The grass slapped his chest as he prowled closer to her. He wanted to be with her. He stopped, shook his big head. For a moment, confusion stirred in him, slowed his steady padding toward her. He lowered himself until he was flat out on the ground. Far off he heard the rumble of an engine. Not from the water. It came from the road. The rumble vibrated the ground as the car approached, passed and stopped some distance up from the driveway entrance.

He waited until the engine died.

Silence for a while—he couldn't tell how long—but he waited, and finally something moved, approached the house quietly, secretly.

The rain had stopped and other creatures were on the move.

Gathering himself, he flexed his powerful leg muscles and jumped, landing soundlessly on her porch and vanishing into dark spaces.

It wasn't time.

Eyes wide, unblinking, he folded himself together and settled, head cocked to the sound of footsteps coming from the driveway, growing louder. The shells popped and crackled underneath shoe soles.

He lowered his head and waited.

He would recognize this intruder the next time.

There would be a next time.

He was certain of it.

* * *

Molly straightened, her thigh muscles shaking. She'd crawled around the perimeter of the kitchen for the last hour, scrubbing the baseboards. She glanced over at the microwave clock. Eleven o'clock. Her shoulders ached, and her back might not ever work right again. Each vertebra felt permanently fused to the one above it as she stood up and looked with enormous satisfaction around her clean kitchen.

Earlier she'd thought she'd seen the cat meandering around and she peeked through the shutters, but she'd been wrong. After two dates, the creature was apparently playing his feline version of "I'll call you." She picked up the bucket of dirty water and unlocked the door.

Pitching the water over the edge of the veranda railing, she stopped and looked around her. It had been a long time since she'd willingly stepped out of her house after the sun set.

The night stirred with life, creatures on the wing and afoot after two days of rain. With the gun riding her spine, Molly breathed in the night air. Scented with orange blossoms and the sweet fragrance of the oleanders that lined the road, the damp air filled her lungs, making her part of the night and its creatures.

In the clear sky, the moon shone down, silvery and huge, turning the white flowers of the night-blooming cereus otherworldly. Hundreds of blossoms climbed up the trellis at the end of the gallery in an explosion of magic after the dreary, rain-swept days.

When the cat didn't stalk haughtily onto the veranda, she shut and locked the door again, but not in fear. Maybe Detective Harlan would arrest her come morning, but in the meantime she felt freer than she'd felt for a long time.

And hungry.

Pulling a box of cereal out of the pantry, she shoved the door shut behind her with her fanny. It swung half-open again as she grabbed a bowl out of the cupboard and upended the box of cereal into it. Sniffing the milk first, she poured it over the crackling, snapping stuff, crossed her legs yoga-style in the chair and dived in.

She didn't even jump when three firm raps at the kitchen door rattled the chain. But unscrambling herself from the table, she sent milk onto her already wet shirt and down her leg. Pebbles of cereal clung to her thigh.

"Hello, Detective Harlan," she muttered through the crack of the door, her right hand firmly at her back.

"You shouldn't open your door this late at night." Propped against the side of her doorjamb, he looked big and dangerous, his lazy pose merely concealing his speed and power.

"I wouldn't have, but I knew it was you."

"Ah."

"I peeked through the kitchen window."

"Ah." He eyed her speculatively. "So you knew I was your late-night visitor? And that it was safe to open your door?" One hand rested negligently in his slacks pocket, the other at the edge of her door where the chain held it fast. His fingernails were blunt cut and clean. "Such courage all of a sudden, Ms. Harris." He smiled. His smile hinted he knew the source of her courage. "I'm very impressed."

"I'm sure you are, Detective." Molly kept her hand on the butt of the Luger. "What do you want?"

"Why don't you ask me in, and I'll tell you?" He tapped the chain and it swung gently for a moment.

Molly edged the door shut. "I don't think so. Not tonight. You've finished your searches in here for the day, Detective Harlan."

"I didn't come to toss your house again, Ms. Harris." He touched the bottom of the door with the toe of his loafer. Its highly polished black surface gleamed. "I want to ask you a question."

"I don't feel like answering any tonight."

His toe blocked the door so that it wouldn't shut. "Do you know how to shoot that gun you're clutching in your ladylike grip?" His expression was, as usual, slightly curious and reserved. Countering his civilized demeanor, the ever-present mockery in his eyes made him seem elegantly barbaric.

"Of course."

"Why did your ex give you the gun, Ms. Harris?"

"What?" His switches of subject left her bewildered.

"It puzzles me that he would let you have a gun, knowing that you were a possible homicide suspect, that's all. Seems a little careless of him, don't you think?"

"Paul told you he gave me my father's gun?" She hadn't thought Paul would betray her in this way, especially after their talk.

"No. I haven't talked with him today." Harlan again swung the chain. "Tell me why he gave you that gun, Ms. Harris?"

"Because I asked him to! I told him I was afraid out here by myself and he agreed to help me."

"Are you sure that was the reason?" Insinuations slipped through his courteous voice. "Don't you think it's a bit—" he smiled as he tapped the chain "—naive to hand over a gun to a suspect? Why would an upright, upstanding citizen behave like that, Ms. Harris?"

"Because we're friends."

"Everybody should be so lucky. To have friends like Dr. Bouler."

Molly leaned her head against the door. "You're implying Paul had some other reason for helping me? What? Spit it out, Detective."

"Ms. Harris, you alarm me sometimes. Three murders have been committed on your property. You've been either on the scene or have come upon it shortly afterward. You insist that you're not guilty, and, in fact, have an alibi for the first murders, an alibi provided by your ex-husband. Did you know that the shattered window glass at the front of your house didn't prove anything about what actually happened that night?''

"Someone broke in. It was a burglary," Molly murmured, tears thickening her voice. "Random. Stupid."

"That lovely etched glass with its patterns of birds and trees could have been smashed after the murders to give the appearance of a burglary. Those murders, like Camina's, Ms. Harris, weren't necessarily random."

Molly rubbed her forehead on the door. "Of course they were. Nothing else makes sense."

"Really?" He moved so quickly she didn't even react. The chain dangled uselessly between them.

He'd managed to slide it off its slot before she could slam the door. She hadn't even seen the quick flick of his finger along the chain until he'd finished. The gun at her back seemed ineffective in light of his speed.

"Ms. Harris," he continued, waiting calmly on the veranda, the partially shut door merely a pretense between them, a pretense he allowed. "The glass showed a concentric fracture—that's where the point of impact is surrounded by concentric, circular tracks—and the side of the glass that formed a right angle with the conchoidal fracture indicated only that the force had been applied from outside."

"That's all technical talk. It doesn't mean anything to me," she said, refusing to open the door even though she knew he only needed to push it and it would swing wide.

"The report didn't help the cops on the case, either, Ms. Harris. I read the report. The guys gathered their evidence real carefully. Your folks being such prominent citizens, I reckon no one wanted to screw up."

"Why are you telling me all this? I don't want to hear the details again! I read the report once. That was enough."

As if he hadn't heard her, Harlan went on, his even voice reciting words that became a grocery list of horror, bringing the smell of blood, the dark splotches into the present. "The evidence gathering was very carefully done, Ms. Harris. The pieces of glass were collected and fitted back together like a jigsaw puzzle. The techs worked hard to keep the surfaces of the broken window separate. They checked to see if dirt layers matched up to indicate the outside of the window, but it had been cleaned too recently for that to yield anything significant."

Lifting her head, Molly swallowed. "I cleaned them that morning." She had polished the delicate tracery of mockingbirds in the windows beside the front door as a favor to her mother, who'd teased her about cheap labor. Oh, God. Molly laid her cheek against the door.

"Not that it would have mattered if the windows had been dirty," he said, watching her face and nudging the door with his foot.

Loose in her grasp, the door moved. The chain pressed into her cheek.

"You and I both know any fool who watches TV knows enough to break a window from the outside if you want it to look like a break-in. Unless the mope's caught with glass splinters in his clothing or shoes, or unless he's caught in the act, we cops are working against the odds and against time. Most crooks are caught within a matter of hours, or they're not caught at all. Most people are killed by people they have some connection with, someone they know. Ms. Harris, anyone could have killed your parents. Anyone could have killed Camina. Someone familiar to them, someone you know. Like your ex-husband, for instance."

Molly jerked her head up. "Why are you trying to make me suspicious of people I care about?"

His voice was as soft as the gulf water sliding against the sand. "Ms. Harris, why aren't *you* suspicious of the motives

of everyone around you? That's what alarms me. If you're
not a murderer, you're way too trusting for your own good.
And that's why I want to talk with you. I saw you leave Dr.
Bouler's office with the gun. Open the door, please.''

Letting her hand drop to her side, Molly opened the door.
''You followed me?''

''Yes, I was right behind you. I watched you go into Dr.
Bouler's office—a very nice setup, by the way, very classy
and expensive, I'm sure. I waited until you left. Your purse
was heavier, you know, with the gun in it. It was the way
it swung against your side when it bumped you that clued
me in.''

There was no point in denying the obvious. If he'd seen
her slipping, running back to Paul's office, Detective Harlan
had known how frightened she'd been. ''You scared me.''

''No. *I* didn't.'' Stepping in front of her, he grabbed a
paper towel and wiped a milk mustache from her mouth
carefully, then threw the towel into the wastebasket. It might
have been her imagination that he lingered at the corners of
her lips. ''You never saw me.''

''Maybe not,'' she conceded, stepping back, annoyed
with him, annoyed with herself. She must have looked like
an idiot, slapping at her face where the *Ficus* branch had
blown across her face and tangled in her hair. ''But I heard
you. Same difference.''

''Not quite. You heard something ahead of both of us.
Not me.'' He reached behind her, his arms grazing the sides
of her ribs as he plucked the Luger from her limp grasp.

Where he'd brushed against her, her skin ached, as if,
somewhere inside of her, the cells of her body were rear-
ranging themselves, turning like a compass needle toward
him. She didn't understand her reaction, and she didn't like
it. The awareness came from someplace other than her conscious mind, which told her clearly and insistently that she

didn't like Detective John Harlan. "You made that noise. It had to have been you. I know it was," she persisted.

"Definitely not me, Ms. Harris." He placed the gun on the counter.

"I—I…" Comprehending at last, Molly sank into the chair he pulled out. His forearm bumped her cheek and her skin burned. "You heard something, too?"

"Yes." Slouching against the sink, he stretched out his legs into her space, his shoes inches away from her bare toes.

"I didn't imagine it?"

"No."

Sick with relief, Molly bowed her head. "I was frightened, so frightened," she whispered.

"You should have been." He was kneeling before her. "Ms. Harris—"

"You're sure you heard that scraping sound, as if someone were waiting for me? And accidentally moved?" She touched his face. His cheekbones were hard and his skin warm. She'd never dreamed there could be such comfort in touching another human being. She longed to let her hands linger against the angled planes of his face, trace the cords of his strong neck and the muscles of his wide shoulders. He had been there. "You're positive there was someone else in the corridor?"

"There was *something* there," he said, placing her hands back in her lap.

"You mean an animal?" Molly couldn't figure out what he was trying to tell her.

"No."

"I don't understand."

"Neither do I. Not yet. But I will." He touched her knee fleetingly, and her skin buzzed under the frayed denim. "Do you believe in evil, Ms. Harris?"

"I don't know. Bad people do bad things. I don't get your point."

"My point is—" and his voice lowered, became sibilant, a hiss that coiled around her and slid down the channels of her hearing to her innermost being "—that evil exists, Ms. Harris. I told you I've seen it, up close and personal. I believe evil takes shape and wanders through the universe."

Her spine prickled with each word and Molly looked uneasily at him. "I believe people are basically good. I don't believe in the bad-seed idea."

Harlan's voice, low and dreamy, whispered, evoking monstrous images. "Sometimes wickedness brushes past us, leaving us untouched. Sometimes, for no reason, it lashes out, annihilating whatever it seizes upon. It's real. It destroys, senselessly, mindlessly. And then it wanders on, finding another victim and striking again. No rhyme, no reason."

"That's the most frightening idea I've ever heard."

"Remember an old Ray Bradbury story called 'Something Wicked This Way Comes'?"

"Yes," she whispered, her mouth dry. "But people aren't bad without a reason. Wickedness isn't random."

"Well, believe in it, Ms. Harris, because it's strolling around. And we know when it passes by us because our most primitive self recoils in its presence. If we're lucky."

He lifted the hair at the back of her neck and lightly touched the top of her spine.

All down her back, fine hairs rose. Along her arms, everywhere, her skin tightened, her stomach, her nipples.

"Ah, yes. That's the spot, Ms. Harris. Fight or flight. Fear or pleasure. The body knows. And if you haven't destroyed all your primitive instincts, you know when you're in the presence of evil."

Molly couldn't have moved if her life depended on it. Fear or pleasure. The dividing line was too fine. Her breathing went shallow as he moved his fingertip one inch, and a flush rose from her breasts to her face.

His voice dropped lower, became huskier. "And you know when it's pleasure."

"Yes," she murmured, shifting, the tension in her crying for release. Even the air circulating from the fan sent buzzes over her skin. Pleasure. This was pleasure. She recognized it at last.

He stood up, his hands dropping to his sides.

She almost cried out. Her breathing hitched, stopped, began again, and she wanted him to touch her once more, wanted his touch more than she could have ever dreamed.

Something must have shown in her face, because he reached out slowly, reluctantly, toward her mouth. Her lips parted under his weightless caress. As if he'd lowered a mask, she saw loneliness in his amber eyes in that unguarded instant, a loneliness so bleak and all-encompassing that it flooded her, drowning her, and she realized as he reached for his sunglasses and covered his eyes that he'd never touched her mouth after all.

"This afternoon at the medical center, Ms. Harris, you were in the presence of something wicked."

Remembering her absolute need to bolt from the rain-swept, deserted corridor, Molly shivered. Her body had known, its visceral response sending her running as fast as she could back to light and safety before she could think. What had been at the end of the colonnade?

The doorbell clanged, loudly, abruptly, and this time she did jump, her body in motion before her brain connected the synapses. She pitched to her knees. Harlan caught her, his arms sliding tightly around her waist, and knee-to-knee they knelt on the floor while the wild clanging pealed through the house.

CHAPTER EIGHT

The insistent ringing was shockingly invasive.

Molly staggered to her feet, collapsed, and Harlan jerked as her mouth slid across his chest. The clamoring of the doorbell reverberated to the noisy beating of his heart under her mouth.

Lifting her away from him, he steadied her as her knees bent once more. "Are you expecting company?"

"No." Her eyes were stretched wide, but she was controlling her fear.

"All right, then. Wait here."

"No! Don't go!" Her small fingers had a stranglehold on his shirt. One finger wound through his buttonhole and scalded his skin. "It could be anyone. Let me call the police."

"I *am* the police, remember?" He pried her fingers loose gently, but he wanted to unbutton his shirt and flatten her hand against him. "I'll check the door. Theoretically, I know what I'm doing, okay?"

"Okay," she said, her voice catching shakily.

He hadn't heard a car, hadn't been aware of anything except Molly and the grief in her face as he'd tried to convince her that she should regard even her friends with a wary eye until Camina's killer was caught.

He moved along the wall, staying clear of sight lines and windows. With every damn light in the house on, his silhouette would show against the shutters, and he saw in a quick scan of the hall and living room, of course, each light was a lamp controlled by a separate switch.

"Stay!" he said in an undertone as Molly bumped against

his back. Not looking at her, he repeated, "I mean it. Don't leave this room until I give you the all-clear. And if you hear anything weird, run like hell out the back door and find someplace to hide. Do you hear me, Molly?" he demanded. "You have to do that."

"Yes. I'll try."

"I know you don't want to stay here by yourself, but we have to split up. It makes more sense." He eased into the living room and reached under his jacket for his gun. Extending it stiff-armed, he circled the room against the walls until he was next to the door.

He didn't see Molly.

With one hand, he thumbed the locks free, imperceptible movements against metal, his fingers wrapping around the front-door chain so that it wouldn't rattle. He checked for Molly once more and threw open the door, leapt to one side and growled, "Freeze right there, you SOB! Don't even think of breathing until I tell you to."

The screeching cat streaked between his legs toward the kitchen, the tall, brown-haired man blinked and said, "What the hell? Who the hell are you?" But he didn't move, not even when Molly pelted down the hall toward him and threw herself against him.

"Reid!"

Harlan set the safety on his gun and slid it back into his holster. He leaned his shoulders against the wall and breathed deeply. Molly's twin. She hadn't expected him. So why had he shown up?

"Hey, Sissy, who's the cool dude in black?" He stepped free of Molly toward Harlan.

"Detective Harlan." Molly's arm was tight around Reid's waist, her hand gripping his belt for dear life.

"I'm Molly's younger brother." Reid's outstretched hand was thin and tanned. "All right, all right, old lady. By only four minutes," he cut in swiftly, forestalling her comment and flashing a smile in her direction.

Harlan glanced at Molly's radiant face and ignored Reid's outstretched hand.

Life on the Costa Rican ranch had evidently been good for her brother. In his tanned face, white smile lines radiated from the corners of his light blue eyes. Reid was drop-dead gorgeous, and his vivid coloring made Harlan's eyes hurt.

But maybe that was only because Molly hadn't left Reid's side.

"When did you get another cat, Sis? Look what your damned watch beast did to my boots while I was trying to get you to answer the door." Reid extended a booted foot. Deep, ugly claw marks gouged the leather. Vertical rips made pinstripes on one leg of his jeans.

"He's a stray I've been feeding. I wondered where he'd gone to." Molly again hugged Reid tightly.

Watching, Harlan wondered if she saw Reid's wince.

Catching Harlan's narrowed gaze, Reid lifted one shoulder tentatively. "Busted my rib a month ago falling off a horse."

"Are you all right now?" Molly stepped away from his side and touched his rib gingerly. The ready sympathy in her face gave Harlan a sour taste in his mouth.

"Son-of-a-gun's still sore. The rib," he said with a wide smile. "Not the horse. But I'm fine. Think we might find a chair somewhere and one of you could fill me in on why a detective pulls his gun on me in my own home?" His genial face acquired a subtle edge that Harlan didn't misinterpret for a minute. "That's right unusual to my way of thinking, Detective."

Reid Harris was telling him to talk fast, make it good or hit the high road.

"Molly?" Harlan inclined his head to her. It was her home, her show. She could fill her brother in on as many of the details as she wanted to. Harlan intended to listen until he was kicked out.

Reid's expression suggested Harlan might not have long to wait.

"I was going to call you tomorrow," Molly said, looking up at Reid. "We've had a problem. Camina."

"She's taken off? What?" Reid strolled down the hall. "We'll find someone else. No big deal." He raised his hands and brushed the door trim as he passed from the hall to the kitchen.

"Murdered, Reid. That's why Detective Harlan is here."

Molly's blunt statement halted Reid. He swung to face them. Harlan had positioned himself behind Molly and to her right. He had a clear view of Reid's stunned expression.

"What happened? She get killed in a brawl over at that dive where she hung out? What?"

"Dive? Camina wasn't that kind of person, Reid."

"Sure she was. Before the folks were killed, Camina and her sister hit Tommy's Golden Gate most every Saturday night." Assurance filled Reid's voice. "What happened, Detective? Tommy overserve someone?"

Harlan touched Molly's back, telling her to finish the story. Her spine curved infinitesimally to his touch. He doubted that she knew her body had responded to him that fractionally. To his dismay, though, he knew his own body had answered that small, feminine response. He folded his arms over his chest and nodded to her. "Go on, Molly. Tell your brother everything. He should know."

Molly's recitation of the facts was concise, unadorned by whatever she must have felt at each stage of occurrences. Harlan sat at an angle where he could watch her and Reid both while they talked. Molly didn't mention that her bracelet had been found under the pier, nor did she mention the incident at the medical center. Harlan found no fault in Reid's reactions—interested, a little detached, but typical.

And his detachment wasn't surprising, considering he hadn't been around except at the beginning of Camina's employment.

When Molly finished, Reid slumped in his chair, his elbows resting on the table. "Damn, Sissy. Hell of a thing. No wonder the detective met me with guns ablazing." He glanced at Harlan. "I'm glad you were here, Detective. I've been trying to get Moll to move into town since the folks..." he drummed his fingers on the table. "I thought, what with one thing and the other, that Moll would be happier closer to town."

"I like it here. Most of the time." She stood up, filled a coffeepot with water, spooned in grounds. "Are you hungry, Reid?"

"Hell, yeah. I could eat a cow."

"Will spaghetti do?"

"If that's the best you can do, Sissy," Reid groaned, making a face. "You and that damn vegetarian stuff. Men need meat, Sissy. Red meat." He thumped his chest. "Lots and lots of thick, juicy red meat."

"Ugh." She grimaced. "Not for me, thanks."

"Hell, Sis, I'm a rancher. What else would I eat? Right, Detective?" Reid shrugged and glanced at Harlan.

"I wouldn't know." Gaze lowered, noncommittal, Harlan studied Reid's scarred boots. The cat had really done a number on that leather. Suppressing a smile, he looked up as Molly slapped her hand on the coffeepot lid.

She plugged in the pot and turned to Reid, smiling. "Oh, Reid, you don't know how glad I am you're home. You couldn't have come at a better time. I've missed you so much. And here you are."

Her smile was incandescent, and for the first time, Harlan could see how she'd been before tragedy had dimmed her. Like a translucent candle with its light shining from inside, Molly's wide smile transformed her. With happiness, her silvery eyes turned pewter blue and her soft mouth curved up at the ends.

Her love for her brother glowed within her, making her terribly vulnerable and completely beautiful.

Impassively, Harlan watched her innocent, glowing eyes. She could be the best actress in the world, but she couldn't fake what he saw revealed on her face and by her body language. She loved her brother. She was friends with her ex. She'd been friends with her maid. She took in stray cats. The woman was a walking, talking advertisement for "nice."

As if lightning had sizzled through him, Harlan straightened, his back sliding right up the wall near the pantry.

Sometime during the hours after he'd left the medical center, his instinct had sifted through everything he knew about the case and reached the conclusion that, perhaps, Ms. Molly was as innocent as she looked.

He'd left the center believing only that something had threatened her. His sense that she was in danger hadn't absolved her of guilt—he knew better than that. Conspirators fell on each other like jackals all the time, ripping each other apart.

Watching Molly's face soften as she talked with Reid, Harlan grasped the exact moment his subconscious had believed her. He'd told her that the smashed windows had been recently cleaned. That insignificant detail had pinched her mouth with grief and turned her skin ashen. Loss and bewildered pain had stared at him from her eyes.

His cynical soul hadn't recognized those emotions until now.

"Detective Harlan? Would you like some spaghetti?" Grains of cereal clung stickily to her faded jeans along the long line of her curved thigh.

His palm would fit—just so—over that delicate curve. His hand flexed, unconsciously shaping itself to her. Harlan clenched his fist tight against the sensation of satin skin beneath his palm. He'd figured he was in command of his thoughts, but images of Molly had been bombarding him uncontrollably since he'd first shown up at her kitchen door.

"Detective Harlan?"

"Excuse me?" He tilted his head to her. She would have had a sweet, milky taste if he'd kissed her as he'd wanted to. Instead, he'd wiped the milk off her mouth, her lips turning pink as he'd rubbed them.

"Spaghetti?" She had to be exhausted, yet, with the appearance of her brother, she looked as if she'd been shot full of a mysterious rejuvenating elixir.

Her lips were rosy, her cheeks flushed, and the sharp desire that cramped through his veins caught Harlan off guard. The need to swoop her up and sprint out the door with her stunned him. Twisting through him, the intensity of his hunger confused him. It must be the effect of adrenaline, that was all. Nothing more.

Leave. Now. The words crackled in his brain. Harlan cocked his head. *Go.* The order counterpointed Reid's slightly impatient tone.

"Oh, come on, Sissy. It's close to midnight. I'm sure Harlan has better things to do at this time of the night, right, Detective?" Reid's expression was ruefully understanding, an us-guys-got-to-stick-together, male-bonding look.

"No. I'm free." Perversely, in the face of Reid's camaraderie, Harlan found he wasn't interested in any male bonding. "I like spaghetti," he said politely to Molly, once again ignoring Reid.

A teasing glow in her eyes, secondhand though it might be, warmed Harlan for a second. "Such manners. But I'll bet you hate vegetables, too, Detective."

"No, actually, I don't." He shot a glance at Reid, whose boots were tapping rhythmically under the table. "I've been known to eat cauliflower."

Laughter bubbled up from Molly. "You're joking, right? I can't see you eating cauliflower, Detective Harlan. You've blown your big, bad image."

"Has he been giving you trouble, Moll?" Reid frowned and turned to Harlan. "Why don't you fill me in on the rest of the details, Detective? Is my sister in some kind of trouble?"

Tension crackled between them.

"Why would she be in trouble, Mr. Harris?" Harlan tilted his head, sorting out impressions.

"Because of Camina's murder, of course." Reid bristled. "I don't want you hassling her. She's been through enough. She almost had a nervous breakdown after finding our—"

"Reid. Stop it." Anger swept over Molly's face. "I've been fine."

"Paul prescribed those sleeping—"

"I said 'enough,' Reid. Detective Harlan knows about the sleeping pills. I did *not* have a nervous breakdown." Her bottom lip trembled. "I was stressed out, that's all. Nothing more."

"Okay, Sissy. Sorry. It's in the past, anyway. No problem. You're fine. Relax."

"I'm okay. There was never a problem." The more soothing Reid became, the more agitated Molly grew.

"I know you're okay now."

Harlan wondered why Reid didn't drop the subject as Molly had asked.

"Listen, Reid, you can either be quiet or eat. Which is it going to be?" Molly plopped a cup in front of him. "Younger brothers. Think they know everything," she chided, affection underscoring the annoyance. "I can take care of myself, you know." She squeezed Reid's shoulders. "I know you worry about me, but don't, okay?"

"Sure, Sis." Reid's expression showed he wasn't convinced, but he patted her hand.

"Give me fifteen or twenty minutes for the spaghetti."
She stood with her hand on the partially open pantry door.
"Okay? Alone?"

"Sure," Reid said.

Harlan nodded.

Molly swung the door open and the large black cat leapt
onto the kitchen table in front of Reid and slashed out with
its claws.

"Hell!" Reid jumped back from the table. The chair
tilted, rocked and clattered to the floor.

Leaning against the wall, Harlan smiled.

Hissing and spitting, the cat arched its back. Front claws
extended, it rose on its back legs like a bear and its fur
stood straight out from its body as if it were electrified.

"Hey, puss. Easy does it," Molly said, walking over to
the cat and picking it up. "Reid's not all that bad, even if
he doesn't like cats," she cooed, laughing over at her
brother. "Shame on you, Reid, scaring a poor little helpless
animal." The cat butted Molly as she went to the refrigerator and pulled out the milk carton.

"Right." Reid's mouth formed a sulky line. "Keep him
away from me, Moll. Damn thing's already ruined my jeans
and my boots, and you're going to feed it?" He sucked on
the scratch along his wrist.

"Relax, Reid, you're bigger than he is. One on one, you'd
have a chance. Maybe," Molly tossed over her shoulder as
she filled a saucer of milk and placed it along the far wall,
away from Reid.

The cat padded around the saucer, his gold eyes with their
black centers alert. Settling himself on all fours facing Reid,
the cat curled his tail around his body and watched them.
When no one moved, he lowered his head and lapped the
milk. He looked up, his ears swiveling as Harlan straightened from his spot against the wall.

"Come on, Detective. Let's wait in the living room. This

room's not big enough for the two of us," Reid muttered, edging cautiously toward the living room.

Looking at Reid, the cat let out a low growl.

Molly laughed and Reid glared.

Harlan unhooked his sunglasses from his pocket and put them on. His eyes were hurting. "When did you arrive from Costa Rica, Mr. Harris?"

"Call me Reid," Molly's brother said as he looked absently around the room.

"When did you arrive, *Reid?*" Harlan sat down on the sofa where he'd covered Molly with her quilt.

"I flew in."

"I reckon you have your passport with you?"

"Why? Do I need an alibi, Detective, or is this idle conversation?" Reid grinned.

"I haven't made up my mind." Harlan crossed one leg over his other knee. He heard Molly murmuring to the cat, her syllables liquid and restful. He liked sitting here in her living room and listening to the sound of her voice from the kitchen. "But I wonder if you'd let me see your passport? If you have it with you?"

"Damn. You aren't making chitchat, are you?" Reid frowned.

"Not altogether, no. I really would like to see that passport, Mr. Harris." Harlan held out his hand.

"Sure. Hang on a sec. I dropped my bag at the door when you opened it and shoved your gun in my face." Resentment turned his cheekbones red. "I'll go get it, but this is stupid." He opened the door, which they hadn't locked, and stepped out onto the veranda.

"I'm sure you're right."

Reid dug around in a small duffel bag and pulled out his passport. Tossing it carelessly to Harlan, he smiled and sat down in the chair opposite. "Everything's in order, Detective."

"I'm sure it is, Mr. Harris." Turning pages, Harlan checked dates, stamps, entry notations. "You travel a lot."

"Part of the job. A lot of red tape when you own property out of the country. And I like to see Moll whenever I can."

In the kitchen, Molly rattled flatware in a drawer. Harlan wanted to be in the kitchen with her, not here in the living room with her twin.

Harlan flipped the passport back to Reid. "As you said, everything's in order."

"Why wouldn't it be?" Reid challenged, his mouth a tight line, nothing like Molly's generous one.

"I have no idea." Harlan tilted his head and observed the man's restless movements.

He'd left the chair and was wandering around the room, his boot heels thwacking against the wood. He couldn't seem to stay in one spot. "Look, Detective—" he brushed against an end table and the pictures on it trembled and righted "—it's late, and I'm plumb out of energy. I've been on the go all day, and I may be giving you the wrong idea."

"I have no ideas," Harlan said. "I ask questions and see what answers I get. I go from there."

"Well, look, I'm not ticked off with you, but I am worried about Sissy. If I could have let the ranch run itself after the folks died, I would have stayed with her, but I couldn't. I know she insisted she's fine and all that, but she's not. She went to pieces. She'd call me at all hours of the night in Costa Rica. I don't think she's been sleeping, even with the pills Paul gave her. She can't go on like this without cracking, and if you're giving her a hard time about Camina's murder, Molly's going to—" Reid sat down heavily in the chair "—I don't know what she'll do. And I have to get back to the ranch."

"Ms. Harris seems to be handling herself," Harlan said softly, watching Reid's troubled expression. "I don't think you have to worry."

"No?" Reid said, leaning back. "Damn, I hope you're right. Sis is all the family I have left." He leaned forward. "You don't think she might..."

"What, Mr. Harris? She might...what?" Harlan asked very, very softly.

"Do something stupid?"

A lid clanked onto a pot. The fan over the stove whirred.

"For instance?" Behind his sunglasses, Harlan watched Reid's anxious movements.

"To herself?" Reid stood up and resumed his pacing, moving quickly around the room.

"No. I don't think she'll do anything stupid, Mr. Harris."

"Really?" Reid lifted his duffel bag, dropped it. "You're sure?"

"I can't read her mind. I don't believe she's...suicidal."

"Good. I hope you're right. But she's been under a lot of strain. It's been too much. I should have figured out a way to stay with her." He tugged the string on the duffel bag. "I'd blame myself if anything happened."

"Would you?"

"Of course. We're family. Blood's thicker than water, and all that." Hoisting his duffel bag, Reid added, "And you know she couldn't have killed Camina. Molly doesn't have a vicious bone in her body. If you're putting Sissy on your suspect list, take her off. Find someone else."

"We'll do our best, Mr. Harris," Harlan said, as Reid headed toward the front staircase. "You're staying here for a while?"

"Tonight. I'm entertaining some prospective investors at my fishing cabin for a few days. I'll be there until I go back to the ranch. Now that I've heard about Camina, I'm hoping I can close out my deal early and come back here to be with Sis. Maybe I can get somebody to cover the ranch for a week or two." The muscles along his arms flexed as Reid swung the duffel bag back and forth. He glanced down the hall toward Molly. "Damn, I wish I didn't have this meeting."

Harlan restrained his sarcastic comment. Everybody had the same twenty-four hours. If Reid wanted to be with Molly, he would be. Harlan rubbed his neck. He'd told Molly she was too trusting, but he was, possibly, too skeptical. His cynicism was too ingrained, tainting even the most normal reactions with a nasty tinge. Perhaps Reid was sincerely concerned about Molly. Perhaps sincerely selfish. Either way, he was going to be here one night.

Reid's flight from Costa Rica would still have been in the air while Molly was at the medical center. Clearing customs would have slowed him down further.

His timing was probably coincidental.

But Harlan had never believed in coincidences, so he watched with narrowed eyes as Reid walked out of the living room. Harlan intended to check the flight time.

He went up the front stairs although his bedroom was closer to the back stairs off the kitchen. Harlan reckoned Reid didn't want any more close encounters of the feline kind.

Leaning back against the couch, Harlan took off his sunglasses and hooked them back into his pocket. Resting, he opened himself to the free-floating impressions he was picking up, letting them flow through him as he listened to Molly's noisy cheerfulness in the kitchen.

He'd gone home to change after leaving the medical center and fallen asleep for a while even though he'd planned on driving straight to her house. Jolted awake by an impulse too strong to ignore, Harlan had decided to pay a call in spite of the late hour. He intended to stay on surveillance outside, but he'd seen her moving around her kitchen through the gap where her shutters didn't quite dovetail with the window. Seeing her, he'd given in and knocked on her door.

If he hadn't fallen asleep, he would have arrived and departed earlier, missing Reid.

The sense of evil that had rushed through him at the medical center swirled around him once more and he turned his head toward the hall leading to the kitchen.

Auras. Impressions. Blood. Death. If he were Molly, he wouldn't be able to stay in this house. It shrieked of pain and sadness. He had to give her credit. Like a willow tree, Molly Harris had an unexpected and resilient strength. Harlan knew he wouldn't be able to sleep in the house, beautiful and gracious as it was. He rolled his shoulders and stood up, suddenly as restless as Reid.

Molly and the cat were eyeball-to-eyeball over the bowl of spaghetti on the counter. "Cats don't like tomatoes. You're being an old bully again. I'll give you a taste—you'll turn up your nose and walk away. Don't pretend you won't, buster. I know your type."

"Do you?"

Molly jerked upright. "Detective Harlan! You startled me. You're always sneaking up on me."

"I'm sorry. I don't intend to be sneaky." Harlan raised his arm and propped himself in the doorway, angled so he could see Reid when he came down the front stairs. Reid wouldn't enter the kitchen from the back stairway, not while Bully Cat was on the scene, and Harlan wasn't through with what he wanted to find out from Molly. "What's his type?" Harlan gestured toward the cat and lifted his eyebrow.

The cat leapt down from the counter and padded to him. Launching himself with a thrust of his haunches, he landed on Harlan's shoulders and draped himself at the back of his neck, his tail curling forward onto Harlan's chest.

"He likes to intimidate people. Like you." Ms. Molly was teasing him. The quirk at the corner of her mouth gave her away.

"Not me," Harlan said lazily. "I only ask questions. There's a difference."

"Maybe to you," she groused, wiping her hands down her jeans. Red streaks paralleled the cereal trail.

"Nice fashion statement," he said, tipping his head toward her food-smeared jeans and indicating the paste. "Goes well with the cereal."

"I make a mess when I cook." She shrugged. "What can I say?"

Harlan saw the opened cans of tomato paste, the colander balanced precariously in the sink, the sprinkles of oregano. "That you're enthusiastic? That you're happy?"

"I am." She nodded emphatically. "I was so surprised to see Reid. It was almost as if I conjured him up."

Harlan stroked the cat's tail. "Careful with conjuring spells, Ms. Molly. You never know what you'll summon."

The widening of her eyes told him she was remembering what he'd said about evil roaming loose in the world.

"I'm safe here with Reid. And I'll be careful when I leave the house."

"I doubt it. I'm learning you're not a cautious lady, Ms. Molly. Even when you should be." Harlan didn't like what he was about to do to Molly and the happiness radiating from her face. He liked seeing her sparkling and shining. But it was necessary. For her sake, most of all.

"I'm cautious enough."

"I don't think so."

Harlan moved away from the doorway.

The cat's tail twitched once. He placed his front paws on Harlan's chest, balanced and dropped to the floor. Sniffing Harlan's feet, the cat flicked his tail and disappeared.

"Reckon he's gone looking for Reid?"

Molly's smile wavered. "If that cat's as smart as I think he is, he'll give Reid plenty of walking-around room."

Harlan lifted one of her black-and-white place mats. "How well did your brother know Camina?"

She wrinkled her nose. The tip of it was dotted with tomato paste. "Only casually at best. I don't think Reid and Camina exchanged more than a dozen words that I know of before I fired her. Maybe he can help you, but I doubt it. What are you looking for?"

"Her habits. People who knew her, knew why she might have been on your dock in the rain. Why did you fire her, Molly?"

Molly pursed her mouth and raised her hands helplessly. "You never give up, do you?"

"I told you I didn't."

"I remember. Does why I fired her matter? Really?"

Holding her gaze, Harlan brushed the dried paste off her nose and nodded. "Yeah."

"You're always handing me paper towels, cleaning up. You're a very tidy man." She was avoiding the subject.

"It's because I like order, and, yes, it's important for me to know why you fired her. Tell me."

Molly's shoulders sagged. "She was stealing. Nothing of importance at first, then some of my clothes, my jewelry. A ring. Things from the house. Some of Reid's things he'd left here."

"Ah." Harlan smiled. "That helps. Why were you so reluctant to tell me?"

"I felt petty. I had so much and Camina so little that what she took seemed unimportant."

"*Things* are unimportant, but *motives* aren't. What did she say when you fired her?"

Rubbing her wrist across her forehead, Molly said passionately, "I hate this!"

"What did she say, Ms. Harris? She didn't admit the theft, did she?"

"No." Molly looked at the floor. She was clearly having

a difficult time telling him the rest of the story. "But by then I had no choice. I found Reid's watch and a pair of my earrings in a plastic bag stuffed in a container in the freezer. Camina always cleaned out the freezer. The container was labeled in her handwriting. *Beef stew.* Way at the back, underneath all the other containers. The damned thing could have stayed there forever before I found it. It was only a fluke that I unearthed it anyway. I wish I'd never seen it! I thought I'd lost the earrings at the funeral, and I'd given up any hope of recovering them. They didn't matter anymore to me!"

"I'm sure they didn't," Harlan said.

"Camina came in just as I opened the container and pulled out the bag. Neither of us said much. We were both embarrassed. That's all. And if I had it to do over, I wouldn't fire her. If I'd known she needed money, I would have given the damn things to her." She gestured helplessly. "But it all happened so fast."

"Did you ever see her again? Did she call you?"

"No. I wrote out a check, she packed her suitcase. She left that afternoon."

"Thank you. That was a help. Why didn't you tell me this earlier?"

"When I saw Camina's body, I couldn't think straight. Nothing made sense to me. I didn't know what was going to happen to me." She glanced away, tugged at her shirt. "You thought I'd killed her, and I—"

"And you were afraid you had, weren't you, Ms. Harris?" Harlan pitched his voice low, letting it ride the air between them. "You thought you'd gone out on the dock and stabbed her with the butcher knife I found on your kitchen floor, didn't you?"

"Yes." Her whisper overrode his last words.

"Until I told you I saw you on the dock last night and followed you back, you weren't even sure how the knife could have gotten from Camina's body back into your tightly locked house, were you?''

"No." She nibbled the edge of her thumb.

"And neither of us knows for sure whether or not you might have killed Camina while you were…unconscious."

"But—"

Harlan shook his head. "No, let me finish. We both know what happened at the medical center. You were the victim there. As for what really happened with Camina, I'll tell you God's own truth, Ms. Harris. I don't know. You might have stabbed her. It's possible. We know you have periods of amnesialike behavior. And unless someone can verify that you didn't kill her, that possibility is still viable."

She looked as if he'd slapped her across the face.

"You have to face facts. I can't rule out that possibility but, frankly, I think it's the least likely explanation."

Her shoulders sagged with relief. "Thank you for that, in any case." Her voice was thin but it didn't quiver. Molly Harris was holding her own.

"So here's why I think you probably didn't kill her. You weren't violent last night when I saw you. In fact, you were extraordinarily passive. That's why I thought you were on drugs."

As clearly as if he could read her mind, Harlan knew she was sorting through the options. He wanted her to. It was a small thing he could do for her. "For a while, I thought you and a cohort might have stabbed Camina because she knew something about your parents' murder. Other people will jump to that conclusion, too, Ms. Harris." He stretched his hand toward her, stopping her before she spoke. "No, I don't believe you killed your parents, either. I do believe, though, that in some fashion the deaths of Camina and your parents are linked. If you didn't kill Camina, you're in danger, too. And you can't let yourself forget that. Because if you're innocent, there's someone out there with a very clever mind who's messing with your head, Ms. Harris. And anyone who would do that is a very dangerous, very evil person.''

Harlan heard the cat's claws clicking against the wooden floor upstairs.

"What if I did kill her and don't ever remember doing it?" She faced him with only a minute tremble in her chin.

"Then that will be between you and your lawyer."

She gained control of the tremble, but the light died from her eyes, and he could tell she was accepting what was in front of her.

That was all he could do for her.

He'd had to wipe out the happiness shining from her eyes. He'd seen that she was on a roller coaster of emotions, but it wasn't prudent for her in any sense to forget that she was in danger. Happiness had a way of blunting the body's gut reactions.

"Ms. Harris," Harlan said, seized with an increasing sense of urgency, "whatever happens with this damned case, it's going to be better for you in the long run if you face the worst that can happen."

"The worst would be if I killed Camina and didn't know I'd done it." Her voice caught, a heartbreaking hiccup of sound.

"All right, but you've got to remember that you might not be safe, either." His hand hovered over her shoulder, but he repressed the urge to comfort her and, instead, with an effort, jammed his hand into his pocket with such strength that the inside seam of the pocket fabric ripped.

What she needed most from him was reality. Harlan frowned. He didn't know how to put his impressions into words, and something was driving him to protect her in spite of his cynicism, his skepticism, in spite of every good reason he could think of for keeping his damned mouth shut and letting events fall out as they would. So in spite of his resolve not to touch her again, he gripped her arm tightly and struggled for words. "Listen to me, Ms. Harris. You can't afford to forget for even one second that you're in danger. From the police, from someone hiding in the shadows—I don't know. But you're not safe."

She nodded, one short dip of her head, her light brown hair swinging forward over her face and catching in the corner of her mouth. Reid's boots thunked against the stairs, and Harlan spoke quickly, "Do you understand?" He gave her arm a light shake, and she nodded again.

She stood there, small and vulnerable in her big house with its history of explosive violence, its scent of blood beneath its fresh paint, and whatever she might have done, she was brave, her shoulders straight, her gaze holding his, and Harlan stooped down to her and took her soft pink mouth in a fierce, hard kiss. She tasted of tomatoes and basil and something infinitely precious that stunned him with its power. "Remember. Not with anyone. Not with people you love and especially not with me."

CHAPTER NINE

"So, boys and girls, is our chow ready?" Reid stepped off the bottom stair and ducked under the cross beam, resting his arms on it as he surveyed the room.

"Yes." Stepping away from Harlan, Molly turned to her twin. In the alcove between the hall and the kitchen, the light threw shadows over Reid's face. Was his expression a little calculating, a little too studied? She wanted to run over to her twin, throw her arms around him and tell him the horrible notions John Harlan had planted in her brain.

She didn't. Checked as strongly as if the detective were still gripping her arm tightly with his agile, narrow fingers, she couldn't move. The overhead light played across Reid's familiar, beloved features. Her brother.

Reid took a step forward and the light angled obscurely across his face, casting it half in shadow, transforming her twin, her psychic link, into a stranger.

Molly didn't like the way Harlan was altering her vision of the people around her. Making a sudden decision to ignore his influence, she contracted her muscles to move toward her brother.

The thought hadn't found completion in motion before Harlan was behind her, so close that his knee pressed the back of her thigh, that small point of body contact an insistent heat that arrowed upward through her and kept her motionless.

"Did I miss something?" The air circulating from the fan ruffled Reid's wet hair, lifted the brown ends turned dark with water. His grin was lighthearted, his gaze shifting from Harlan to her and back to Harlan, speculation gleaming in his light blue eyes. "Anything important happen while I was showering?"

"No," Molly said, not moving.

"Could have fooled me. Sure looks like I interrupted a mighty important conference." He ran his hands over his wet hair. Water flew and his arms sent long, spidery shadows creeping across the kitchen floor.

Reid would never harm her. He loved her as much as she loved him. And he had no more reason to kill Camina than she did. He certainly had no motive to kill their parents. Molly gasped. The idea was appalling, beyond belief.

"No, Reid, you didn't miss anything. Detective Harlan was telling me he couldn't stay for supper." She pivoted toward him, severing their physical contact. "I'm sorry your beeper interrupted us. Reid was right, after all, Detective. You do have more important things to do. Maybe another time."

"Don't forget—"

She interrupted him. "I'll think about what you said."

And she'd think about the way he'd kissed her, too. Her mouth still ached. Maybe she was lucky she didn't remember the encounter with him at the bayou. There had been power and hunger in the quick way he'd taken her mouth, something desperate in the hard pressure of his body against hers.

She tasted the loneliness she'd only sensed earlier, a loneliness so all-consuming it had rushed like a wave over her, engulfing her, sweeping her to a barren plain on the near side of a chasm too wide to be bridged. And he was on the other side, reaching out, calling to her with the touch of his body in a language she didn't understand.

She understood the hunger, though, and she'd recognized the latent power in John Harlan before she'd let him through her door the first time.

Recognized it and feared it. Because he was a policeman and because...

Because there would be no holding back with a man like him.

He had lifted his head, releasing her, and as he did, she traced the corded muscles of his stomach, suddenly needing to be closer, yearning—oh, it had been only for that brief, immeasurable second—but *yearning* to throw him a rope across the abyss.

Instinctively she recognized that marriage to Paul had not prepared her for a man like John Harlan. Compared with Paul's pastel blues and greens, Harlan was Chinese red and ebony.

She went to the kitchen door and unlocked it. "I'm sure I'll hear from you."

He rested his hand against the door. "You will." He opened it. The moon, waxing full and silver, shone over his shoulder. Harlan's eyes darkened, the gold deepening and glowing as he looked at her. He wanted to stay.

During the night when she couldn't sleep, she would remember his loneliness, remember his unspoken appeal.

Interrupting the moment, Reid walked quickly to the counter and picked up the bowl. He pulled out a sauce-covered strand of pasta and swallowed it. "Can we eat?" he asked plaintively as he carried the bowl to the table.

"Eat," Harlan said, never looking at Reid. "I'm leaving. As your sister said, I have business, and I find I've lost my appetite for spaghetti." He looked edgy and uncomfortable. "Besides, I'd hate to disrupt a family reunion." Glancing over his shoulder, he frowned and rubbed the back of his neck.

Reid yanked a tray of ice from the freezer. "Whatever. But I'm not waiting any longer, folks." He popped the lever on the tray and plopped ice cubes into a tall glass. "Got anything worth drinking, Sissy?"

Distracted by Harlan's reaction, Molly murmured, "Look in the pantry."

With the metal cube divider in one hand, Reid shook his head. "Not unless I know where the beast of the bayou is. I last saw him skulking around your room, Sis. Did he come back down here?"

"No." Molly opened the door wider, silently urging Harlan to leave. With him on one side of her, Reid on the other, she was pulled, her attention split in some fashion between the two men. "Is there anything else, Detective?"

Reid opened the pantry door and disappeared behind it.

"Molly—" Harlan's voice lowered to a rasp "—lock the door behind me." He shot a glance toward the pantry. "And lock your bedroom door, hear?"

His voice sandpapered her skin. "I'll do what I have to do," Molly said, despising what he was suggesting.

Rough and fast, he added, "Tomorrow, get a portable phone."

She nodded. "I will. It's a good idea." She wouldn't be isolated if the lines were cut. "Good night, Detective."

For half a second, indecision flashed across his face and he tapped the edge of the door. Molly thought he might not leave after all, but he ran his finger along the dangling chain, nodded abruptly and departed.

Clicking the locks behind him, Molly unaccountably wished he had stayed. The chain was warm from his fleeting touch.

After Harlan left, the room seemed to expand, Reid appearing small and far-off, as if she had turned a telescope around to look at him. Like a thin gray mist, Detective Harlan's presence hovered between her and her brother, tainting her joy at having him home.

Catching up on Reid's news and filling him in on what had been happening took less time than she'd expected. They were both too tired by then to be coherent, and conversation went in spurts and non sequiturs. It was good to have him home, but she wondered why she'd stood at the doorway and listened to Detective Harlan's quiet footsteps cross her veranda, why she'd waited for the rumble of his car's engine before she'd gone to sit with Reid.

Shoving strands of spaghetti around his plate, Reid finally swallowed one last bite, said, "Sorry," and gave in to exhaustion, leaving her to clean up. She heard him moving around restlessly in his room for a long time before he fell asleep.

She took the Luger out of the waste basket where she'd shoved it after Reid and Harlan had left her alone to cook.

Molly didn't forget to check the locks before she went upstairs, and, although she made a face at her paranoia, she left all the lights on behind her.

When she reached her room, the cat was curled at the end of her bed, his unwinking gaze watching the head of the staircase. He stretched as she entered, arched his back and settled down, folding his front paws under his massive chest. His eyelids drooped to half-mast as he stared at her with the same sleepy-lidded gaze Harlan had fixed on her in her pre-dawn kitchen.

The cat's intention to stay exactly where he was couldn't have been clearer if he'd spoken out loud. It was fine with her, as long as he didn't leave her room and decide to confront Reid.

For the first time in months, Molly shut her bedroom door and locked it.

She knew cats. She'd had a tiny gray female once, Ms. Riffraff, who flushed the toilet in the middle of the night until Molly would give in and play with her. "You wouldn't have any trouble flipping the doorknob until you opened it, would you, buster?" She told herself she was locking the door because there was no reason to have Reid throw a conniption fit if the cat decided to leave the bedroom before morning.

"You'll be fine for three or four hours, won't you? No urge to be a midnight rambler? I promise I'll let you out if you ask, okay?"

Coiling his tail around himself, the cat closed one golden eye, then the other, and rested his head on his folded paws.

She stuck the gun under the edge of the bed, the edge that faced her door, and crawled under her covers.

During the hours before morning, he worked his way up her bed. Drifting on the edge of sleep but not finding it, Molly faced her locked door, her knees drawn up to her chest. When she thought she'd never fall asleep and was ready to go downstairs to heat a cup of milk, the cat padded close to her, circling her and nudging her gently but insistently until she shifted and made room for him in the cove between her knees and chest. Kneading her hip, his broad paws flexing and pushing, he finally settled, curling up to her with his long, lithe spine a comforting weight against her.

Molly wrapped her arm around him and went to sleep, surrendering at last to the cape of her demon lover.

And she dreamed, oh, she dreamed such wonderful dreams. Safe and unafraid, she wandered down golden halls that led somewhere, somewhere she yearned to be. With the brush of a finger, she pushed open shimmering glass doors to sunshine and star shine and heat, a heat that coiled through her, around her, melting like liquid gold into the cells of her blood, dissolving her bones and beating in the pulse of her wrists, her neck, her heart until she thought she would die of the wonder and the ecstasy of the slow thrumming running through her, through her, pulsing.

Nahual. In his grandmother's voice, the word wove through his sleep. *Nahual,* she'd said, over and over. Harlan stirred, tossing the light sheet off his sweat-glazed skin, and slept, a moan caught buried in his throat. *Nahual*.

When Molly woke up, the cat was facing her. His eyes were open, their golden gaze fixed on her, his silent purr vibrating against her breasts. His hooked nose was under her wrist, against the slash in her palm. As she opened her eyes, he tapped her chin with a paw, once, and waited.

Molly scratched his chin and patted him from head to tail. His body rumbled under her stroking. Not too hard, she thought ruefully, to understand the source of her dreams. "That's enough for now, buster. I have things to do, places to go, a phone to buy." Certainty ran deep and strong in her that she hadn't been wandering through her house last night.

A line of sunshine showed under the edge of her door as she stretched lazily, dislodging him. He gave a low chirrup of protest and stalked disdainfully to the door. Rising on his back legs, he smacked the doorknob and looked back at her. The knob rattled as he banged it a second time.

"Hush up, you fool. You want to wake Reid?" Molly climbed out of bed, yawning. The wound on her hand no longer hurt, she felt great and the world outside her window gleamed and sparkled.

But Reid had already left. On the table, his note anchored under an egg-yolk-sticky plate explained that he'd knocked on her door, she hadn't answered and he hadn't wanted to wake her up. He'd try to finish his negotiations and stop back before he returned to the ranch. He'd scrawled "love ya, Sissy" across the bottom of the paper.

The sun rising over the bayou blinded her. Reid had opened the shutters. The dead bolt on the kitchen door was thrown and above it, the chain dangled from the second lock. Well, that was Reid for you. At least he'd closed the door after him and its push lock was in. Molly threw open the wooden door and stood at the screen. The cat wound between her legs, bumping her calves and making a pest of himself until she opened it. He sat upright at the edge of the door and flicked his tail when she gave him an encouraging shove forward.

He tilted his head, and the look he sent her was, at best, condescending.

Molly laughed. "Beast. Who crowned you king?"

From the veranda down to the bayou, the lawn was a brilliant green in the sun. Even the tag end of the crime-scene ribbon lost its power in all the bright sunshine and color. Yellow hibiscus, purple hydrangeas, pink morning glory—color everywhere catching her eye and filling her with delight after days of endless rain.

Her toes curled with pleasure.

The cat made up his mind, licked his paw and sauntered down the gallery steps to the lawn. The hedge along the driveway swallowed his lean, muscular form.

During that first day of sunshine, Molly half-expected Harlan to arrive with an arrest warrant. When he didn't, she went about her errands. She wrote lists, she made phone calls and she bought a portable phone. She set up appointments with her customers, she bought groceries and she bought a 20-pound bag of dry cat food.

It was the best day she'd had in months.

When the sun dropped behind the horizon, leaving streaky pinks and greens against the sky, though, she went inside and banged her shutters tight against the windows.

Harlan phoned her while she was eating a grilled-cheese sandwich and told her that the lab reports weren't in yet and wouldn't be for a few days.

"Did you buy a portable?" Over the phone his Florida drawl was more noticeable, its sand buzzing in her ear and prickling down her spine.

"I hate to give you the satisfaction, but, yes, I did."

"Good. That was smart."

"Oh, thanks," she said, pulling a string of cheese from the bread. "Golly, I'm so glad I have big, strong you to help lil' old me." The sarcasm slipped out, the result of too much sun and sleep and dreams. And, maybe, the result of the way he'd kissed her. It was sarcasm that bordered on flirtation and she flushed as she realized what she was doing.

"Smart mouth."

Molly thought of how he'd made her mouth tingle, and she couldn't answer him, bravado fleeing before the knowing in his gritty voice.

"You there, Ms. Harris?" At his end of the line phones rang in the background, and he raised his voice when she didn't respond. "Not going to play?"

Sitting straight in her chair, she poked her finger through the sandwich. "Was there anything you wanted, Detective?" She made her voice as prissy as her Sunday-school teacher's had been.

"Ms. Harris," he chided, amusement running like honey over the grit of his voice, making it smooth and golden, "you have a way of walking right into these little double entendres, but you don't really want me to answer that question, do you?"

The wire hummed between them, and Molly shifted on her seat.

"I could answer you." Amusement vanished. "There are a lot of things I want. Taking you to bed is one of them. But you already know that." He tapped a pencil against the receiver, its rhythmic drumming continuing as he talked. "Ms. Harris, most of the things I want, I can't have. That's life, isn't it?"

"Yes." She placed her knife and fork at right angles on her plate.

"You there by yourself?" *Tap, tap.* Pause.

"Yes."

Tap.

Loneliness washed back and forth between them in those humming moments.

"I saw Reid leave."

"You did?" She jostled her plate and the flatware slid to the table. "Why?"

"Why did he leave? Why did I see him? Which do you want to know?"

"Were you here when he left? Did you talk to him?" She hadn't heard Harlan's car. Her room fronted the driveway, and even with her windows closed, she should have heard him driving up.

"I don't know why he left. I know what he told me last night. Perhaps he was telling me the truth, but I didn't follow him to the cabin, so I can't say for sure. I didn't talk to him this morning because he didn't see me. I..." he paused "...wanted to take another look at the dock, and morning seemed like a good time. Before I got tied up with paperwork. And if you're wondering, he left around six. In a rental car." *Tap.*

"You make it sound like a report."

"It is. That's what I'm doing. Typing and taking notes. Ms. Harris," he said, his manner becoming more formal, "I need to ask you a question that's probably going to make you slam the phone down in my ear. So let me get it out before you hang up, okay? And if you can bring yourself to tell me the answer, you'd save me a trip to the courthouse tomorrow. Could you find it in your heart to do that? I surely would appreciate it."

"Go ahead." Every time she let down her guard, he zipped in with the real point, drew blood and was gone. She sighed. "But drop the good-ol'-boy routine."

"Of course." A file drawer slammed, metallic and heavy.

"I'm waiting."

"Did you make a will after your parents died?"

"Me?" Molly stood up and walked to the kitchen window over the sink. The cord trailed behind her, tautened as she crossed the kitchen, went slack, its coils pulling together, as she paced back. "I already had a will. I didn't need a new one."

"Hold your horses for a sec, okay?"

"All right."

Quickly, his words rushed over the line. "Who's your beneficiary?" *Tap. Tap. Tap.*

"You don't pull any punches, do you?"

"I can't."

"Are you suspicious of everyone you know, Detective? Don't you trust anyone? Not even people you love?" She wasn't angry, merely curious. After all, he'd told her not to trust anyone, not to trust him.

A phone rang in the background. Someone yelled, and Harlan answered her. "Yes, I suspect everyone. Even my friends. My family."

"That makes for a lonely life." She thought she understood a little of what his life must be like.

"I'm used to it."

Molly didn't think so. She'd been overwhelmed by the desolation behind his hungry kiss. "Are you?"

She waited for him to answer, but he didn't.

He zigged back to his question, ignoring her comment. "So who did you name in your original will?"

"Paul. Reid. My cousin in Texas, Susie Warrin. A bequest to Camina." She swallowed. "A charity."

"But you and Dr. Bouler had divorced before your parents' death. Didn't you need to update your will to include your inheritance from them?"

Molly twirled the cord around her fingers. Why hadn't she changed her will? "I can't remember what I was thinking back then, Detective. Paul and I divorced. Too much happened all at once after that, and I guess I didn't think it was important to make a new will. For whatever reason, I didn't change it.''

"Perhaps you should think about updating it, Ms. Harris. You're a reasonably wealthy woman now. What with one thing and another.''

"You may be right," Molly said slowly, "but it would be basically the same. Maybe more to the charity. I don't know. Reid is all the real family I have left, and Paul is still my best friend. Susie and I haven't seen each other in a couple of years, but she's my father's brother's daughter. That counts for something. Who else do I have? It's only money. It's not important." She thought of Camina and the earrings.

"It's not important unless you need it, Ms. Harris," Harlan returned softly. "Perhaps you need to think about who needs money.''

"Only Camina." All the sweetness of the day was seeping out of her.

"Are you sure about that?''

"Paul has buckets of money. He's so busy he can't keep up with his schedule. Reid has all kinds of investors interested in his projects in Costa Rica, and the ranch supports itself. He sure doesn't need money.''

"Ahh." His sigh was long and drawn out. "Well. It's been a long three days. Thanks." His indrawn breath was a mere hiss of sound along the wire. "I really expected you to hang up, you know.''

"Yesterday I would have." Her admission was painful. She didn't enjoy thinking about Reid or Paul or Susie in the same breath with greed strong enough to drive someone to murder. "You sure you don't want the name of the charity?" She managed a laugh. "Maybe someone on the board of the hospital has been shuffling numbers, running two sets of books. Anything's possible in your world.''

"Well, in fact, it is. People have committed murder for money, for reputation, for territory. The name of the charity was my next question. I'll send Ross to the hospital on a fact-finding mission."

"I wish you wouldn't." Molly leaned over the sink and adjusted the bottom of the shutter.

At the far end of the gallery she thought she saw something moving. The cat. She pressed the shutter tight and walked back across the kitchen. Leaning against the counter holding the microwave, she faced the bayou.

"I know. But it's my job. Speaking of which, Ms. Harris, you were very tricky last night. You thought fast, getting your brother and me out of the kitchen. I didn't expect you to react that quickly. I meant to take your gun with me, you know."

"That's what I thought." Molly tried to disguise the smugness in her voice.

"Proud of yourself, are you?"

"A little." She grinned.

"Don't get overconfident. You hid it, and if I'd had time to look, I would have checked—let me see..." He was teasing her. "Oh, I would have checked that wastebasket under your sink first." When she kept silent, he added, "Gotcha."

"Why didn't you ask about it before you left? I was surprised you didn't." Molly took her dish and utensils to the sink and rinsed them, stacked them neatly in the dishwasher.

She was enjoying talking with Harlan. She could handle him over the phone. All that intimidating presence was muted by the distance—except for the sly way the sound of his voice sort of rumbled through her, buzzing across her skin and inside her, way, way down in her innermost self.

His answer was a long time coming, and while she waited, Molly realized she didn't want him to hang up.

"That's a good question, Ms. Harris. I don't know why I didn't mention the gun in front of your brother. The human mind doesn't always work rationally. But then, you're the one who doesn't believe in an irrational world, aren't you?"

"And you do?"

"Oh, yes, Ms. Harris. I most emphatically do," he said, and hung up.

As the week passed, each day filled with sunshine, Molly permitted herself to believe that her life would right itself. Harlan called her every day. He said he was calling to keep her up to date on the investigation, but their conversations, if that was what they were—she herself thought that they were an elaborate minuet of approach and retreat—never lasted more than ten minutes.

She let the cat in every night and out every morning. Most of the time the animal slept at the foot of her bed, his large presence facing the stairwell, keeping watch over her.

Sometimes she slept, sometimes not. When she couldn't, she walked through the upstairs halls, peering through the shutters at the world outside her house.

In that night world made silver by the waxing moon, she sometimes saw the shape of John Harlan walking around the perimeter of her property. His shadow blended and merged with the hedges, the trees, the corners of her lower gallery. He never rang her doorbell. He never knocked on the kitchen door and demanded entrance.

But she saw him.

And once, as she moved the shutter in Reid's room, Harlan was walking up from the bayou and looked up sharply, his gaze drawn to the flick of the shutter and to her, caught between shutter and glass.

He moved closer, smoke in the moonlight, his dark form growing larger, his black shirt and pants and hair fading into the night. He stopped at the foot of the veranda.

The moon touched his pale face and left a silver glow that glittered in his eyes. He raised his hand slowly, so slowly that she couldn't take her eyes from him, and with his palm toward her, he swayed his hand, outlining the shape of her in the window, moving his palm from her throat all the way down the center of her body.

Before she knew what she was doing, she pressed against the window, laid her hot cheek against the cool glass. Her white satin nightshirt was heavy on her skin, heavy over the heat of her blood roaring through her body and turning, like the tides to the moon, to him.

And the glitter of the moon in his eyes was the glitter of an increasing hunger that found its echo in her.

Silver and gold filled her sleep that night as she followed him in dreams, wandering through the gleaming halls behind him, his black shape vanishing and reappearing behind glittering glass, never close enough to touch, yet drawing her on.

Molly woke the next morning aching, aching as she had never ached and burned for anyone. She was feverish with need.

All day she raced from appointment to appointment, her body driving her into movement, and she found no ease for the fever that burned in her, filled her lips, swelled her breasts until they hurt.

She would have thought she was coming down with the flu, but she knew better. There was no cure for the fever that burned her to the bone.

On the fourth day, at noon, on a miracle of a Florida winter day, he came to her house with Ross Whittaker.

The low-slung sports car rumbled slowly up her driveway, and she heard it before she saw it. As he had that first time, he came to the front door and rang the doorbell. When she opened the door, she noticed his rigid posture, the silver-rimmed sunglasses masking his eyes. A thin silver watch on his wrist caught the sunlight.

"Detective?"

"Ms. Harris." He tipped his head. Sunlight was lost in the darkness of his hair and clothes.

She needed to see his eyes. If she could see his eyes, she would know if he were going to arrest her. She gripped the door and waited. "What is it?"

He hesitated. He was ill at ease. "There's a problem. At your brother's river cabin."

She couldn't begin to fathom what he meant. "Problem?" She shook her head. "What kind of problem?" She peered around him. "Is Reid with you?"

"No." Harlan placed his hand over hers. "The cabin's burned to the ground. We think your brother was inside when the fire started."

"An accident?" she whispered, pleading for the only explanation possible in a rational world.

Keeping her grounded with his touch, he shook his head and shoved his glasses to the top of his head with his free hand. She'd thought it would help her to see his eyes. It made everything worse. "Someone was smoking and fell asleep?"

"No. The fire was set. It—" he touched his glasses, started to lower them, left them where they were "—was arson. Kerosene. Accelerants. It burned for thirty-six hours. There's not much left of the building—some beams on top of the rubble. Where the ceiling crashed."

"I don't believe it. Reid must have left. He *couldn't* have been inside!"

"Have you heard from him? Has he come back home at any time since he left?"

"You know he hasn't been here. He hasn't called me."

"Oh." Harlan touched his sunglasses.

"Someone could have broken into the cabin after Reid and his investors left."

"That's possible. Except his rental car is in the shed."

Reid could have taken off and changed plans without telling her. He was thirty-four; he'd been used to functioning independently since he was thirteen and in military school. He might even have cancelled his meeting at the last minute. He wouldn't have told her if he had. "Reid doesn't give me his itinerary, Detective. He could have left with one of his friends. Maybe that's why he left his car behind." Her voice shook.

"We don't know who he was meeting there, so it's possible he left with one of his investors and intended to return for his car. We don't know for sure about Reid, but the investigators have found torso fragments, some longer bone fragments. Someone was in the cabin. It may not have been Reid. We'll know when the investigators finish. We've called in a forensic odontologist to help sift through the rubble. If any teeth are left after a fire this intense, we may get an identification that way."

She wouldn't accept that Reid, her twin, could have met disaster and she didn't sense it. She couldn't accept that Reid, with all his energy and enthusiasm, was gone, and that she'd never see him again. She couldn't accept that the last memory of her brother she'd have would be that scrawled, "love ya, Sissy."

The world couldn't be that cruel. Life wasn't that irrational.

CHAPTER TEN

"We'll be there in a few minutes, Ms. Harris. Hang on." Harlan whipped the wheel to the left and spun it back to the right, skirting a tree limb.

"You all right?" He steadied the car.

"Fine, thank you."

"Yeah? Could've fooled me." He shot her a quick look.

Maybe she only imagined the narrow-eyed look behind his silver-rimmed sunglasses.

Sitting tensely beside him as he drove the unmarked beige four-door, Molly tried to shut out her awareness of his frequent glances in her direction.

With each glance he crowded and confused her.

She was angry with herself for being aware of him, angry with him for riffling her nerve ends until she was vibrating inside, her emotions twanging and clanging to his glances, to his touch, until she wanted to lash out at him and tell him to leave her alone and let her grieve for her brother.

Since the day John Harlan had rung her doorbell, her emotions had played crack-the-whip with her, and she'd been the tail end, cracking back and forth, hanging on for all she was worth while her hands slipped free and she whirled crazily into the unknown.

He'd been one step ahead of her from the first minute she'd met him. From the beginning, she'd been driven to throw up walls against him, to resist him. She'd wanted to shield her thoughts, her feelings, her... Balancing her arm on the car door, she shaded her eyes.

She needed privacy to collect her thoughts and emotions.

Harlan saw too much. He understood more about her than she wanted him to.

He understood how close she'd come that night to running down to him. If he'd lifted his hand to motion her forward, she would have walked right out of her house and across the moonlit lawn to him.

Emotions dormant for too long had burst forth, going wild, and she'd felt alive, alive for the first time in... She took a deep breath. Maybe she'd never felt that alive, that frantic with need.

She couldn't grasp how it had happened, but Harlan had made her feel again. He'd given her a glimpse of what life in the sunshine could be like after months in a gray, cold world.

And then, when she'd dropped her guard, he'd told her her brother was probably dead.

His news about Reid had been the emotional equivalent of a pitcher of ice water.

Gasping, her heart pounding, she'd surfaced, honeyed heat draining from her in the face of this latest catastrophe.

Molly closed her eyes. She wanted to hate John Harlan for taking away the numbness.

With each glance he reminded her of what had almost happened between them. He kept his distance physically, but she couldn't keep him out of her head.

It was as if he were slipping inside her mind, opening doors and walking in on her naked soul.

They had unfinished business.

And, regardless of what occurred with Reid or with Camina's case, she was beginning to understand that John Harlan had changed her.

Ross Whittaker sat in the back, behind Harlan. They were on one side of the line, she on the other. Cops. Civilian.

She was the outsider.

But as the thought flicked through her mind like the dry

rattle of a diamondback, Harlan shot her a sideways glance
and touched her elbow fleetingly with his right hand while
he steered the car with his left. "I told you once not to trust
anybody. No matter what happens, whether we find Reid or
we don't, you still can't let down your guard with anyone.
Nothing is ever what it seems."

"I listened to you once. I was wrong." She frowned and
looked out the side window, avoiding him.

"We'll see." The car bounced and settled. He turned to
concentrate on the road. His mouth was grim and tight-
lipped. He was angry.

She didn't care. In fact, she relished seeing the evidence
of strong feeling on his austere face.

But he stayed on one side of the line, coldly dispassionate
at the scene of other people's pain.

Observer.

Cop.

She'd been on one side of the window, he on the other.

And it was because of him that she had actually doubted
Reid for a few minutes in her kitchen the night before he
left. John Harlan had planted that suspicion. Maybe if he
hadn't poisoned her view of her brother, those last hours
with Reid wouldn't have become strained and uncomfortable.

Molly turned to the window, staring at vines and scraggly
clumps of grass along the road. She'd blamed her reactions
on fatigue. They'd been the result of Harlan's insinuations,
though. She'd allowed herself to be carried along in the
riptide of emotion he drew forth from her with every look,
every touch, and she'd let herself think for a second that her
brother had suddenly become a stranger to her.

Mesmerized by John Harlan, she'd been wandering in
dreams while Reid had been out here in the woods dying.

Dropping her hand, Molly picked at the metal strip under

her window. If Reid were dead, Harlan was partly responsible.

Because she'd listened to him and tuned out her brother, because she'd let Harlan's suspicions become hers that last night, she bore the heaviest guilt.

Harlan had only been doing his job. He'd been playing cop.

She was the one who'd looked at Reid and hesitated, letting those vague suspicions root her at the opposite end of the kitchen.

She was angry with herself, with Harlan, with fate.

And even while admitting that it was unfair of her, she blamed Harlan most of all.

After so many months of operating on automatic pilot, she could feel an explosive mix of emotions roiling through her like lava. Molly scratched at the metal on the car door.

Harlan had said she was like a volcano.

With a quick sideways check, she noted the tiny ridges of tense muscle along the side of his mouth. His glance met hers in a long, considering look that said he knew exactly what she was feeling. Thinking.

She was the one who looked away.

All right. She dug her fingernail into the gap between window and doorframe. All right. She was overreacting. She knew that.

Harlan hadn't made her do anything.

No matter how much she told herself that she was wrong to react the way she was doing, she couldn't stop herself. She couldn't hold back the resentment licking through her like a line of angry fire moving forward toward a keg of black powder.

And even resenting him, Molly couldn't stop her gaze from returning to the strength in his broad shoulders, the solid column of his neck where the glossy black of his hair was a straight line above the fabric of his charcoal shirt.

He'd thrown his jacket on the seat next to her, and his scent, elusive and faint, surrounded her.

His lean hand, negligently guiding the car, was strong, and she found herself aggravated by the deftness with which he drove. Resenting his effortless skills used up her energy and kept her from thinking about her brother. She wanted Harlan to hit every pothole, lose command of the car, lose his polite reserve. She wanted to see him wracked by the kinds of emotions she was experiencing.

She wanted to rip past his powerful control, to see him without his mask. She wanted to see him as much at the mercy of his emotions as she was.

In a still, quiet part of her brain, she knew what she was doing, knew she was using Harlan and his strength to get her through the coming hours, knew she preferred resenting him to imagining what she would see at the cabin.

And the part of her that reasoned through her careening emotions accepted at a primitive level that Harlan's shoulders were wide enough to bear the weight of her anger and grief.

She needed to nurse her resentment.

After the brief exchange between her and Harlan, Whittaker occasionally leaned forward and murmured to Harlan, but neither talked to her. The lines were drawn, and all three were suspended in the bubble of the car, waiting for the moment of arrival, when time would hurtle them forward into irrevocable events.

In this bubble of sunshine and suspended time, though, she allowed herself to hope that Reid was laughing somewhere, that someone in her life wasn't systematically wiping out her family, one by one.

Shielded inside Harlan's anonymous cop car, she pretended that evil wasn't hidden by a face she knew.

Ross leaned forward. "Half a mile farther."

With resentment popping through her, hope still alive,

Molly was in no hurry to reach the cabin. Half a mile could be eternity.

At the cabin, she would face whatever she had to.

The quiet warmth of the sun coming through the car windshield onto her arms and face was a gift, and she let it seep into her.

Seeing her lift her face to the sunshine streaming in the windshield, Harlan rolled his window down and rested his arm on the car door. The wind flattened the sunshine-brushed fabric of his black sleeve against the hard curve of his biceps and forearm, and his hand draped to the inside of the car, his thin fingers forming a C against the brown door.

The rutted road leading to the cabin ran through stands of pines down to the Palmetto River and was nothing more than a lane of washboard bumps and holes, jarring Molly against her seat belt in spite of Harlan's expert handling of the sedan.

When they stopped several yards back from the ruins of the cabin, Molly smelled the lingering odor of smoke first, and underneath, the sharp cleanness of the pines. She took a shallow breath, pain splintering her.

In the rich, late-winter sunshine, the delicate pale blue blossoms of the plumbago blurred in front of her. Reid had always called them the lumbago bushes.

She took another breath.

"Let's see what they've discovered." John Harlan unclipped her seat belt, and his shoulder bumped hers as he reached over her to open her door. "Perhaps they've found an item of your brother's that you'll recognize." His words were low in her ear as he added, "Not knowing is the worst part."

Several men in nylon Windbreakers labeled with huge orange letters, their movements efficient and concentrated, sifted through grayish black ashes. The heavy beams of the two-story cabin, charred and broken, lay over black lumps that had been appliances and furniture. Tall and stooped, an older man was clearly directing the activities. He looked up as the car doors opened. The bill of his Florida Marlins cap shielded his face as he waved them over.

"Ross and I will talk to Dr. Franklin," Harlan said to Molly. "He's the forensic odontologist we called in as a consultant. It would be better if you waited here." He touched her cheek, a light, transitory contact that flowed through her and left her lonely as he dropped his hand and picked up his jacket.

He shoved his sunglasses on top of his head as he stared at her. In that second, his pupils were contracted until his eyes were all gold, their color deepening and swallowing her. "I'll come back for you."

"Whatever you say. You're the detective."

The skin over his cheekbones tightened, and his slow exhalation was a drawn-out hiss shivering over her.

She swallowed and tried to look away.

He *was* angry.

Before he opened his door, he stared back at her over his shoulder. "This doesn't make a damned bit of sense to me." He flipped his glasses down and slammed the door behind him. The car rocked with the force of his exit.

Maybe he meant the arson. Maybe he meant the hunger that hovered like an almost-visible shape between them.

She rubbed her cheek. It was an emotion more compelling than hunger. Stronger. She'd glimpsed his loneliness.

Molly slid out of the car and waited by the headlights. She was as close as she wanted to be to the melted and charred remains of the cabin.

Whittaker loped off in the direction of the men with their different-sized sieves. The man in charge wiped his face with a grayed handkerchief, lifted his turquoise cap and resettled it as Whittaker poked at chunks in a sieve with a stick.

Ash drifted on the wind, bits freckling her arm.

Molly stared at the flecks and couldn't look away. Her vision hazy with unshed tears, she touched one of the bits and watched it crumble and blow away.

A smudge so small she had to strain to see it dotted her finger.

Wrapping her arms around herself and letting her hair tumble into her eyes, she watched Harlan take a pen from his pocket and stir the contents of the older man's sieve. The man hunched his shoulders and nodded as if to say "Who knows?" and Harlan gestured for one of the men to cart over a large black plastic bag. Through the open back doors of the white van, she saw four more bags.

Molly didn't know what she had expected to feel on seeing the burned cabin. Numbness, overpowering grief, an awareness of evil. But after that first, wrenching sight of the plumbago, she could have been looking at any cabin anywhere.

And she was glad.

Any lingering sense of Reid at this desolate ruin would have been too much to bear after everything else that had happened.

With the breeze blowing her hair into her face, she thought about Reid and the ties that had bound them over the years. Flattening strands of hair, she tried to recall the last time they had spent hours together, laughing and joking. Teasing, the way they had as children alone on the bayou.

In one panicky beat of her heart, she realized she couldn't remember.

She'd been so certain she would know if anything had happened to him. Maybe that certainty had been her own wishful thinking, creating bonds that no longer existed.

They hadn't spent much time together in years. She'd

gone off to college, while Reid had finished military school, entered and dropped out of a different college, joined the army and eventually taken over the ranch in Costa Rica with their parents' encouragement. Had she and Reid become strangers, and had habit become their link as adults?

Molly frowned.

Maybe she wouldn't know if her twin had died.

Molly doubled her fists. None of that mattered. She wanted Reid to saunter over, punch her on the arm and shake his head, his handsome face screwed up in unholy amusement at the thoughts she'd had. She wanted him to hoot and rag at her for being a dope.

But most of all, she wanted him safe at her side.

Looking at the collapsed roof and walls, the blasted remains of the cabin, Molly thought about the circumstances. One way or another, her parents, Camina and maybe Reid had become victims. Their murders hadn't been a random series of events, an irrational glitch in the universe. She knew that now.

Someone had planned and set these events in motion. Someone had meant for her to be blamed for Camina's death. Harlan had tried to make her accept that, and she hadn't.

Someone she knew, smiling and affable, thought there was gain in death.

Anger ramrodded her spine and she walked over to Harlan and Dr. Franklin. "Is there anything you want me to take a look at?" She hardened herself to memories, sentiment, to everything except the necessity of doing what had to be done to uncover the monster behind the smiling mask.

"So far, all we have is a heap of stuff in garbage bags. Some tear-shaped things that might be plastic with ash corroded on 'em might also be teeth. Can't tell 'til we X-ray 'em. We'll run the whole bag through and see if teeth or—" Dr. Franklin looked at Harlan's forefinger pressing his arm.

"Whatever. But nothing looks like anything anybody would recognize at this point, ma'am."

He turned away from her and drew Harlan to his side, but Molly heard the muttered comment, "Problem is, John, this sucker's been burning so long that even if we find teeth, they may crumble right to pieces. Folks think teeth'll survive anything, and usually they do. But this was a bitch of a fire, I'm telling you. Intense and long lasting. We may find nothing."

"Reid had a crown on one tooth," Molly said. She imitated Harlan and stepped away from pain, moved across the dividing line. "Gold and porcelain."

"You sure about that?" Franklin squinted at her. "That's real precise. I'm damned if I'd know what my wife has in her mouth by way of dental work unless I saw the X-rays."

"I sell dental supplies. My ex-husband, Dr. Paul Bouler, is an oral surgeon. And Reid lorded it over me because he had gold in his mouth and I didn't. I'm positive. If Reid..." She cleared her throat. "If Reid's in there, you might find the crown. No fillings. No other dental work for either of us. Paul's his dentist. He'll have Reid's records." She looked hard at the sieve in the odontologist's hand. It held shiny, melted black objects, chunks of wood or something else.

Harlan had moved toward her with her first words and cupped her elbow. "Good." He beckoned to Ross, who loped over. "Get on the cellular phone. We need Bouler's records." His fingers slid against her wrist and she stifled the impulse to hold onto his hand. "That's a real big help, Ms. Harris. You've saved us time."

"Good," Molly said. "May I see his rental car?"

Harlan shrugged. "It's been dusted? Checked out?"

Franklin nodded. "The records from the rental agency and the odometer match with his trip from the airport to your house and up here. We've accounted for the mileage. The car wasn't driven anywhere else, apparently.''

The door to the shed creaked when Harlan opened it and stepped in before her, moving to one side as she followed. ''So? What do you see?''

Hesitating, Molly scanned the dilapidated interior. ''It looks the same. It's been years since I was here.''

Separate from the two-story cabin, the shed had been built to shelter the boat when they took it out of the water. Lawn chairs, an old bicycle and a wooden raft hung on hooks along the wall. Oars and bait buckets filled one corner. Dust covered the gasoline cans and stacks of old magazines along the shelves. The interior of the shed was hot and stuffy. The small, square windows, grimy and smeared with wasp droppings, kept the shed dim, ghostly in the waning light.

''Take a good look. I'm in no hurry.'' Jamming his glasses once more on top of his head, Harlan rubbed his neck. Fine lines radiated from his eyes.

Sadness crept into her. ''I don't know what I expected. I thought…'' She shrugged. The urge to involve herself and not wait helplessly for the next disaster had made her ask. She walked over to the rental car and opened the driver's door.

The car was empty, smelling a little of stale air and cigarette smoke. ''Reid doesn't smoke,'' she said absently, running her finger along the steering wheel.

''No?'' Harlan reached in front of her, she stepped back against the metal doorframe and he pulled open the ashtray. Two quarter-inch-long marks showed where the techs had removed cigarette ashes. ''Someone did.''

His arm lay beneath her breasts, but in that hot, still, dusty moment, as they stared at the ashtray, Molly couldn't move. She leaned forward, resting her head briefly on his shoulder. There was comfort in the solid strength under her forehead. Then, like an old woman, she straightened. ''Or the rental agency was careless about checking the cleaning crew's work before renting out the car again."

"Yes." Harlan shut the tray and stepped back, giving her room to move away. "That would explain it, too." In the dusty dimness, where the smell of smoke lay like a pall over them, he said, "Molly, I promise you. If your brother is dead, I'll find out who killed him."

She rested against the car. "You think he's alive?"

He lowered his gaze and moved away from her. "I don't think anything at this point." He pivoted and placed his hands flat against the car roof on either side of her and bent his knees until he was eye-to-eye with her. "But I know this case is going to get nastier before all the answers are in." Lowering his head, he nudged her forehead with his, just as she had lain hers against his shoulder, and said, "The blood on the knife was Camina's."

"Oh." Molly shut her eyes.

"You knew it would be. It's no surprise."

"I expected it." She had, but her stomach churned.

"As of today, an arrest warrant hadn't been issued." Sliding closer to her face, his palms moved along the metal, making a shushing sound, until his broad hands cupped her face and his fingers spread over the back of her neck. "I think one will be, though. Especially now. You should prepare yourself."

"All right. I will." Molly opened her eyes. "I wondered why—"

He interrupted. "You're one of Reid's beneficiaries. The situation doesn't look good for you—all these coincidences joining together like a spiderweb with you at the middle. And it's been a week since Camina's murder. The department honchos are getting antsy. An arrest would look good."

"For you?"

He nodded. "Of course. It's my case, after all." Under

her hair, his fingertips traced the curve of her ear. "But it's in the department's hands. They'll make the decision with the state's attorney."

His thumbs slid to the corners of her mouth, touching, stroking, the rasp of his thumb somehow an overwhelming comfort.

"At least you know I couldn't have killed Reid." She touched his chest, whether by accident or on purpose, she didn't know, but under her hand his heart thundered, speeded up. "Everyplace I've been this last week, you've been right behind me. You've been at my house every night, prowling and circling and watching. You're my alibi, Detective, aren't you?"

"Perhaps." His mouth was so close to hers that his breath buzzed over her lips and made them tingle. "I'm going to do something incredibly stupid right now, Ms. Harris."

"Don't," she whispered, lifting her face. "We don't even like each other."

"I have to," he murmured against her mouth and kissed her, his mouth slanting over hers. He never moved his hands from her face, where his thumbs pressed lightly at the corners of her mouth. His bent knees bumped hers awkwardly as he lowered himself to her. "And liking has nothing at all to do with it."

He nipped her lower lip and she took a breath to tell him no, this was a bad idea, no, she didn't want this at all.

But she was lying to herself and she knew it. She wanted the wild taste of him, wanted the weight of his chest against her, the race of his heart. Oh, it was stupid, foolish, for both of them.

"Yes," she said and curled her arm around his neck and pulled him closer, because here in this dusty shed she was alive, he was, and death was far away in this moment of heat and pounding blood.

"Come on, sweetness, open for me," he muttered, trailing his lips down her neck and up again, his mouth fierce and hard against her. "Let me taste you, please."

"Yes," she said, because this was what she wanted—him touching her, helping her forget. She *wanted*. She slid her fingers through his thick black hair and opened her mouth to him, kissing him back as hungrily as he was kissing her, needing his touch to keep the demons at bay.

Her choice, to run her open mouth along the cords of his strong neck. Her decision, to slide her hand inside the silky fabric of his shirt. Her choice, to press her mouth over his thundering heart, to taste the skin burning there and to sink into his heat.

Her choice.

He tilted her face toward him once more and held it for his sipping kisses, for the butterfly flick of his tongue against the lobe of her ear. He groaned, shivered, and then his arms were around her, lifting her off her feet, pulling her into the cradle of his legs. He turned and rested against the car frame, pulling her left leg over his hip.

Against the nylon of her panties, his belt buckle was cold, hot, and she pressed closer restlessly.

And that was her choice, too.

He was right. The river of heat sliding through her had nothing to do with liking and everything, everything to do with craving and obsession and need.

She needed *him*. Her body craved him, melted against his hardness, chest, thigh, groin.

One arm anchoring her to him, he cupped her breast, curling his hand over her nipple and plucking the small nub until she rubbed anxiously against him, needing.

Her mouth was full and aching, needing the flick of his tongue over it. Her skin ached with need, and she forgot everything—resentment, grief—forgot everything as he lowered his head and took the tip of her breast in his mouth, everything flowing to that pressure of his teeth and lips against her, pleasure a burning blackness behind her eyelids.

She whimpered.

And he stopped. But not easily.

He was shaking against her.

Need, like hers, was raw in his unmasked face. Hunger, like hers, glittered in his eyes.

But he stopped. "Well, damn me to hell," he said, leaning his head back against the car but not releasing her. "I said I was going to do something stupid. Stupid, dumb, irresponsible. I didn't mean to be this damned stupid, though." He swore fluently, filthily and earnestly, cursing himself in a flat, unemotional tone that made the curses even more powerful. His breathing slowed, but his nostrils still flared. "I thought I had more control. I was wrong."

"If you say you're sorry, I swear I'll kill you," Molly muttered. Not her choice, this unsatisfied aching.

His laugh barreled up from his chest, rumbled against her breasts, and the spring unwinding inside her tightened, hitched, uncoiled. "Ah, Ms. Harris, you might want to rethink your choice of words...under the circumstances." His chest shook against her again as he let her slide to her feet.

She stumbled on the concrete floor.

He rubbed the back of his neck as he looked around the shed. "This is, without a doubt, the worst idea I've ever had in my life." He glanced down at her, his eyes narrowed and ruthless. "And, no. I'm not one damned bit sorry."

"Good," Molly said and brushed her hair back from her face. "Because I was as much responsible for what happened as you were." Thinking through the urgency of her response, the rush of adrenaline that had slammed through her as she'd seen Reid's abandoned car, she added slowly, "I used you, you know."

"Oh, you did, did you?" His voice was silky soft. "Used

me for your pleasure—is that what you're trying to tell me?''

"Yes," Molly insisted, trying desperately to be honest with him and to make amends for her earlier, unwarranted resentment. "I wanted what happened between us. I've had enough of grief and death. I *wanted* to kiss you. And I'm not sorry, either." She stepped forward and tried to slide the top two smoke-colored buttons of his shirt into the buttonholes.

"Ms. Harris, you are something else." One side of his mouth lifted. "But don't get the idea I'm easy, you hear?" Once again Florida sand roughened the easy smoothness of his voice.

"Believe me, Detective, that's the last idea I would ever have about you." Molly bit her lower lip as she tried to button his shirt in the dusty shed.

"Listen, I'm serious. I didn't mean for this—" Harlan frowned "—*this* to get out of control." He watched her shaky fingers twist the slippery buttons through the buttonholes and tried to ignore the quick graze of her fingers against his skin as she worked the pieces of slate firmly into place. Forcing himself to stand there under her touch took every ounce of his willpower. Tremors tightened and torqued inside him, shivered slowly to a halt.

He took a deep breath.

He'd meant only to distract her from what was happening. He'd understood the way she'd withdrawn in the car, understood, but hadn't liked it, and wasn't sure why not until he'd taken her mouth with his. He'd meant only a quick, casual hum of sex, not the swamping need that had taken him to the edge. He'd been out of control completely, and for the first time in his life.

Out of control. The thought was terrifying. He couldn't afford at this point in his life to lose control.

Anything could happen. Anything.

Nahual came the whisper. Harlan cocked his head and frowned.

Molly hadn't heard anything. Head lowered, she worked the second button through the silk-bordered hole. She finally looked up at him, her gaze holding his. In the triangle of her face, her delicate chin trembled, firmed. "I lost control, too. And I'm not sorry that I did," she added stubbornly. "But it doesn't mean anything. It's just—" she raised her hands, searching for a word, but he refused to help her "—sex. Or the life force. I don't know." She stepped back. "Something."

"Oh, it's *something,* it is, Ms. Harris. And I don't know any more than you do what it means," he lied, trying to forget the feel of her against him.

She might not understand what had happened between them, but he did.

And knowing, he longed to smooth the flyaway strands of her hair, to pull her close and keep her beside him through the long night.

But it was impossible.

Not for him the timeless, lovely twining together through night into morning, the waking up in luxurious heat and reaching out to find himself in her.

It couldn't happen, not for him.

His control was slipping, day by day, and he couldn't indulge the craving growing in him for Molly Harris.

Nahual, his grandmother whispered, and he tilted his head, almost expecting to see her appear in front of him. He saw only the outlines and forms in the shed, the rental car, Molly's bent head in front of him, the sweet curve of her neck within stroking distance.

Afterward, when he drove up the driveway to Molly's house, his skin crawled. The windows of the house were like hooded, secretive eyes, and he insisted on walking through the house with her, checking doors and windows.

Though the hairs on the back of his neck rose as he paced through the rooms, he saw nothing to alarm him, and so he said nothing to her. At the front door he started to tell her he would stay the night. He even opened his mouth to say the words. "Ms. Harris?"

"You'll let me know if anything shows up when they X-ray the bags?"

He shut his mouth tightly, holding in the words that would bring disaster on his head. "Yes. When. If."

"All right."

He wanted to stay and wouldn't allow himself to, so instead he cautioned her, "Keep your portable phone handy."

"I will."

"Give me the gun. I can't make you give it to me—but, believe me, you're safer without it."

She'd hesitated. "I feel safer with it."

"It's an illusion." He held the screen door open and swung it to and fro. "Guns don't make anybody safer in the long run."

"I'll think about it. Maybe you're right."

"I am. Your phone will do you more good than that gun." With those words, he left.

On the way home, Harlan stopped at a filling station, called Ross and told him to schedule a squad-car check on her house every hour during the night.

Later, the picture of Molly's even, white teeth against the pink swell of her lip was the picture that lingered in his head as he watched the reflections on his bedroom ceiling shift and flow. He imagined her satiny hair under his chin, catching against his rougher skin.

Harlan turned on his side. The sheets tangled in his legs and, swearing, he jerked the top sheet free.

He was sweating, his skin hot and damp despite the fan.

The scent of Molly lingered in his nostrils, on his skin. He turned to the other side, seeking a cooler spot on the sheet.

He wanted her.

Sweat beaded along his forehead. He flexed his fingers and stretched out, letting the air from the fan waft over him, giving it a chance to dry the sweat and cool him.

She had wanted him.

Her body had told him that as it softened against him, and she'd been honest enough to admit it. She hadn't turned coy or teasing. She had been straightforward about her feelings.

When he'd gone through her house, checking it before leaving her, he'd almost let himself believe he could stay. He'd seen the acceptance in her eyes. She would have let him.

The calves of his legs twitched and he stretched, arching his toes.

The shadows on his ceiling blurred as the moon passed through the night sky. She would inherit whatever estate Reid had. Reid and Bouler would have inherited her estate. The hospital would get its part. And so would the cousin in Texas, Susie Warrin.

Molly carried the gun with her into her bathroom and put it on the back of the toilet while she bathed. When she went to bed, she placed it carefully on the floor under her bed. She put the cordless phone next to her pillow.

Through her closed windows she heard the hunting call of an owl.

She couldn't shed tears for Reid. There would be time for grieving when she felt safe. Until then, she would do what she had to stay alive and find Reid's killer. To see the face that had taunted her with madness.

Because of John Harlan, the miasma that had lain over

her for most of the year had dissipated. She was determined never again to be a victim.

Before he rang her doorbell, she'd spent a year in limbo, grief flowing through her and creeping slowly forward until she'd finally been encased in ice, feeling nothing, not pleasure, not pain.

Nothing.

She'd turned her home into a prison whose bars were grief-forged. She would have stayed there, too—falling deeper and deeper into that place of midnight ice where she was no longer herself—if John Harlan hadn't showed up on her doorstep.

Confronting her, not allowing her to retreat from him, he'd dragged her out of that limbo of black ice. He'd bullied his way past her door with his impeccable manners and not-going-to-take-no-for-an-answer attitude. Oh, he'd only wanted to solve the mystery of Camina's murder, but he'd cracked the shell Molly had sealed around herself. He'd threatened her, irritated her and agitated her until she hadn't been able to stay numb.

He'd dragged her, kicking and screaming, back into the land of the living, because he'd forced her to see that she could spend the rest of what was passing for her life in a real prison with real bars made of steel.

She'd created her own prison, but he'd made her see that she didn't want to go back there.

Harlan had forced her to see that life with all its pain and heartbreak and loneliness was better than the half life she was drifting through.

After all the months of not sleeping, of not dreaming, of wondering if she were losing her mind, he'd forced her to see that she had to save herself, find the strength to face what was happening around her.

And then, through the sheer force of his will, he'd pulled her to the window of her house and kept her there, pulled her to the brink of utter surrender and made her *want* to surrender to the hunger he evoked.

Her hand on the cordless phone, Molly finally slept.

He stirred, the hunting instinct flowing through him. Arching to his feet, he padded to the door. The night was rich with prey, the smells strong and powerful, drawing him into the night. Moving slowly, stealthily, through the night and the cool moonlight, he came to her. The grass was damp against his face as he neared the big house.

The house shimmered with light. The moon turned the hedges into secret lairs. He cocked his head. Other predators were about in the moon-bathed night.

Settling himself, he listened for a long time.

The night grew quiet around him.

He heard her turn in her bed, sigh.

The moment of truth had come. He sensed it.

Long, long ago he'd known that she was the one, and he'd waited patiently all these months.

It was time.

What would be, would be.

It was out of his control now.

Harlan was drenched in sweat when he bolted from his bed, his pulse racing and his heart banging against his ribs so hard he couldn't catch his breath. Bending double and gasping, he touched his toes and arched his back.

Moonlight banded his face and belly when he straightened and waited for his pulse to return to normal. He ran his hands down his sweat-slick body. Moonlight and Molly. Molly, alone in her house behind locks that weren't keeping out the evil stalking her.

He'd been dreaming about Molly.

* * *

Moonlight bathed her face and she turned to it in her sleep.

In her dreams she followed him, his indistinct form shifting and flowing through the corridors. Suddenly, like a rush of wind roaring through a tunnel, he whirled and came to her, his heavy cape swirling, concealing his shape and face. Luring her with promises of a darkness beyond sleep, a darkness beyond anything she'd ever known, he came, her demon lover.

The sound at her front door jerked Molly out of a profound sleep.

Disoriented, still lingering in her dream, she held the cordless phone in her hand.

CHAPTER ELEVEN

Harlan was surprised to find himself on her doorstep.

He shouldn't have been.

He'd known from the beginning that this moment was inevitable.

Where the lawn gave way to overgrown bushes and cabbage palms, he heard the annoyed chatter of a raccoon. Moonlight lay across Molly's yard in wide patches broken by shadows, and the grass down at the edge of the bayou moved gently in the night wind, a gray-and-silver flow of light. The leaves in the hibiscus hedges and on the vines growing over the gallery rippled as if something had brushed past only seconds earlier.

He cocked his head. A scent of nastiness, faint and elusive, teased him. His nostrils flared. Old, that persistent scent? Or new?

His eyes dilated in the darkness, but he saw nothing in the deep hedge shadows, the dark spaces under the veranda.

A hunting night.

Harlan wiped his hand across his face. His sweat was drying in the cool air, but the heat burned in him, incandescent and white-hot. He jammed his shaking hand into the pocket of his jeans.

The chain on the lock rattled as she cracked open the door. "Hello, Detective." One cheek was pink and creased from her pillow. Her face was soft and drowsy and unguarded in the wedge of space between door and frame.

"Good evening, Ms. Harris." The band around his chest ached. His body felt stretched and tight, too big for skin and bones, pummeled, as if he'd been beaten with a two by four and left by the side of the road. He flexed his fingers.

"I didn't hear your car." She glanced down the driveway.

"It's—" he gestured vaguely to the road "—down there."

"Has something happened?" Strain showed in the corners of her eyes and the circles underneath, showed, too, in the lift of her chin. But moonlight lit her face with radiance, and in the light from the house and the porch, her hair glinted golden brown. "Have you heard anything about Reid? Do you know if—"

"No." He placed his palm on the other side of the door from hers.

"No news?" Strain pinched the fullness of her bottom lip.

"No. Not yet." He wanted her to ask him in. She had to open her door to him.

"This isn't an official visit?" She gripped the door. Her knuckles were white and the sleeve of her nightshirt fell back from her elbow. He saw the tender curve of her underarm, the skin fine textured and delicate.

"No."

White on pearl, the colors of Molly Harris standing in her nightshirt next to the wood and glass of her front door. Light to his darkness in this place where violence had burst through her etched windows, and he craved her with a longing beyond his understanding.

"You're off duty?"

Words locked in his throat, he nodded.

"I don't understand. What are you doing here?"

He breathed in the night air, let it fill his lungs, breathed out and found words after all. "Damned if I know, Ms. Harris." He didn't move. "Call it an impulse."

"An impulse, Detective?" Her face was sweet and inviting. Or perhaps it was the moonlight deceiving him.

Down near the road, a stone in the gravel driveway shifted and crunched at the pressure of something moving over it.

Harlan touched the knuckle of her little finger. "An irresistible impulse. I can't stay away from you."

Her eyes widened and she inhaled sharply, but she didn't move.

"I couldn't sleep. It's winter, but I wake up hot, smothering with heat. Naked under the ceiling fan, and I'm burning up." He stroked her knuckle. It was smooth, the small bones pressing against the covering of skin. He wondered if she had any idea how fragile she was. He hoped not. He did, though, and it terrified him. "I wake up dreaming of you."

"Do you?" She looked helplessly at him.

"Yes. I can't sleep without dreaming of you."

"I'm sorry." Her social skills failed her, and he was amused.

"Don't be." He smiled gently. "They were very pleasant dreams. I enjoyed them."

She jerked, her hand flew to her mouth and the chain rattled.

The chain, no barrier at all, not really, stayed between them. If necessary, he could have been inside her house within seconds. But tonight, trapped in moonlight and shadows, he needed her invitation. She might not understand, not yet, but the real power lay within her. She had drawn him here. He hadn't wanted to come, but he hadn't been able to stay away. He'd fought against the need winding within him so tightly that he couldn't eat, couldn't sleep. Couldn't stay away from her.

He'd lost.

He'd told himself he had to protect her.

He hadn't lied.

What pulled him to her porch at this time of night,

though, was more than the need to keep her safe. As a cop, he'd protected her with the resources at his command. He'd arranged for the patrol car to monitor her house.

Her face was pink and creamy warm. "What do you want?" she whispered, as if a crowd were around them instead of night creatures and solitude.

"Ah, that's easy. What I want is simple. I want you, hot, wild, under me, over me." His voice lowered, becoming guttural. "Me in you."

In the silence, he heard the satin shirt slide over her skin with her breathing.

"But I'll take whatever you choose to give me tonight. Nothing more." He coiled the chain around his index finger, released it, and it shortened, grew taut again. "One night. That's all." He managed to smile.

The scent of her, sleepy and woman-warm, drifted to him through the partially open door. He saw the answering loneliness in her eyes, which darkened to blue-gray. "You're blunt."

He nodded. "I want you. As I said, it's simple. I believe you want me." Down at the bayou, water slapped quietly against the pilings of the dock and the silence lengthened. "Is that speaking too directly for you? Do I—" he shrugged, not finding the word "—offend you? With my bluntness?"

"I'm not sure." A vein throbbed, blue in the moonlight, at the side of her throat.

"Ah. Well." He yearned to trace that gently pulsing vein. It seemed he'd waited for her throughout eternity, waiting longer than she could ever imagine. "The real question is, what do *you* want?"

"You told me I shouldn't trust you." Her voice had gone husky and shaky.

Harlan shifted more fully into the light and gave her a clearer view of him. His sunglasses dangled from the edge of his jeans pocket. "It was good advice. You'd be smart if you followed it. Nothing has changed. But I keep reminding you of that, don't I?" He knew his smile was rueful.

Yellow porch light pooled at the entrance to her home. Warm, inviting in the space between them, a space no larger than could be crossed in two steps. But he wouldn't take those steps, not yet, not until she gave him permission. If she chose to.

Light trembled in her hair, across her smooth skin. She looked away, back at him and hesitated.

He sensed the confusion and ambiguity in her, her need, and he wanted to end it for her.

He could have seduced her at any point with words. He knew his power, and it took the last of his immense control to stay silent in the face of his hunger. He could have pretended that he had news for her. Oh, there were words he could have said that would have made her unlock her door and let him in.

But he hadn't. He wouldn't.

He was trying to be as honest with her as he was with himself, when what he wanted was to place his fingertips against her door, press and shove the damned thing against the wall.

But he wouldn't do that, either.

She had to open her door and invite him into her home, her body, her soul.

Finding himself in front of her door, he had opened himself and allowed her to see his need. With eyes narrowed against the moonlight and porch light, he watched her as she read the intensity he no longer hid from her.

Her eyelashes fluttered. They were pointed with gold in the light.

She pushed her hair away from her face, and the tip of one earlobe showed through the shining brown strands. A shudder rushed through him like a wave crashing onto the beach and rushing back out to sea. He craved the taste of that delicate lobe. It would be sweeter than peaches, softer than silk. It would taste of gold and sunshine and life everlasting. He wanted to take it between his teeth and scrape it lightly, gently until she shivered.

Instead, he said simply, "May I come in?"

Her gaze locked on his, she nodded and unhooked the chain. She moved to the side and the door swung slowly open, but it was still a barrier between them.

"Are you sure?" He waited. He wouldn't take that first step through her door until he believed she was certain she wanted him in her home.

He couldn't. Because there would always be tomorrow.

"Oh, yes." Her voice quavered, and he could hear her pulse beating in her veins, crying to him with its hunger. "I'm sure."

Against his mouth that pulse would be hot, strong. He could make the blue-veined line at the base of her neck clamor against his mouth with yearning and need and pleasure, until she craved him the way he craved her.

He knew how. But not without her permission, and so, giving her a final chance to turn him away, he asked her once more, "Are you sure, Ms. Harris?"

"Yes."

"Why?" His curiosity surfaced, as always, even now. "Why me? Why tonight?"

She drew herself up to her full five feet something. Light flashed in her eyes as she said fiercely, "Because there's been enough fear and death in my life to last me forever. I want to feel alive again, even if it's only for tonight. I need to remind myself that life goes on, that I'm a part of it." Her voice shook with her vehemence. "I *need* to be alive again."

"You want to use me?" he asked, drawing on politeness to cover the aching bleakness.

"Isn't that why you showed up? So that you wouldn't be alone tonight? Who's using whom?" She stood erect, tension and strain pulling her skin tight over her face, her intensity matching his as she played with the words she'd used earlier.

"Two lonely people clinging together in the face of death and disaster? Is that why you're letting me in? Is that what this would be? Charming," he said, mockery tingeing his voice despite his effort.

"Would that be horrible? To—" she raised her hands helplessly "—share the loneliness, to get through the night? Together?"

"I would be honored." And he would be. It wasn't what he wanted from her, but it would do for tonight. He sketched a bow.

"Honored?" She frowned. "How formal you are, Detective. Your language, your manners.... Old-fashioned, almost." She reached toward the door, and he wondered if she might shut it in his face after all, even at this point.

"My mother and I lived with my grandmother after my father died. My grandmother didn't speak English until she was an adult. She was Guatemalan Indian. Old-fashioned in her own way. I learned English from her." He thought of the threshold as a line of demarcation between the gallery porch and her living room, and he stayed on the gallery side, wracked with need, waiting.

"But under those old-fashioned manners, you're also relentless, ruthless and dangerously persistent." She took a deep breath, and the satin fabric shimmered over her breasts and dipped into the soft indentation of her belly button. "Had enough compliments, Detective?" Her face, pink and white and radiant, shone with gentle mockery of her own.

As impossible as it was, in that second he liked her as

much—no, *more*—than he craved her, and so, surprised once more, Harlan answered her in kind. "My ego can handle it. I'm not a boy. I haven't been for a long, long time." He paused and smiled as her eyes widened. "I don't need someone blowing smoke at me. Go on, Ms. Harris. Please. You have my attention."

"There's something merciless about you, too, Detective."

"Yes." He dipped his head in acknowledgment of her hit. "I'm that, too."

"I have no doubt that no matter what happens between us tonight, you could arrest me tomorrow or the next day and it wouldn't make any difference to you." Her eyes, with that innocence shining in them, begged him not to lie.

He wouldn't have, anyway.

"Yes, no matter what we do together, I wouldn't hesitate to arrest you if I had to." He knew it sounded curiously like a promise. At last he let himself touch her face, a reward for honesty when lies would have been easier. "But," he said softly, "it *would* make a difference, Ms. Harris, believe me."

"You could have lied. I wondered if you would." Behind the innocence and loneliness, sadness surfaced in her face.

Wondering if she knew how much he'd revealed with his answer, he slid his palm down her neck, over her collarbones, down the slope of her shoulder and caught her hand loosely, letting it lie in his. "But you haven't answered my question. Why me?"

She looked at their joined hands.

"Because you can't 'help yourself?'" He gave a derisive spin to the words.

"That would be the worst reason, wouldn't it?" She couldn't look at him. "To be so enthralled that you were helpless, all rational thought and control gone, vanished, leaving you at the mercy of another?"

"Yes." He willed her to look at him. When she did, he added, "I wouldn't want you helpless and at my mercy. I want you involved, as needy as I am, both of us lost in each other but knowing the way back."

"I want you for all the reasons I said. And because, God help me, some primitive part of me trusts you. Isn't that crazy? I insult you, and then I tell you I trust you!"

"I will give you whatever I can, Ms. Harris. But I won't lie to you."

"I know," she said, and closing her fingers over his, she drew him over the sill. "But under the circumstances, Detective, do you think you might call me Molly?"

"Molly." He left his hand in hers. "Will you share tonight with me?"

"Yes, John Harlan, I will." Slamming and locking the door behind him, he was three strides into her house before she finished, "Because I don't want to be alone tonight. Because I need you. And because I choose to."

Wrapping his arms around her, he swept her up against him and felt her slim arms slide around his waist. A hard lump in the pocket of her nightshirt bumped against him as he lifted her off her toes and pulled her legs tight against him.

Blindly, eyes shut, his face buried in the sweet-smelling tendrils of her hair, he made his way across her living room and to the stairs. He wanted to go slow, he wanted to stretch out the moments and he couldn't.

His control snapped.

Frenzied with the need to take her, to close her around him, he lowered her, her back against the wall of the staircase. His skin, where it brushed hers, seemed to sink into hers, to meld and become one with her cool skin that warmed, heated, burned as he touched. He needed to be within her, have her body grow soft and supple around him, accept him. Only then would he find ease from the desolate loneliness that invaded his soul. Knowing he shouldn't, knowing that what he was doing was wrong, knowing he'd fought and lost against the hunger driving him to Molly Harris, Harlan thought perhaps a merciful god would find pity and forgive him.

And if there were no mercy in heaven?

Her skin was hot under his palm, the feel of her belly softer than velvet.

Sliding his hand over her thigh, he pushed the satiny nightshirt to her waist. The shiny fabric of high-cut white panties gleamed against the matte white of her skin. Her right leg, bent at the knee, rested on the stair tread, her left sprawled below him as he bent to her.

He glimpsed the butt of the gun, dark against her nightshirt, and, not turning her loose, closed one hand around it. With his arm still wrapped around her, he lifted it free of her pocket, the butt between his fingers and her back.

"The Luger," she said, running her fingers over his mouth. Her other hand pulled at the waist of his jeans, stopped, tugged again, popping the metal stud. Her words rushed forward on a long, drawn-out breath as he cupped her supple calf and stroked the underside of her knee. "I took it with me to the door."

Light dazzled him, and he blinked, lifted his head from the satin-covered buttons at the neck of her shirt.

Molly's eyelids were half-closed, her eyes dilated. Her hair caught on rough spots in the white wall behind her and fanned out in a shining, golden brown halo around her face.

They were collapsed on the stairway, lights blazing, and in full view of the squad car that would make its rounds. The waistband of his jeans gaped where the snap lay open and he had one finger hooked under the thin elastic of her panties, her shirt shoved up above her waist and draped in folds over one pale breast.

"This won't do," he muttered, his voice thick and harsh with urgency.

"No," she agreed, pushing at her shirt.

"Don't." He stopped her fretful movements with the brush of his tongue over her hard pink nipple. Still gripping the gun, he lifted her in one arm and slid his other under her knees. Her toe caught in the open V of his zipper, grazed his belly, and he flinched, pierced with pleasure.

Straightening against the clenching in his groin, he took the stairs two at a time, carrying her folded against him. "Molly, Molly," he whispered against the corner of her mouth. He couldn't get enough of her. He felt as if he were dying of thirst, smelling water when he couldn't drink it. "Molly."

Reaching her room, he flicked off the light. He held her a moment, motionless, letting his senses fill with her in the darkness.

When he let her slide down against him, her hair tangled around the gun and he slipped his fingers through the silky strands, letting them fall into his palm as he straightened her hair.

She turned, watching him as he placed the Luger on her dresser.

Their gazes locked in the mirror. Their reflections overlapped. In his dark jeans and shirt, he was a shadow at her back, while she, a shimmer of white and pale pink reflecting back to him, was small and luminescent in the dim room, her head coming to below his chin. She moved, he did. In the mirror, their arms collided, slid together, his over hers until she was drawn back against his darkness and lost in the shadows of his form. He touched the pulse thrumming in the bend of her elbow and brought her arms and hands back against his hips.

She flattened her hands against him, and in the mirror, Harlan saw the pleasure in her face, felt her pleasure as she softened against him. Above her, barely visible, his eyes were dark. Only the gold rims showed.

He lifted the fall of hair at her neck, baring the nape, and bent to the small, delicate spot where her spine joined the base of her skull. With the tip of his tongue, he flicked it once. Her skin smelled of her bath soap, spicy and clean, and she tasted of milk and honey. Then, his mouth firm against her silky skin, he bit gently, a careful claiming. Held in place with his mouth and body, she shivered, a long, rolling tremor against him as she moved her hands convulsively down his thighs and up again.

And all the while, his teeth sharp and careful on her skin, Harlan watched her, as much a prisoner of her pleasure as she.

Keeping her hair to one side, he trailed kisses over the curve of her neck and down to her shoulder, nudging aside the satin fabric to find skin softer than any satin ever made.

"You make me weak with need," he whispered against her skin. "Strong with hunger. For you, only you." Releasing one of her arms, he traced the line of buttons, flicking them open as he went until his hand rested at the final one at her stomach. In the mirror he saw his forearm lying over the sharp point of her hip and his wrist against the supple, bare skin of her belly. His index finger was at the rim of her navel. In the opened front of her shirt, her skin from belly to breasts glowed rosy and warm. Her nipples were delicate rose points in the mirror as he slipped his hand lower and cupped her against the nylon of her panties.

She jerked against his hand and her eyes flickered shut, opened, closed as he pressed the heel of his hand against her. He absorbed her response with his watching eyes, with the strength of his chest at her back, with the palm of his hand. He trailed his fingers back up the middle of her torso, all the way to her neck and back down to her left breast. Circling the ruched tip, he watched the hectic flush burn under her quivering skin. Slowly, slowly he edged his finger around that point until she twisted and turned against him, gently scraping the soft skin until she whispered, *"Please."*

"Here?" He slipped his hand lower.

"No. *Yes,*" she said as he slipped his hand inside the elastic edge of her panties and touched her. Startled, she moved violently against him, and as she did, he slid his left hand to her breast and cupped it, flicking his thumb against the hard point.

Holding her there, watching her glow against him and respond to him, Harlan thought he would die with the need to have her and he shook inside until he didn't know anymore which tremors were his, which hers.

Like clouds passing over water, their reflections shivered in the mirror.

"Molly, I can't wait," he groaned. "Not any longer. I want to, for you, but I..." He stroked against her from behind, and touched lower, parting her, tracing her slickness until his eyes shut and nothing existed for him except the pleasure of touching Molly Harris and wanting her and knowing she wanted him. Tension flattened his lips across his teeth.

"You don't have to wait. I don't want you to." Her words were a thready sound in the darkness, the final invitation.

"May I?" he asked and skimmed her panties down with the back of his hand.

"Yes, you may," she said, her laugh shaky and her movements restless, agitated. She dropped her head to his shoulder and reached up to curve her arm around his neck. She slid her fingers into his hair and his scalp buzzed with her touch.

Harlan bent his knees and lifted her leg to the edge of the dresser. His jeans slithered to the floor. His belt buckle thudded against the wood and foil caught the light, twinkled to the floor as, with an urgent thrust, his knees bent to accommodate her shorter height, he brought her down onto him and held her, controlling their movements while he watched them in the mirror, watched her spine arch her forward, her breasts lifting and falling as he took her, as she took him, watched the play of light and shadows in the mirror and in her silvery eyes until something beyond pleasure rocketed through him and took him into darkness where he was lost, lost, his eyes shut against the wonder, and only her hand shaping his face in the dark splendor could bring him back.

Her. Molly.

When Molly turned to Harlan, he was still shuddering, his broad shoulders under his shirt bunched and tight. She stood on tiptoe and took his hard, angular face in her hands. A dark flush slashed his cheekbones, and his chest was sweat-sheened as she unbuttoned the slate buttons of his shirt. Those buttons had pressed into her spine, their cool hardness a perverse pleasure against her heated skin.

Dropping his shirt on the floor, she walked to the edge of her bed, glancing at him over her shoulder, her eyes filled with mischief. She'd wondered what he would look like without his mask. She'd wondered how emotion would transform his austere, remote expression. And now she knew.

His naked hunger was there for her to read in every line of his harsh face, his tough body. She was responsible for his loss of control. He'd yielded the force of his body to her, letting her find a sensualism in herself she'd never dreamed she possessed, enabling her to forget everything except the intensity of what he was sharing with her.

When he stepped to her side in a flowing, smooth movement that made her blink, she stroked his face and watched his eyes dilate. Her hold over him turned his gold eyes dark with need.

"You like knowing how you turn me on, don't you, sweet Molly?" He lifted an eyebrow and grinned at her. "You like having me—" he gestured lazily along the length of his body "—at your command, don't you?"

She nodded, her heart in her throat as she stared at him. He was all primal male and he allowed her to see how much power her touch, her glance had over him. Even as she stared, he responded as if she had touched him and stroked him intimately.

"See what you do to me? See the power you have, Molly?" He shrugged. "I can't hide how you make me feel."

"Good," she said with feminine satisfaction and wonder. She slid her hand across his slick, smooth chest and watched the ridged muscles of his abdomen tighten. Filled with awe at the miracle of him, she slipped her hand to his hip, down his tight flanks, up the curving line of his spine until she tangled her fingers in the heavy silk of his black hair. He stayed still under her touches, his hands at his sides, but Molly had the oddest sensation that where she touched him, his skin buzzed, vibrated, hummed with an electrical pulse.

He made a noise almost like a low growl in his throat as she ran her fingernails down his spine to the cleft of his buttocks. "Molly," he said, claiming her with a kiss that curled her toes and left her limp against his hard chest. He swung her up into his arms and onto her bed. "I need you again. Now."

Flinging her arms out to the side, she whispered, "Be my guest," offering herself to him and knowing in the deepest part of her self that the power she had over him, he also had over her, knowing that what she gave him was more than her body.

"Until morning."

"All right," she said, and opened her mouth to his as he lowered himself over her, blotting out the light.

And in that moment it seemed to her that he changed, blurred, shifted, and she couldn't find him. She had the strangest sensation that she was grasping smoke, air, but then, suddenly, she was stroking his ribs, the solid muscles of his back, and he was inside her, driving, thrusting, until lights burned behind her eyelids and he became her entire universe. "Who are you, John Harlan?" she whispered, rocking to his thrusts and lifting higher, yearning for the light-spangled heat he was promising with each thrust. "Who are you?"

His rhythm slowed. "Only a man. A man who needs you tonight, Molly. Nothing more. Take me. Let me take you. Please." Then, faster and faster he drove her, drove himself, and she took him with her to that place where darkness burned golden, as gold as the gold of his eyes.

Once, much later during the night, Molly found herself on top of him, her thighs gripping his flanks, her head arched back as she sought release from the tension again building within her. She had never understood before Harlan that passion was a state of being, an actual place, and, having discovered it with him, she longed with all her being to go there again.

As she strained toward that end, his voice, low and gritty, urged her on, encouraged her to go where she needed to, told her that he would find her there. He lifted his head and took her breast in his mouth. His teeth grazing the nipple, scraping, he took her deeper into his mouth until the spring inside her burst, twanging and whipping through her, and she collapsed, spent, onto him, her hair falling like a curtain over his face as the moonlight turned the sheets to silver and his pale face to marble. Against her cheek his hair was damp and warm to her touch.

She fell into sleep, her arms curled around him, his

wrapped around her, and, held safe next to his powerful heart and chest, she didn't dream and she didn't think about death and dying and blood-spattered walls.

When she awoke, he was gone.

He'd drawn the sheet over her and placed the cordless phone on the pillow he'd picked up off the floor and returned to the bed.

Sitting upright, Molly lifted the edge of the sheet and crumpled it. She'd taken a risk, letting him into her house, her bed, her heart. She'd thought it would be all right because he was taking a risk, too. But she hadn't known that she wouldn't be able to separate her body from her heart, her soul. She hadn't known the risk would be so enormous.

She would never again have a lover like him. Whatever happened from this night forth, she recognized that he'd claimed her in some primitive way and no one ever again would touch her, not in the ways that John Harlan had. With his leaving, he'd taken part of her with him.

She hadn't expected that when she'd opened her door to him. That was a risk she'd never thought of.

And even knowing she would take it again.

When she went downstairs for breakfast, she saw that he had bolted the doors behind him.

The chain on the kitchen door felt warm, as if Harlan had slid it into the slot only moments earlier.

The cat was curled in front of a bowl of milk in the sunlight streaming through the open shutters. Reaching down to pet him, she ran her hand along the length of his sunshine-warmed spine, and he arched into her hand, rumbling silently under his sleek black fur, the vibrations passing into her being.

John Harlan had left.

He'd taken her gun with him.

And all the locks were in place.

* * *

When he came, shortly before noon, she knew he'd returned this time to arrest her. He didn't need to say the words. His face was bleached white, pain splintered the gold of his eyes and his mouth was a thin, angry line.

"This is an official call, then?"

"Yes. Arresting you wasn't my choice. The order came from the state's attorney's office. I said there wasn't enough evidence. But there was your bracelet, you see. And your fingerprints on the knife with Camina's blood. And, finally, your fingerprints were found on a gallon container of gasoline half a mile into the woods from the cabin."

His words were worse than a nightmare. None of what he was suggesting was possible, and yet his words were so logical, so sane. "We always kept gas cans in the shed. For the boats. Of course my finger prints would have been on the cans. That's not proof of anything!" She rubbed her eyes.

He didn't hide behind his sunglasses and she saw his anguish. He didn't have to tell her he was at her doorstep unwillingly. Tired lines scored his mouth, the crevices around his eyes. Underneath his flat tone, she heard his frustration. "There's more. This morning Dr. Bouler identified a crown found in the rubble at the cabin as one he'd made for your brother. They figured you killed him for the rest of the estate."

"I see." And she did. But this time she *knew* she hadn't done anything. Could *prove* it. "Didn't you tell them you'd followed me around for most of this week and that I couldn't possibly have killed my brother?" She asked, but she would have bet her life that he'd even admitted to what had happened between them last night.

"I told them. Everything." His mouth was tight. "I've been officially reprimanded."

She nodded. Reid was dead, she was going to jail, but

she wasn't going to go down without a fight. "You'll say the same things in court? If I'm put on trial?"

"Yes."

"And you're still investigating the murders? Even with the reprimand?"

"Yes." He frowned. "The prosecuting attorney believes there's enough presumptive evidence to charge you and take it to trial. And the department wants closure." He started to reach out to her but let his hand drop.

"All right. Can you give me time to change and call my lawyer?"

Ross Whittaker stayed in the car. Molly was glad. Somehow she found the strength to face Harlan, her memory of the previous night filling her and keeping her chin up as she listened to his perfunctory recital of her rights.

While she dressed, she called Bob Nolan and asked him to meet her at the county jail. Harlan snapped the handcuffs around her wrists without saying a word and led her out to the unmarked car.

As he placed his open palm on her head to keep her from bumping it on the car, Molly looked at him and said, "It does make a difference, doesn't it? All the risk wasn't mine alone?"

His fingertips flexed in her hair. "I couldn't have imagined what a difference." Pain was a jagged edge underneath his drawl. He leaned down so that only she heard his final words as he shut the car door. "I thought last night wouldn't harm you. I never reckoned it would destroy me."

CHAPTER TWELVE

Bob showed up with Paul in tow as Harlan parked the car in back of the jail. The three men stayed by her side until Harlan, with a scowl at Paul, disappeared. His last glance at Molly seared her with its reminder of the night, and the chill that had begun creeping back vaporized.

The crown was definitely Reid's. Paul said it was unique and easily identifiable as the one he'd made for Molly's brother. Paul posted bail for her, and couldn't quit explaining about the stupid crown. Molly let his words roll over her.

"God, Molly, I don't know what to say. This is a mistake. Everybody in the county knows you didn't kill Reid. Or Camina. Hell and damnation." He tugged his mustache. "I knew the damned crown was Reid's the minute they brought it to my office. There was that millimeter shoulder all around the tooth, the gold collar at the bottom. The rest was porcelain. I knew it was my work. I pulled Reid's records. I wouldn't have involved you, but what else could I have said?"

"It's going to be okay, Paul." Molly would have laughed if she could have found an extra ounce of energy. She was the one facing jail, but she was reassuring Paul. She was suddenly struck with the memory of similar times while they'd been married. She'd forgotten how often he'd left the hard decisions to her and avoided confrontations and unpleasantness.

He was still her friend and he'd shown up to post bail for her. That counted for a lot.

But he was a rumpled, worried teddy bear when what she

needed was a dangerous panther. She glanced around the pea-green station walls and wondered where Harlan had vanished to. She thought she saw his broad-shouldered shadow down a hall, but it turned out to be someone else. Harlan would find her when he was ready to.

"Can I go now?" she asked Nolan.

"Sure, honey, but God almighty, I never expected you to be pitched into the middle of a mess like this." Nolan scratched his bald head. "I'm thinking you're gonna need a better lawyer than this old country legal beagle, Molly." He took her by the elbow. "Come on, sugar, I'll drive you home."

Turning away from Paul, who hovered at her side, Molly said, "I want to go to your office first, Bob. Okay? I need to talk with you."

"Sure. Hey, Paul?"

"Yep?"

"Molly and I are going to stop at my office, so you can go on along."

"Paul, thank you. For being here. For posting bail. You know I'll pay you back when all this is cleared up." She reached up and hugged him. Instead of his burly chest, she felt Harlan's hard planes and muscles.

"Hey, don't sweat the small stuff. It's only nickels and dimes. What else are ex-husbands for, if not to have deep pockets? What's mine is yours, babe."

Molly shook her head. "And what's mine is yours. I know." She should have been exhausted, but adrenaline was keeping her fueled at such a pitch that all her senses seemed sharper. Colors were almost painfully bright, sounds unpleasantly loud to her acute hearing.

After Paul left, she collected her belongings. She was overwhelmingly grateful that she hadn't had to spend the night in jail. She didn't want to think about the several hours in the room with flaking green paint and no privacy.

She rubbed her ink-stained fingers against her cream-colored skirt. She would throw the skirt and blouse and jacket away as soon as she got home. She never wanted to see the outfit again.

There would be an explanation for what had happened.

She would find it.

Or John Harlan would.

In the meantime, she would take steps to protect herself.

From the corner of her eye, she thought she glimpsed him once more as she and Nolan left, but she didn't look in that direction, not wanting to be disappointed once more.

She needed him, and she didn't understand it. Like the cat, Harlan had come into her house, her mind, and made himself at home, entering and leaving as he chose. She needed him, but not because he could save her from what was happening. No, she needed him because during the long hours of the night, he'd become part of her. If someone had told her that the cells of her body had merged and become one with his, their DNA blending into one whole, she would have believed it, because that was how she felt.

She was incomplete without him.

At Nolan's office, she told him to draw up a new will while she waited. She would sign it before leaving.

"Honey, you don't want to rush into something like this." He'd always been overly cautious, and her father had respected that quality. It was one of the reasons Nolan had been their family's lawyer ever since her father had gone into business. Nolan had drawn up every document anyone in their family needed. He knew everything about the Harrises. "Let me think about this first."

"No. The police think I'm guilty of murder. I know I'm not. But someone is. Someone who can profit from my death or by making me look guilty. I want my will changed. Today," she insisted stubbornly. "I'm not leaving your office until you do what I'm asking, Bob. I know you'll have to go through all the legal steps, but at least you can get the intent down now and I can sign it. That will count for something.''

"I don't like this, Molly. It's very irregular." He glared at her. "Your dad wouldn't want you handling the situation like this. With Reid dead, there's the ranch to consider. His will to be probated. You inherit all that."

"Look, Bob, keep it simple, okay?" She leaned forward on his desk. "Draw up an instrument that leaves anything I have as of this date to the hospital cancer fund." No matter what Harlan had implied, she refused to believe that some far-reaching conspiracy could involve the whole hospital board. Nevertheless, she changed her charity bequest.

Straightening, puzzled, she looked out the glass door of his office. She'd heard Harlan's gritty drawl, almost as if he'd spoken in her ear. She shook her head.

If she eliminated the hospital board as suspects, that left her with Paul, Susie or Susie's husband. Molly didn't know Susie's husband. It was easier to think he'd been behind what happened to her even though she couldn't figure out the why or how of it. All she knew was that she didn't want to think Paul was the one who had plotted against her.

But she was taking precautions as fast as she could.

She was going to survive.

When Nolan reluctantly shoved the hastily typed document in front of her, Molly read it thoroughly and made one change. "I want Camina's family to be included. I didn't think of them until now. They're still in Costa Rica."

Nolan made the alteration and had her initial it. All the way back to her house, he nagged her, until she wanted nothing more than to walk into her house and shut the door behind her, locking out all noise and interference.

When he finally left, she stripped off her clothes and carried the cordless phone with her into the bathroom. Alone in the white room, she left the shower curtain open and wished briefly that Harlan had left her the gun. Scrubbing her back, she decided that maybe it was better he'd taken it with him.

Heaven help her if someone else got hold of her gun. She didn't even want to think about how her situation would look if that happened. Her gun. Found somewhere in suspicious circumstances. If that happened, she'd have no chance of ever digging her way out of the hole she was in.

Molly scrubbed her body with the washcloth until her skin was blotchy and almost raw. She wanted the smell of the jail out of her nose, off her skin.

Harlan drummed his fingers on the wadded up sheet of his bed as flipped through the pages of reports. The initial call from the fishermen. The blood matches. He raked his hands fiercely through his hair. He wanted to be with Molly. He should never have made love with her last night. But he had. And now, his soul merged with hers, he sensed even more powerfully than ever before the nature of the wickedness that stalked sweet Molly with her innocent, trusting eyes.

He tried to hurry, but the pages stuck together, flew apart, scattered onto the floor. "Damn!" He gathered them with one fist, pages out of order, and stilled as he saw three sentences on one of the reports.

She was alone in her enormous, unsafe house, alone on the bayou in the dark.

He would never reach her in time.

She dragged a long white muslin nightgown over her still-damp skin and raked a comb through her shampooed hair. With its long sleeves and squared neckline it looked more like a dress than a nightgown, and, like her nightshirt, it had pockets. She slipped the cordless phone into one pocket and went downstairs. For the first time in a week, she planned on making a cup of hot milk and taking it upstairs with her to bed.

Defiantly, Molly slammed the shutters closed while the milk was warming on the stove. When she dumped in a spoonful of Ovaltine, the milk in the cup foamed over onto the counter. Wiping up the sticky mixture, she thought again about the morning she'd come to on the floor after Camina's murder. She'd been asleep then, right here in the kitchen. She hadn't been walking around in a daze.

Remembering that, she considered all the ways of drugging people. The pills Paul had given her hadn't even made her drowsy. She stirred in the last of the Ovaltine slowly, the milk turning beige-brown as she let the powder dissolve. Who knew about drugs?

Well, she did, of course. Through her job as dental supply salesperson, she could think of several ways she could have managed a tidy little drug trade on the side if she were so inclined. She would have been caught eventually, though. But what would have made her walk in her sleep and never remember it? Who else had access to drugs?

Her spoon clicking against the cup, Molly wished Paul weren't so obvious an answer. Was he in financial trouble? *Click, click.* The spoon trembled in her hand. Paul had always overextended himself. But surely, if he'd needed money, he would have come to her and asked for some. Wouldn't he have?

She sipped from the cup. The milk was too hot, and she left the spoon in it for a minute to hasten the cooling. Tapping the spoon against her teeth as she carried the cup and pot to the sink, Molly thought about her curious amnesia and the description Harlan had given of her behavior. No wonder he'd thought she was on drugs.

But she hadn't been. She didn't remember taking one of the sleeping pills the night Camina had died. If she didn't buy the idea that she'd been in the grip of a weird sleep-walking episode, like those people who found themselves going on nocturnal binges, there had to be another, rational explanation. One she hadn't found yet.

Flexing his fingers, Harlan shut his eyes, tried to concentrate. And for the first time couldn't. Now, when he needed to focus his energies more than he ever had in his life, he failed. He swallowed. Wiping away the sweat dripping into the corners of his eyes, he blanked out everything. Into that emptiness, Molly's face, thoughtful, washed clean, hovered for an instant.

Disappeared.

Harlan slammed his fist against the edge of the rosewood and growled.

Lifting the skin off the milk with her spoon, she dropped it onto a paper towel and threw it into the waste can. For one whimsical second, she looked to see if Harlan had left the Luger there, but the waste can was empty.

Just at the edge of his senses, he saw her. Sweat poured off him. He could hear his skin sliding, popping. If he could...

In her heightened mental state, Molly was aware of the cat before he leapt up onto her shoulder, perching there as he had on Harlan's much-wider shoulders. "Ow, buster." She reached up and lifted him down onto the counter. He hissed as she lowered him. "Hey, don't get mad at me. Your claws need clipping." A thin red line showed in the low square of the neckline. "Well, look what you've done." She turned on the faucet and soaked another paper towel. When she lifted the towel to her neck, water drops arced and sprayed onto the cat.

Leaping straight into the air, all four legs stiff, he came down next to her cup and the pan with the extra milk, and the tip of his tail dunked into the pan like a doughnut. His expression was so offended that Molly laughed. "Sorry. I know you're not clumsy. No, you're not. You're the most magnificent beast around." Thinking of another magnificent male, she rolled her eyes and scratched the cat's chin as he flicked his tail back and forth.

Suddenly he went still and his tail fluffed out. His back arched and stiff, his hair standing on end, he backed up straight into her cup. The cup teetered and clattered into the sink, spilling her drink down the drain. The cat leapt to the floor and stalked to the pantry door, where he folded his paws underneath him and stared arrogantly at her.

"I take it all back, beast. That *was* clumsy. Or deliberate." She scowled at him and rinsed her cup out before shoving it into the dishwasher with the pan. "Thanks a bunch, buster. See if I let you curl up on my bed tonight."

Walking up the back stairs from the kitchen, Molly felt the cat brush against her bare ankles. "Oh, all right. Hey, you already know I'm a pushover." She reached down and lifted him to her shoulder. With his sandpaper tongue, he licked her chin. "What? I have milk on my chin?"

Her bed seemed empty without Harlan next to her. Even the cat curled close at her side left her lonely.

She wanted Harlan.

Tapping her hand, the cat waited. When she frowned, he pushed his head against her fingers, placed his nose next to her wrist and finally wrapped his tail around his body. But he faced the stairs, and that realization sent a small, unwelcome shiver over her.

She thought about calling Harlan, but she didn't.

A week ago she wouldn't have been able to sleep. But with the large cat a solid, breathing presence at her side, and with the phone next to her, she drifted in and out of sleep at last, some knowledge at the edge of her conscious thought teasing and taunting her.

Something to do with drugs and amnesia.

Her scent was all around him, and he was helpless to warn her. He tried, God knew he tried.

She turned in her sleep away from the door and back

again, restless. She wasn't dreaming, she knew she wasn't; but Harlan was there, touching her, whispering to her, telling her to wake up.

Molly opened her eyes and stared around the quiet room. She must have been dreaming after all.

The house was still.

No boards creaked, no breeze lifted a branch and scraped it against the house.

Downstairs, from the kitchen, the refrigerator motor kicked in and the vibration carried upstairs to her, a familiar sound, nothing to wake her.

The cat was watching her, his eyes enormous, the gold only a rim around the black. He looked toward the staircase and back to her, waiting expectantly.

She was too tired to go downstairs and look for food for him. She yawned and her eyelids drooped.

Ketamine.

It was used as an anaesthetic. It could cause disassociative disorders if administered incorrectly. Nightmares. Flashes of hallucination. A patient under the influence of Ketamine could have wide-open eyes, could sleepwalk and never remember. Without another drug to counteract its effects, Ketamine, in high doses, would cause the reactions she'd had.

Paul used Ketamine in oral surgery. She'd ordered it for him.

Her heart pounding and her stomach queasy, Molly ticked off the symptoms she'd had. Ketamine would account for all of them. But Ketamine was administered intramuscularly or intravenously. It wasn't a drug that could be slipped into her food.

Leaning back against her pillow, Molly thought about her reactions each time she'd found herself on the floor of her kitchen. With each passing second, the queasiness in her stomach increased. She was sure she'd been given Ketamine. And Paul was the only person who could have given it to her.

Her stomach turned over and she almost threw up. Clutching the phone, she raced to the bathroom. The cat padded behind her, staying clear of her feet but keeping near. She was glad of his company. "Hey, puss, Paul wouldn't try to kill me, would he? He wouldn't kill Camina, right?"

Standing at the sink and looking at the vase of wilting, bloodred flowers, Molly thought about Paul and his inability to be faithful. What if he'd had an affair with Camina?

And Camina had threatened to tell Molly?

With that thought, she lost control of her stomach.

Afterward, she brushed her teeth; her stomach still roiling, she lay down, pulling the sheet up around her.

The cat prowled in a triangle from the bathroom to the bedroom door to her bed, on guard duty as she lay there, thinking and not liking any of her thoughts.

Wouldn't she have changed her will if Camina had come to her before the divorce with a story of Paul's unfaithfulness? But after the death of her parents, she hadn't even thought about her will.

Could Paul have killed her parents—Paul, who didn't like guns? But he had always gone along with Reid and their father on hunting trips. Paul, who hated confrontations and who always seemed to have expensive toys. Molly pulled the sheet tighter.

She'd lived with Paul. Made love with him.

No, she hadn't made love. Harlan had shown her what was possible between a man and a woman. She and Paul had only played at making love.

Air swirled against her cheek.

The cat stopped and faced the door. His mouth drew back over his teeth and a low, savage growl came from his throat.

The hairs on Molly's arms and neck rose straight up.

Primitive, gut level, this fear.

Someone was in her house.

Someone had come past her locks and bolts and was moving quietly, carefully through her kitchen.

John Harlan had left her house earlier today, leaving it locked and bolted behind him.

Her hand shaking, she reached for the cordless phone, and her fingers spread out against the pillow. She'd left the phone in the bathroom.

Reaching for the phone beside her bed, she knew even before she heard the silence in the earphone that it was dead, but she wasted seconds listening before she laid the receiver down and slid out of bed.

And the whole time, the cat's low growl filled her ears.

Making no sound, her feet slipping easily over the wood, she made her way backward to the bathroom, never taking her eyes off the open doorway of her room. She realized she should have shut and locked her bedroom door. Too late.

She was coming out of the bathroom, phone in hand, when he entered her bedroom. The cat howled, long and low, a nightmare sound of fury as the man stepped into her room.

He stood in the doorframe and frowned at her. "You're supposed to be asleep, Sissy. You drank your milk—I know you did. Now you've messed everything up for me." His hand was in the pocket of his jeans.

"Reid?" Molly recognized the bloodred shirt. It was one she'd given him for his birthday two years ago, two years ago when everything had been exactly what it seemed. "Reid?" She couldn't believe her brother was standing in front of her, alive.

"What, Sissy?" He was annoyed, and his light blue eyes glittered with anger.

She sagged against her chest of drawers. Shaking her

head in confusion, she realized that, no, the shaggy-haired man in front of her couldn't have been the loving twin she'd believed in. There was no love in his face, nothing but emptiness. Emptiness and determination. "I thought you were dead."

"Of course you did. I meant for everyone to. You, that damned, snotty detective. Everyone had to think I'd been killed."

"Why?" The face and form were the same, but the being glaring at her from her brother's eyes was not the brother she'd known and loved.

"Shut up, Sissy. I need time to think. Be still while I figure out what to do now. You were supposed to be asleep," he accused. "Why aren't you? I know there was enough sedative left in the Ovaltine for one more time. I only needed tonight to make everything work out, and you've ruined it. I should have known you would." He glared at her. His mouth was working furiously as he chewed his bottom lip. "It would have been easier if you'd been asleep. Easier for *you*. It's your fault. That's all there is to it."

Giving her no time to punch Harlan's preprogrammed number into the phone, Reid strode toward her. The cat leapt for his face, clawing and hissing and shrieking. Reid screamed and dodged to one side, but the cat dug into his shoulder, spitting and striking out with extended claws and teeth.

Molly flung the phone at him and it bounced off his chest as he whirled and knocked the cat off of him. Landing with a thud, the cat was a still, unmoving shape on the floor.

Grabbing her arm, Reid dragged her out of her bedroom and down the stairs. Pulling back against his maniacal strength, she clutched the banister until he knocked her fingers loose with the back of the Luger.

She'd thought Harlan had taken it.

But Reid had. He was the one who'd left her shutters open, not Harlan.

"Reid, stop. What are you doing?" Molly felt no fear, only a cleansing anger that suddenly roared through her, burning away everything except her resolve to live.

Stronger than she, Reid twisted her arm behind her and frog-marched her to the kitchen door. She thought she might have a chance to make a run when he had to turn her loose to throw open the bolts and chains, but keeping her hard against him, he lifted one foot and battered the door until it hung crazily on its hinges. With each kick, he tightened his hold on her until she was afraid he would break her arm.

"This doesn't make sense," Molly panted as he shoved her through the ruined door and onto the veranda. "I can help you. Tell me what's wrong. We can fix it," she babbled, everything in her world turned upside down in the face of his violence.

The grass was wet on her bare feet and clouds were moving across the face of the waning moon. She stumbled and tried to slow his mad race across the lawn. "We can fix it, Reid," she said again as he twisted her arm.

"No, you can't. *We* certainly can't. Sissy," he said, and for a moment she heard an old echo of her twin, "it's so bad. I'm in such trouble. And it keeps getting worse. I try to fix it and nothing works."

She touched his arm. "But I can help you. Let me."

He was dragging her, inch by inch, to the pier where Camina had been killed.

He moved toward her, his body aching. He'd known it was impossible but he'd gone to her anyway. He'd done everything within his powers to protect her, and he wasn't going to be in time now to save her. The grass hid him as he slid closer. He'd made a mistake, and she was paying for his carelessness, his self-indulgence. He'd found her, found heaven, and he was losing everything. He cocked his head, listening to Reid's ferocious voice.

Reid would kill her.

When he did, Reid would die, too. He would see to it, and then he'd return to the shadows. But they would be unendurable now that he'd tasted the sunshine, walked in the light.

He needed her. She was the beat of his heart, the pulse of his blood. He needed her.

The smell of evil lying over Reid was acrid, sour. Reid's sweat rolled off, dropped onto the grass, and he followed it like a spoor.

Molly saw a shadow at the edge of her vision, and she kept quiet, not wanting to alert Reid. If she could keep him talking, she would have a chance. If she could get the gun from him, she could... Could she shoot her brother?

"Come on, come on, Moll. Step up here. It has to be the dock. That ties everything up nice and tidy for the cops. They'll think you killed yourself because you were afraid to face the music."

"Reid, you disconnected the phone. You broke the door. Nobody's going to think I killed myself," Molly added reasonably, desperation fighting old habits, old love.

Reid scowled. "You're confusing me, I had it all worked out! But you weren't asleep!" His voice was shrill and frantic.

"Reid, give it up," she whispered.

"I can't!" He gripped her tighter. "Okay, okay, so they won't believe it's suicide. But I can make them think Paul killed you. I can still do that! Remember? I'm dead. I can't be a suspect. Yeah, our detective will keep poking around, and he'll think it's Paul. Then when they arrest Paul, I can control of the money. I changed my will, Moll. I'm my own beneficiary! With a different name, of course." He laughed.

"I'll have to stay in Costa Rica permanently, but once I have the money, I can straighten out things down there. It'll work." He smiled, the old, beloved smile of her twin.

"Harlan will figure it out," Molly said, knowing he would, but it would be too late for her—too late for them—and now she knew how much she wanted to be with him forever, now that time was running out. She pulled hard against Reid's grip, anger giving her strength she didn't know she had. "Harlan will know what you've done."

Reid's calm words were terrifying. "I saw your detective at the door last night. I didn't think you'd let him in, though. He was there at Paul's office that afternoon, too."

"That was you? In the corridor?" Molly dug her fingernails into his hand.

"Stop that, Sis." He struck her hand with the gun. "Yeah, that was me. I only meant to scare you a little. Keep you on your toes. I had to get another vial from Paul's office, and I saw him leave. I thought the office was empty except for his receptionist."

"You stole Ketamine from him, didn't you?"

He stopped. "How did you know?" He sounded petulant, and she had a flash of Reid at five, frowning and scowling because she'd found his hidey hole and he hadn't fooled her. "It was easy. Paul's my buddy, and neither he nor his pretty receptionist suspected I'd walked off with a couple of vials of his anesthetic and syringes."

His breathing was loud and harsh. He was having a hard time dragging her deadweight behind him, but Molly had no intention of making his plans easier. She found a perverse satisfaction in realizing that she'd surprised him once more. "I knew. After the last time. I don't know how you managed it, though."

Holding her with one hand, he pulled out a syringe with the hand holding the gun. "When you went to sleep, I injected you. It was too easy, Moll. All I had to do was wait for you to drink your milk, and then crawl through the pantry window.''

"But it was locked.'' Molly made herself go limp. Dropping to the wooden pier, she wrapped her hand under the edge, as far as she could reach, and dug her fingers into the barnacles and splintered wood.

His smile was boyish, all charm, and her heart turned over with memories. The point of the syringe was thin and small, not in the least frightening, not threatening at all. This was *Reid*, after all. She couldn't believe he would hurt her.

Reasonably, she added, "I checked. Harlan checked. The windows were all locked."

"No, right after—" he stopped and frowned, as if the sudden thought disturbed him "—about four months ago, I started making plans. I cut off the back of the lock and painted over it. You'd never know the lock was there only for show unless you tried it from the outside. And no one did. All painted over, it looked as if it hadn't been moved in centuries, and I didn't think you would put a rod across the top. There was no reason to, was there? No one ever opened that window for air. It was caked with years worth of thick paint. That was how I got in and out, even after you changed the locks on me. The window slides open quick and quiet.'' He grinned.

He lifted his head and turned his right ear toward them. Reid's voice was filled with satisfaction and greasy with self-congratulation. Now was the time.

Molly gripped a barnacle in her fingers. Her hand was bloody where the sharp shell had cut into her. Rising, she slashed down with the razor-sharp barnacle at Reid's hand holding the gun. He jerked, and the gun skittered across the dock.

* * *

Leaping toward her, flowing in one long shadow from the side of the pier onto it, he tried to reach her, but she stood up as he leapt, her hand arcing down to Reid's and she stooped and picked up the gun as he stepped to one side of Reid, not near enough to grab him, not close enough to Molly to save her.

"What the hell?" Reid turned to him, throwing up his hand. The syringe somersaulted into the bayou. "Detective Harlan? Where the hell'd you come from?"

"Harlan!" Molly's voice rang in his ear, and he longed to leap toward her, catch her in his arms and vault off the pier with her safe against him.

Standing at the edge of the dock with the Luger gripped in her hands, she was everything he'd craved all his life. Sweetness and softness, with vinegar under the sweetness, steel under the softness.

And Harlan saw no way he could save her. Reid was at one point of the triangle, Harlan at the other. Reid could reach her before he could get to her.

"Moll," Reid said, turning to her, but keeping Harlan in sight. "Let me have the gun. You know you would never shoot me, Sis." He reached out his hand, and Harlan edged toward her. "That's far enough, Detective." Reid smiled at Harlan. "Don't do something stupid now. We don't want Molly to be hurt, do we?"

"No," Harlan replied, watching him. "You can relax. I'm not going to do anything to hurt Molly." Primitive rage churned his gut.

Molly hadn't dropped her arms, and the gun wavered between Reid and Harlan. He wondered if she even realized she was pointing it. From the way she gripped it, he could tell she'd had experience with guns, but the situation had eaten at her reactions, and she couldn't be expected to react normally with her brother risen from the dead.

"Hey, Sis, put the gun down, will you?" Reid teased her. "This is all a mistake. Let's sit down, like you said, and I'll explain everything. You said you'd help me. You said it wasn't too late to fix things, make everything okay. Put the gun down, okay? So we can talk?"

"Molly." Harlan sent his voice low to her, willed her to hear him. "Molly, give me the gun. Don't put it down. Don't give it to him." Not naming her brother, Harlan hoped to distance her from the light-haired man playing on her familiar memories, on the patterns of a lifetime. She'd told him she was linked closely with her brother. He hadn't believed it. He hoped she didn't think of those links, any links, in these seconds as a bank of clouds licked away at the edge of the moon.

He would have one chance. Only one.

"Hey, Sissy," Reid wheedled, "who you going to listen to? Your twin? Or some stranger? Let me have the gun, Sissy, please. If you don't, he'll kill me." Truth was a knife edge in his voice.

Harlan heard it.

Molly heard it.

"Molly, sweetheart, Reid killed Camina. And your parents. If you put down the gun, he'll kill both of us."

Molly's hands were shaking and the gun swung wildly between them. "What do you mean, our parents?"

"I had to, Moll. I needed money. For the ranch. Dad threatened to cut me out of the will because he thought I was losing money, throwing it away on schemes. They weren't schemes, Sissy," Reid added earnestly. "They were *plans*. Business arrangements. It wasn't my fault that the hurricane wiped out one crop, or that two of the biggest investors pulled out of that shopping plaza I was building. Everything would have worked out if Dad would have given me more time, but he wouldn't. He was going to take everything away from me, Sis. The ranch, the farm. Everything in Costa Rica. I would have been nobody.''

"Oh, Reid, how could you?" Tears glistened on Molly's pale face. "You killed them? For money?"

"I *needed* money, Sis." Reid took another step toward her. "You know what the kicker was? I didn't know until too late that Daddy had already changed the will and left everything except the Costa Rica property to you. I had to have money, Sis, but I didn't want to hurt *you.* You're my *twin.* But I had to. You can see that, can't you?"

"And Camina, Reid? Why did you have to kill her?" Harlan asked, watching him, watching Molly's stricken face, watching the slow drift of clouds over the moon.

"She found the vial of Ketamine. She tried to blackmail me." Reid's voice was growing tired and petulant. "I didn't want to hurt you, Sissy. I only needed to get control of the money. At first I thought maybe I could make you think you were having a nervous breakdown—that's why I started with the Ketamine. I could have gotten power of attorney then. Nolan, the old fool, wouldn't have thought twice about it. But then Camina tried to blackmail me. I tricked her into meeting me. I was going to pay her off, but she hit me! With the oar! I had to kill her. She didn't give me any other option."

"Oh, Reid." Molly's voice died away.

"Well, she didn't, Sissy." Reid scowled, justifying himself. "So I thought maybe if you were accused of Camina's murder, *you'd* be sent to jail. I stuck your bracelet under the dock and smeared the kitchen with blood and washed it down so that it would look like you were covering up what you'd done. Jail wouldn't have been so bad, would it? But that didn't work, either. That's why I needed everybody to think I was dead. You can see I had to make the police do something, and they didn't seem in any hurry to arrest you, thanks to your tame cop here," he said, motioning contemptuously to Harlan. "I thought the cops would think Paul was lying about the crown, and they'd suspect him of trying to kill you and me. Or suspect you and him. It didn't matter. It *was* my crown—I had it replaced in Costa Rica. I had an associate fly me in so that my passport would be stamped for the right time and I'd have an alibi. It was all planned, but everything went wrong right from the get-go, Sissy."

The clouds swallowed up the moon.

In that second, Molly heard Harlan's voice. *Move, Molly, get away, get away!* She turned, confused, not able to see anything in the sudden darkness, her eyes not adjusted to the lack of light.

Reid grabbed her arm, wrenching the gun from her.

As he did, an enormous shadow leapt toward Reid, over him, blanketing him.

She saw Reid, Harlan, Reid, twisting and turning, fighting for the gun. In blurs as the shadows thinned over the moon, she saw Harlan, his shape wavering, changing, and she trembled as if she were standing in icy rain.

Run!

But she couldn't. Her brother. Her lover. Their shapes mingling with a third that she couldn't believe. Reid had the gun in his hand when the clouds thickened over the disk of the moon and the shot cracked, shattering the night. A second shot cracked, and Molly ran toward the shadows that coalesced, condensed, separated.

Her brother lay on the ground, his fingers gripping the gun. Kneeling next to him, Molly touched his face, heard him sigh, felt his light breath like a mist. "Aw, Sissy, it wasn't supposed to end up like this." He turned his head away from her.

The mist drifted away, vanished.

Molly saw Harlan crouched at one side, holding his shoulder. As she stared, he blurred into shadows, seemed to move, and yet he was unmoving in front of her, his great golden eyes watching her, filled with desolate need as she stayed by her brother's side. She wanted to call his name and she couldn't.

His sleek black head tilted, turned, and the shadows drifted and vanished, taking him with them.

Molly.

Her name lingered on the air like a sigh.

There was blood on the ground where Harlan had been. Tracking the blood spots, dark against the blades of grass, Molly made her way in the fitful light of the clouds and moon to the hibiscus hedge by the driveway. Under the hedge, his sides heaving and laboring, the huge black cat lay. Blood coated his fur, and, as she stroked his head, tears dripping onto his matted fur, his golden eyes dimmed and closed.

Molly.

She patted his great black head for a long time in the dark until finally, her throat closing against tears, she returned to the house and phoned the police, using the cordless phone Harlan had insisted she purchase.

CHAPTER THIRTEEN

When Molly saw Harlan's dark, low slung car nose its way up the driveway, she was too dazed with grief and loss to understand the meaning of his appearance as he stepped out of the car and stopped three feet away from her. His hair was rumpled and his face was grim and withdrawn as he looked at her. Parallel grooves tightened the corners of his mouth.

He didn't touch her. When she remained on the porch steps, her arms around her waist, he spun on his heel and strode away.

Ross Whittaker was beside him, the two of them began the procedures that would categorize and label the events that had happened. As she watched, uncomprehendingly, a helicopter from the local television station appeared within minutes and hovered above them, casting an eerie light over the scene as the blades whomped and whomped in the air.

Harlan had been with her at the dock.

The cat had been with her all these nights.

The cat had been with her at the dock.

She had followed the trail of Harlan's blood to the dying cat.

Molly jumped as Harlan glanced up at her from the dock's edge. So far away, yet he'd turned to her as she'd thought about him.

His head tilted, he slid his sunglasses to the top of his head and studied her for a moment.

A van from the county morgue screeched up and halted, the driver and attendants waiting for the moment they could wrap up Reid's body. Harlan, who'd walked up to the van, said nothing, his dark presence just *there,* watching her.

She didn't know how to explain her brother's last moments, but she heard Ross say as he looked at the Luger and her brother's wound, "The fool tripped and fell on the gun. He shot himself."

She let it pass. Anything else would have been impossible to explain.

For one dizzying second, everything flashed to the moment she'd awakened to find the knife in her hand, and she thought she'd imagined those moments on the pier, that Harlan had never been there, twisting and turning in the shadows with Reid, but suddenly Harlan, kneeling next to Reid, glanced up at her and when he did, everything was in his unshuttered eyes.

He flipped his sunglasses down and turned away.

When they left, she walked back down to the hibiscus hedge, but the black cat's body had vanished.

During the week that followed, when she was awake, Molly thought she saw Harlan everywhere. Asleep, she dreamed of him, dreamed of the cat and his glowing eyes, of golden corridors with twists and turns and her lost, needing him and unable to call his name.

She cried once for Reid when she remembered his last words, "It wasn't supposed to turn out like this." She tried to remember him as he'd been before greed had turned him into a stranger, into something evil that walked the earth in disguise.

And every night in her dreams she sought Harlan, called to him, yearned for him, and wept silent tears as the image of the cat blurred and merged with Harlan's dark shape.

One night, close to morning, she awoke to find Harlan sitting at the foot of her bed. Dark jacket, dark slacks, hair smoothed back, he was as she'd first seen him.

Her heart labored with the need to tell him everything she felt, her lungs strained for air, and, transfixed by his glowing eyes, she couldn't speak. The heat radiating from him wrapped around her, made her long to touch him.

But she couldn't move. Too much had happened. Too much wickedness and strangeness. Too much she didn't understand because it turned everything rational inside out.

He finally spoke, his words rough and urgent, tormented, their rasp like a scrape against her skin. "You asked me that night who I am, Molly."

She remembered.

He was utterly still. "Do you still want to know?"

At last she moved. Pulling the sheet up to her chin, she said, "Yes, John Harlan, I do."

He shrugged out of his shoulder holster and unclipped the beeper and handcuffs from his thin belt. "I'm a cop. I'll always be a cop. I love what I do. I like hunting down evil and destroying it." He laid the holster on the floor, the handcuffs next to them.

"I know." She was shaking with fever and excitement and the hunger that he aroused in her. And something more, something she recognized only in bits and pieces until now.

He unbuttoned his shirt, draped the black silk over the end of her bed. "I'm a man." He unzippered his expensive slacks, letting the belt slither to the floor, the pants crumple over them. "I'm a man, Molly. A man who needs you and who wants you so much he can't breathe without you."

He slid out of his black silk boxer shorts and tossed them to one side. Naked, he stood before her. "I am what I am, Molly. A cop. A man. And what you see before you."

He was the most magnificent creature she'd ever seen, sleek and smooth, his thighs muscular and powerful as he stood, waiting for her acceptance or rejection. He tilted his head to one side as he watched her with his golden eyes and let her reach whatever decision she would. In all his power and beauty, he waited for whatever she would say or do, offering her himself, naked and vulnerable, placing himself absolutely in her power.

And she *knew* him. Had always known him in her heart, in her soul.

Rising on her knees, Molly crawled the length of the bed to him. Before she reached him, though, he stretched out his palm to stop her.

As she watched, his shape changed, expanded, contracted, and in the shadows blurring before her, she saw the cat that had come to her house that morning long ago, the cat that had stayed by her side and kept her sane, the cat that had saved her, protected her through the terrifying nights. Harlan appeared, the edges of his shape blurring, shifting, in a constant state of change.

"I know," she said softly. "I don't understand, but I know. And, knowing who you are, I want you, John Harlan." Before he could stop her again, she wrapped her arms around him, pulling him to her.

He arched back. "Wait, Molly. You have to know everything before you decide. There are no guarantees."

"I don't need guarantees," she murmured against the heat of his chest, his neck.

Keeping his arms at his side, he said, "I don't understand everything that happens to me. All I know is what my grandmother told me. *Nahual.* The Guatemalan Indians believe that every child has a *nahual.* It's your shadow, your spirit, and it goes through life with you. It's your double, your animal counterpart. It's supposed to be a secret until you're grown, but my grandmother wouldn't tell me what my *nahual* was until she was dying."

"But that doesn't explain this—" Molly motioned toward his blurred shape that altered even as she watched and held him. She heard his voice but it drifted to her from the shadows in her arms.

"I watched my brother's execution." Harlan's voice was soft and she had to strain to hear him. "I loved him so much that I couldn't stand what was happening. I believed he was innocent, and I was wrong, but I couldn't understand that my brother had a core of evil inside him that had let him kill, callously, carelessly, and lie to me." Harlan's face contorted with loss. "And I still loved him. Even as I watched them fit the hood over his face, looked at his eyes for the last time, I still loved him and I screamed his name. And in that instant, when I lost control, something happened to me. I was myself, I was him, I was the person standing next to me." In the shadows of her bedroom now, he became himself, the shape holding under her stroking hands.

Molly clung to him, afraid that he would vanish and she'd lose him forever.

"It only happened that one time, but I began sensing things that I didn't understand, that I had no way of knowing rationally. I hadn't allowed myself to care about anyone after my brother died. I was afraid of what would happen if I lost control of my emotions. But then I saw you at your parents' funeral. I was driving by. I'd heard about the murders and I couldn't resist checking out the people at the funeral. I saw you."

He stretched out his hand to her, let it drop back to his side. "Your head was bent and I only saw a brief glimpse of your face, but I couldn't get you out of my mind, and the incidents began happening more and more frequently. I had no control over them. Things began to happen at night when I slept and I would have dim memories of having gone places, learned things that I didn't know how I'd learned. Nonlanguage things, just and *understanding*. And, finally, I understood that my spirit self and physical self had joined in those moments when my brother died, in those moments when I lost control and opened myself. After your parents' funeral my subconscious somehow believed that you needed me." The intensity in his voice shattered her.

"Oh, I do," she breathed against the shadowy form that was Harlan.

"And I wanted you more than I'd wanted anything or anyone in my life." His voice rose from the smoke in front of her and was the loneliest sound she'd ever heard. "But it's your decision, Molly." He was there, in front of her, the shifting shapes stilled as he waited. "I am as you see me."

She stroked his smooth hair and tried to find words for what she felt.

"Molly, I don't know what the future holds for me. For you if you let me become part of your life."

"You already are," she whispered, holding him, holding him, finding the words at last. "You're part of *me,* my flesh, my *soul.*" She pressed her mouth to the skin covering his thundering heart. "I could never let you go. Never again."

Letting her face brush against his chest, Molly stroked him in wonder, let her hands trace the sleek muscles that had given her pleasure, let her mouth slide against the miracle of him and she knew that whoever, whatever he was, he was *hers.* She dipped and picked up his handcuffs together, linking her wrist to his, "and don't you dare forget it. Not for as long as you live."

His laugh rumbled through his chest as he flicked the lock open and tossed the handcuffs aside. "I need both hands, sweetheart." He lifted her over him and twined his fingers in her hair, angling her face as he bent and kissed her, his kiss a claiming of his own, deep and consuming, sending her spiraling into pleasure before she could tell him that nothing mattered except him, that she loved him more than she could ever say, so, with her hands skimming over him, speaking for her, she told him of her love in a language beyond time, her body speaking to his, answering the need in him, answering his hunger, giving to him as he gave to her in the morning sunlight streaming into her room.

As she sank under him, surrendering as he surrendered to her, Molly heard in the distance a cat's curious yowl.

And then Harlan kissed her, touched her, and there was only silence and him, John Harlan, her lover from the shadows.

* * * * *

SPECIAL EDITION™

From *USA TODAY* bestselling author

SHERRYL WOODS

comes the continuation of the heartwarming series

Coming in January 2003
MICHAEL'S DISCOVERY
Silhouette Special Edition #1513

An injury received in the line of duty left ex-navy SEAL
Michael Devaney bitter and withdrawn. But Michael hadn't
counted on beautiful physical therapist Kelly Andrews's healing
powers. Kelly's gentle touch mended his wounds, warmed
his heart and rekindled his belief in the power of love.

Look for more Devaneys coming in July and August 2003,
only from Silhouette Special Edition.

Available at your favorite retail outlet.

Where love comes alive™

LONE STAR
LCC
COUNTRY CLUB
EST. 1923

Where Texas society reigns supreme—and appearances are *everything*.

On sale...

June 2002
Stroke of Fortune
Christine Rimmer

July 2002
Texas Rose
Marie Ferrarella

August 2002
The Rebel's Return
Beverly Barton

September 2002
Heartbreaker
Laurie Paige

October 2002
Promised to a Sheik
Carla Cassidy

November 2002
The Quiet Seduction
Dixie Browning

December 2002
An Arranged Marriage
Peggy Moreland

January 2003
The Mercenary
Allison Leigh

February 2003
The Last Bachelor
Judy Christenberry

March 2003
Lone Wolf
Sheri WhiteFeather

April 2003
The Marriage Profile
Metsy Hingle

May 2003
Texas...Now and Forever
Merline Lovelace

Only from

Silhouette®
Where love comes alive™

Available wherever Silhouette books are sold.

Visit us at www.lonestarcountryclub.com   PSLSCCLIST

Have you ever wanted to be part of a romance reading group?

Be part of the Readers' Ring, Silhouette Special Edition's exciting book club!

The third title in the promotion is

THE ACCIDENTAL PRINCESS

by Peggy Webb

Silhouette Special Edition
#1516 (January 2003)

Encourage your friends to get together to engage in lively discussions with the suggested reading-group questions provided at the end of the novel. Also, visit www.readersring.com for some exciting interactive materials related to this novel.

Available at your favorite retail outlet.

Where love comes alive™

USA TODAY bestselling author

LINDSAY McKENNA

**brings you a brand-new series
featuring Morgan Trayhern and his team!**

WOMAN OF INNOCENCE
(Silhouette Special Edition #1442)

An innocent beauty longing for adventure. A rugged mercenary
sworn to protect her. A romantic adventure like no other!

DESTINY'S WOMAN
(Silhouette Books)

A Native American woman with a wounded heart. A strong, loving
soldier with a sheltering embrace. A love powerful enough to heal...

Available in Feburary!

HER HEALING TOUCH
(Silhouette Special Edition #1519)

A legendary healer. A Special Forces paramedic in need of faith
in love. A passion so strong it could not be denied...

Available in March!

AN HONORABLE WOMAN
(Silhouette Books)

A beautiful pilot with a plan to win back her honor. The man who
stands by her side through and through. The mission that would
take them places no heart should dare go alone...

Where love comes alive™